Sovereign
Acquisition Series Book 3

Celia Aaron

Sovereign
Acquisition Series, Book 3

Celia Aaron

Copyright © 2016 Celia Aaron

All rights reserved. No part of this book may be reproduced, scanned, or distributed in any printed or electronic form without prior written permission from Celia Aaron. Please do not participate in piracy of books or other creative works.

This book is a work of fiction. While reference may be made to actual historical events or existing locations, the names, characters, places and incidents are products of the author's imagination, and any resemblance to actual persons, living or dead, business establishments, events, or locales is entirely coincidental.

WARNING: This book contains sexually explicit scenes and adult language and may be considered offensive to some readers. Please store your books wisely, away from under-aged readers. This book is a dark romance. If dark romance bothers you, this book isn't for you. If dark, twisty, suspenseful, and sexy—or any combination of those words—interest you, then get the popcorn and enjoy.

Cover art by L.J. at mayhemcovercreations.com

Editing by J. Brooks

ISBN: 1532860196
ISBN-13: 978-1532860195

OTHER BOOKS BY CELIA AARON

Counsellor
The Acquisition Series, Book 1

Magnate
The Acquisition Series, Book 2

***

The Forced Series

***

A Stepbrother for Christmas
The Hard and Dirty Holidays, Book 1

Bad Boy Valentine
The Hard and Dirty Holidays, Book 2

Bad Boy Valentine *Wedding*
The Hard and Dirty Holidays

F*ck of the Irish
The Hard and Dirty Holidays, Book 3

***

Zeus
Taken by Olympus, Book 1

Sign up for my newsletter at AaronErotica.com and be the first to learn about new releases (no spam, just send free stuff and book news.)

Twitter: @aaronerotica

CELIA AARON

CONTENTS

Chapter One STELLA	Page 1
Chapter Two STELLA	Page 7
Chapter Three STELLA	Page 17
Chapter Four SINCLAIR	Page 25
Chapter Five STELLA	Page 37
Chapter Six STELLA	Page 43
Chapter Seven SINCLAIR	Page 51
Chapter Eight STELLA	Page 61
Chapter Nine STELLA	Page 67
Chapter Ten STELLA	Page 77
Chapter Eleven SINCLAIR	Page 83

Chapter Twelve STELLA	Page 89
Chapter Thirteen SINCLAIR	Page 99
Chapter Fourteen STELLA	Page 103
Chapter Fifteen STELLA	Page 111
Chapter Sixteen STELLA	Page 117
Chapter Seventeen SINCLAIR	Page 131
Chapter Eighteen STELLA	Page 135
Chapter Nineteen STELLA	Page 143
Chapter Twenty STELLA	Page 151
Chapter Twenty-One SINCLAIR	Page 159
Chapter Twenty-Two STELLA	Page 169
Chapter Twenty-Three STELLA	Page 181

Chapter Twenty-Four STELLA	Page 187
Chapter Twenty-Five STELLA	Page 197
Chapter Twenty-Six SINCLAIR	Page 203
Chapter Twenty-Seven STELLA	Page 211
Chapter Twenty-Eight STELLA	Page 221
Chapter Twenty-Nine STELLA	Page 231
Chapter Thirty SINCLAIR	Page 237
Chapter Thirty-One STELLA	Page 241
Chapter Thirty-Two STELLA	Page 251
Epilogue STELLA	Page 259

CHAPTER ONE
Stella

THE GROUND RUSHED UP to meet my face, but I turned my head just in time to avoid a busted nose. I wheezed as all the air was crushed from my lungs by the impact. Rolling to the side, I barely missed a large boot that stomped the grass where my torso had been.

I got to my feet and backed away toward the house, trying to catch my breath and ignoring the pain in my ribs. Sweat stung my eyes, and the warm sun peeked from a behind a cloud.

I focused on the massive man who rushed me, his arms spread wide and ready to capture me in what I already knew would be a painful bear hug. Ducking under his right arm, I turned, giving him a hard kick in the ass.

He grunted and took a lunging forward step to avoid falling.

"That's a point for me." I bounced on the balls of my feet.

"No *Krasivaya*. I no fall." Dmitri pointed to the grass and squared up with me again, the tapestry of tattoos on his bare torso rippling as he moved.

"You will." I grinned and ran at him, jumping at the

last moment and landing a vicious elbow to his chest.

He grabbed for me and managed to get one of his bear paws around my ponytail. I landed on my feet and tried to back away, but he whipped my head around and placed his other hand at my throat. He squeezed, attempting to force my submission.

I brought my knee up and slammed my heel down onto his foot with all my strength. He yowled, but didn't let me go. The air in my lungs was trapped there, and Dimitri made sure I couldn't get any more oxygen. I struggled—kicking, punching, and clawing. I wouldn't submit. I'd fight until he choked me out rather than tap out.

Lucius clapped. "All right. She's had enough."

Dmitri released me and slapped me hard on the back as I bent over and took in huge gulps of air.

"Sorry, Krasivaya." Dmitri had made clear ever since we started training that he took no joy in hurting me. All the same, the past two months had left me bruised, strained, and exhausted. But I was better, faster. I could escape him, though I wasn't able to take him down. Not yet.

"It's your hair." Lucius ignored my sputtering and walked up behind me. "You may have actually had a chance this time if he wasn't able to grab hold of you so easily." He yanked my ponytail.

I whipped around and threw my leg out, swiping his feet out from under him so he landed on his ass.

"Ow, fuck." He looked up at me with his light blue eyes, irritation and amusement mixing in the quirk of his lips. "Uncalled for."

"Good." Dmitri patted me on the back one more time, his palm slapping on the exposed skin above my sports bra. "But he is correct. Your hair. It is weakness."

"I'll tie it up in a bun. Hell, I'll cut it." I didn't care. Winning was more important than my vanity.

"No way." Lucius got to his feet and brushed the grass off. "Cal loves redheads. It's an asset. Trust me. Besides, I wouldn't like it if you cut it."

"Thanks for your input." I arched an eyebrow at him.

The sun bore down on the back of my neck like a warm weight. Or maybe the vines tattooed there were growing, getting bigger and thornier every day I spent as an Acquisition. "Your approval of my looks is really key for figuring out how to win this fight."

He shook his head. "I think I liked you better when you were scared."

"I think I never liked you." I crossed my arms over my chest and stared him down.

He smirked. "A woman not liking me? Impossible." He stepped closer, almost within my reach. "Besides, I think it's pretty obvious you like me quite a bit."

Dmitri put his hands on his hips. "Leave her alone."

"Fuck off, Russian." Lucius flipped him off without even looking in his direction.

"This isn't helping." I brushed past Lucius and walked to the little water cooler set up under the oak tree. Pouring myself a cup, I sank down onto one of the collapsible chairs and replayed the fight over in my mind. Where had I gone wrong, other than my hairstyle?

"I could take you." Lucius pointed at Dmitri.

"You always say this. You always lose." Dmitri cracked his knuckles.

"Depends on your definition of losing."

"You flat on back like good little bitch."

They circled each other and then tangled, wrestling before separating and doing it again. Like animals butting heads, both too stubborn to back off and call a truce.

It was the same dance the three of us had been doing for the past two months. I trained. Dmitri taught. Lucius played. Sin… I didn't know what Sin did. After the night of his mother's revelations, he spent all his time in town, not even visiting on the one weekend when Teddy came home from school.

Though he maintained his distance, I knew he kept tabs

on me. I could feel it whenever Lucius took a phone call and glanced my way before leaving the room.

It was Sin. Skirting around my periphery, always watching. He'd chased me, caught me, and trapped me in his web. Once I was snared, he ran.

The last time I'd seen him was stuck on repeat in my mind. That night. I shook my head. The last night before he'd left the house for good. I rubbed my upper arms, a chill rushing through me despite the warm breeze.

He was gone, but I haunted his room, sitting on his bed and staring at my paintings. He'd seen every bit of me, all of my weaknesses, my dreams, and my thoughts. Each piece of whatever made up Stella Rousseau was spattered across his walls like blood at a crime scene. I'd seen him too. Knowing there was a splinter of a good man left beneath all his darkness had done me no favors. All was revealed, the masks gone. He still shut me out.

There were no secrets anymore, not from me. I roamed the house as if I belonged in it, as if it were mine. When Lucius was gone on business, which was often, I had the run of the entire estate. A prisoner with the keys to the castle.

The only place I didn't set foot was the third floor. I'd had enough of its occupant for a lifetime. Sin's mother's revelations were freeing, but they were also a cage, one Sin had been living in since being chosen for the Acquisition. Now I could see the bars clearly, examine each one for a weakness.

After the initial shock of what she'd told me, I'd become focused. Sin would win the Acquisition. Teddy would live. I would do everything in my power to protect him. Endure what I had to do and survive. My sacrifice for my father had been made through deceit. The one I'd make for Teddy was of my own choosing. I would fight for it. I would see him live a long, happy life. Then I would set my sights higher. Dismantling the Acquisition was no longer a wish; it was my true goal. The reason I still drew breath.

Dmitri flung his arm out in a vicious jab, catching Lucius in the mouth.

"Fuck." Lucius darted back and spit a wad of blood into the grass. "That's cunt shit."

"Come closer. We see who is cunt." Dmitri lumbered toward Lucius, the men unevenly matched in almost every way possible.

"Hang on." Lucius held up a hand. "It's hot out here."

Dmitri stopped and waited. "I tire of hitting this clown. You ready for another round, Krasivaya?"

"Almost." I sipped the cold water as Lucius unbuttoned his shirt and pulled it off one arm. He began to pull it from his other arm then rushed Dmitri when he was halfway through the motion.

Lucius' trick worked, and Dimitri groaned as the smaller man's fist collided with his ribs.

"*Blyad!* Little prick." Dmitri whirled and thundered after a retreating Lucius.

Lucius tried to spring back, but it was too late, Dmitri tackled him. They fell with a thud and Dmitri pinned him.

"Who is bitch now, eh?" Dmitri grinned and slapped Lucius playfully before squeezing his cheeks.

"Get the fuck off! You're crushing my nuts."

The Russian sat back and got up before offering Lucius his hand.

He took it and stood. "You need to lay off the fucking protein." Lucius craned his head and tried to wipe the stray grass off his naked back.

"Protein make man strong. You too skinny."

Lucius may not have had the larger build of Sin or the hulking Dmitri, but he wasn't a small man by any means.

"Skinny huh? I'll still kick your commie ass. Come on. Let's do this." He put his fists up, his abs and chest glistening with a light sheen of sweat.

"Again, then?" Dmitri shook his head but squared his shoulders.

"Okay, that's enough of a pissing contest." I stood and stretched, my muscles aching. "I need to get back to training."

"She just doesn't want you to get hurt, comrade." Lucius dropped his fists and walked past me, plopping in the chair I'd just vacated.

I pulled the elastic from my hair and wrapped the strands around in a tight ball before re-tightening the band. Once satisfied it wouldn't serve as an easy grip, I walked back out into the sun to take position.

I bent my knees and pulled my hands up. I was too small to win a straight-up brawl, but Dmitri had taught me to grapple and strike just enough to get my enemy into a submission move. Get them to tap out. But first, I had to get close enough. So far, I'd only gotten close enough to Dmitri to get my ass kicked. Bruises colored my legs, and no amount of warm baths and massages could erase the tenderness in my muscles from day after day of training. It was worth it. I had something to fight for. Something I would fight until my last breath to keep safe, as well as something to destroy.

"Ready, Krasivaya?"

"Bring it."

CHAPTER TWO
STELLA

TEDDY DIES. THE WORDS lingered as I woke in a sweat. Like I did most mornings. Another dream—blood on my hands and screams in my ears. I rose from the bed, not content to stay where my fears manifested in my subconscious. Stripping, I walked to the bathroom and climbed into the shower.

The warm water rushed down my body, waking my senses and washing away the terror of the dream. It was always Teddy. His innocent brown eyes staring at me, lifeless. His blood coating my hands, seeping into my white dress from the last trial. I swore I could even taste it, coppery and hot.

I leaned my head against the cool shower tiles, willing the feelings away. Instead of fear, I put resolve in its place. I had a month.

One more month of training. One more month before the spring trial. What would it be? I wasn't sure. All I had to go on was Renee's memories about her year—a physical competition of strength and stamina. She never told me how it ended, only that I needed to be stronger and faster than she had been.

And so I trained. Weights, swimming, running, and sparring. I couldn't guess what Cal had cooked up for this year, but I knew it would be worse than what happened to Renee. Cal always made it worse. I could see why Rebecca had chosen him to reign. He was the perfect Sovereign, cruel and calculating. The system needed a firm hand to rule it, and Cal didn't hesitate to crush anyone who stood in his way.

I finished showering and dressed in what had become my uniform—a sports bra, t-shirt, and gym shorts. Snagging my tennis shoes, I pounded down the stairs to the breakfast room.

Laura served my usual fare of eggs, smoothie, and a flax seed waffle. Dmitri was already seated and powering through an immense pile of sausage. He'd stopped shaving his head since he'd moved in, and his dark hair was finally laying flat. It made him look younger and a little less intimidating. But it didn't matter. I already knew he was a big softy, with or without hair.

Lucius strolled down the hall, his voice carrying as he talked business. "No, I don't give two shits what the distributor charges, the price of sugar doesn't change based on some dipshit middleman. I'll handle it."

He walked into the sunny breakfast room dressed for travel in a navy suit, light blue shirt, and dark tie. His medium brown hair was cut neatly and smoothed back. Professional and suave, he fit perfectly as the business head of the family. Sin was wilder—something in his eyes, or maybe his bearing, gave him away as a threat.

Like water circling a drain, my thoughts always found their way back to Sin.

I shook my head slightly, as if that could erase memory of him, and took a drink of my banana, strawberry, and protein smoothie. "Where you headed?"

"New Orleans for the next few days." He sat across from me and flipped his tie over his shoulder as Laura served him. "Contracts and lawyers and shit. Nothing interesting."

I pointed at him with my fork. "Don't forget Saturday."

"I won't. I'll be back with bells on."

"Bells?" Dmitri stopped mid-chew and drew his thick brows together.

"Just an expression. He means he'll be sure to be here for Teddy's birthday." I reached behind me and felt along my left shoulder, the tenderness bothering me more than when I woke.

"Why don't you go easy today?" Lucius texted with one hand and ate with the other.

I stopped rubbing my shoulder. "Because I can't."

"You haven't had a break since…" He stopped texting and looked up. *Since Sin left.* "You need a break."

"No, I don't. I need to keep getting better. I'm still not strong enough. What if I have to climb, what if I have to swim for hours, what if—"

"Stella." Lucius glanced to Dmitri and went back to texting.

We'd told Dmitri I was training for a triathlon and wanted to throw in some self-defense just to help with coordination. He went along with it, though I often felt he suspected there was more to it, especially when he ran his hands over the scars along my back.

"Just think about it, okay? You can't keep going like this. You're a rubber band that's about to break."

"I'm not going to break. That's the last thing I'll do."

Lucius stopped texting again and caught my eye. "I know the heart inside you believes that, but you're just a person. You're a body, a mass of organs and muscles and whatever the fuck else Teddy studies in school. Your heart may stay strong, but the rest of you—" He let his gaze slide down my body then back to my eyes. "—doesn't have the luxury of whatever it is that drives you. Your body can be broken."

I downed my smoothie and stood, pushing my chair back with a harsh scrape. "I know my limits. Dmitri, you ready?"

He gestured to his half-full plate.

"Fine. I'll get a head start on stretching. Meet me on the porch when you're done." Without giving Lucius another look, I strode through the hall and into the foyer. The chandelier caught the morning sun and sent fractals of light glinting in all directions.

Lucius followed, and it wasn't long before he grabbed my shoulder. I turned, staring up into his sky blue eyes that never seemed to give me any hint of truth.

"What?"

"Why are you doing this?"

"You know why." I swiped his arm off my shoulder.

"No. This isn't for Teddy." He gripped the collar of my t-shirt and pulled it to the side, getting a look at the bruises along my shoulder from sparring. "You don't have to run yourself into the ground."

"Stop." I shrugged him off.

"No." He stepped closer and glared down at me. "You're acting like an idiot."

"Trying to save your brother's life is me acting like an idiot?" I tilted my chin up, giving him nothing but disdain.

His jaw tightened, the sinews in his neck thrown in sharp relief. "That's not what you're doing."

I could have fought him. I didn't. Something about his words disturbed the numbness I'd drawn around myself like a cloak.

He grazed his fingertips up my arm and gripped my chin lightly between his thumb and forefinger. "I know you. I've seen you. I…" He paused and leaned closer. "You aren't mine. It was foolish to think you could ever belong to me. Even so, I don't want you hurt, self-inflicted or otherwise." His gaze bored into me, and he let his hand drop to my waist. "Lay off for a day. Please. That's all I'm asking."

He was pleading with me as if we were equals, as if he had some say in my life other than the simple illusion of ownership.

I fought the urge to slap him, claw him, make him hurt just so his cries could blot out the turmoil that ruled in my mind. "How many times do you think Gavin or Brianne begged 'please' while your friends violated them? Care to hazard a guess?"

He cocked his head. "Is that what this is? Don't blame yourself for all that, Stella. You didn't—"

"Shut up!" I exploded, his words like a match to a barrel of gasoline. "You don't know what we did, what happened. You weren't there. You didn't leave Brianne behind. You didn't send Gavin off alone. You didn't—" My voice cracked and I quieted.

His expression softened and he put his palm to my cheek. "No. I don't know. I wasn't there in the woods. But none of this is your fault."

"Whose is it, then?" I challenged. "Sin's? Your mother's? Whose—"

His phone rang in his pocket. Biting out a curse, he pulled it out and checked the number.

Glad for the reprieve, I sat on the bench by the front door and pulled my shoes on. "I'm training. You can either help or stay out of my way." I tied my laces, not even looking at Lucius as he answered.

"Yeah. Hang on." He turned and strode down the hall to Sin's study. I knew who was on the phone. It was as if I could sense his presence even across the miles separating the two of us.

Dmitri hadn't emerged from the breakfast room yet. I opened the front door and slammed it shut, though I still stood in the foyer. Then I crept down the hall toward the sound of Lucius' voice. The runner quieted my steps, and I eased to the closed study door.

"It's taken care of. I just have to go make a show of negotiating, sign the final contracts, and then I'll be done... No more than two days." His voice quieted, as if he were pacing away from me.

I pressed my ear to the door.

"Fine. Well, not fine. I mean she's training, but she's not being smart. It's like she, like she wants it to hurt. I don't know... Yes. Saturday." His voice grew nearer and I side stepped, hugging the wall.

"Do you think that's wise? I fucking don't." Lucius voice turned darker. "I'm not telling her shit. You need to sack up. I'll put her on the phone right now... Coward. You know what this is going to do, right? You know what Stella will... Fine. I *know* she's yours. Jesus fucking Christ how many times... Yeah, go fuck yourself, too." Something crashed, and then the room fell silent.

I slipped back the way I'd come and quietly left the house.

I swam one more lap, pushing myself until the tips of my fingers and toes tingled. Pulling myself up on the edge of the pool, I took in breath after breath. Dmitri lazily swam in circles, floating on his back and keeping an eye on me.

"Running, you okay. Swimming, you good. Fighting, you worst." He splashed me before flipping under the water so I couldn't retaliate.

I glanced to the clock above the door leading back into the house. It was time to start setting up for Teddy's birthday party. He was a grown man, so it wasn't anything too over-the-top, but a small family to-do was well deserved.

Laura spearheaded the cake, and all I had to do was decorate a little and show up.

Dmitri surfaced and began his leisurely circle again.

I rose and wrapped a towel around me. "I'm going in. You coming?"

"Soon."

"Okay. We're done for the day, but I'll need you in the dining—"

"Yes, yes, Teddy's birthday, Krasivaya. I know. Every woman in house cannot stop talking about that *malchik*."

"He's a good malchik. He deserves a special day. When's your birthday?" I padded around the pool, leaving wet footprints on the grainy concrete.

"Real men no have birthdays."

"Here we go again." I laughed. "We'll continue this later. See you inside. And put on a happy face for the party."

"My face always happy." He frowned.

"Yes, I'm convinced." I pushed through the side door into the house and took the back stairs up to my room.

After a quick shower, I dressed in jeans and a black, flowy blouse. I dried my hair and applied minimal makeup before heading down to the dining room.

My decorations—a simple happy birthday sign and silly party hats—were laid out on a sideboard. I grabbed the sign and, after a trip to the library for tape, I climbed up on a chair and started to hang the sign over the wide windows.

"This seems familiar. Like the first time we met. Though that time you weren't wearing so many pesky clothes."

I glanced over my shoulder at Lucius. "I was standing on the table, not a chair."

He shrugged, his black polo and jeans giving him a casual but put-together air. "Still a nice view, all the same."

"Grab the other side and help." I secured the 'H' to the window casing.

Lucius leaned backed against the table and darted his tongue out to his bottom lip. "I prefer to watch."

"Suit yourself." I dropped to the ground and pushed my chair to the right before climbing back onto it.

"I still have your panties from that morning."

My hand faltered and I missed the 'Y' with the tape. I tried again and got it pinned.

"That's gross." I dropped to the floor and pushed the chair back to the table.

"They smell like you, you know?" He moved around so he stood at my back. "I only had a little taste that night at the cabin, but it was enough... And it wasn't."

I turned, the heat in his eyes impossible to miss as his gaze flickered to my lips. "Lucius, we aren't doing this. I thought I'd already made that clear. I'm done playing this game with you."

"You say that now." He towered over me and ran a finger down my jawline.

Slight tingles rushed through me at his touch. "Stop." I slapped his hand away.

"We'll see. You might have a different answer for me later. I can't wait to hear it." He gave my lips one last look before he turned and walked toward the hall.

I gave Lucius credit for his single-mindedness, but not much more than that.

Laura pushed through the door from the kitchen and carried a two-layer cake to the table.

"That looks amazing." I walked over and helped her center it. It was done in a sky blue, with navy piping, and a white doctor's coat design on the very top.

"You think he'll like it?"

"He'll love it. I just don't know what we're going to do with all the leftovers."

She smoothed down her black maid's uniform. "Well, I was told to make enough for the family and two guests."

"Guests?" I asked.

"Yes. Those were the orders from Mr. Sinclair. I have to get the hors d'oeuvres set out." She retreated to the kitchen.

"No, go. That's fine." I walked to the powder room off the main hallway and ran my fingers through my hair, just to make sure I looked presentable.

After all, company was coming.

CHAPTER THREE
STELLA

THE STEADY RUMBLE OF a motorcycle told me that Teddy had arrived. I peeked out of the music room window and saw his sleek black form cruise down the oak-shrouded lane and into the garage.

"He's here," I called, loud enough for Laura and Farns to hear. Excitement welled up inside me. I hoped Teddy would enjoy his sweet surprise.

Glancing back up the drive, a black limo moved slowly toward the house and parked out in front. Luke, the Vinemont driver, got out and opened the back door. A heeled foot hit the ground, and then Luke helped a woman from the rear of the car as Sin exited the other side and came around.

Curiosity turned to something slimy in my gut the moment Sin's hand touched the small of her back. He led her forward, smiling and gesturing at the house as if he were some sort of salesman. The smile never reached his eyes. His dark gray suit created sharp, masculine lines against his broad shoulders and trim waist, and his dark hair shone in the sun.

The woman was tall and willowy, her long hair

cascading down her back in ebony waves. Her sapphire wrap dress accentuated her long legs. She raised her perfectly arched eyebrows at the house, but had a smile for Sin. He led her up the stairs as another car pulled down the drive, the polished metal glinting in the noonday sun.

Farns walked past me as I stood motionless and unseen in the music room. He opened the door and greeted Sin and his guest with a "welcome." The woman didn't speak, only walked to the center of the foyer and turned her head back and forth, sizing up the elegance in every fine detail.

She swept her gaze into the music room and narrowed her eyes when they met mine. Something about her was familiar. Not her face, in particular, but her eyes. I'd seen them before, though I couldn't place where.

Sin walked up beside her and placed his hand at the small of her back again. He followed her gaze and froze, his eyes locking on mine for a split second before he turned away.

"I believe I saw Teddy riding ahead of us. The dining room is this way. If you'd care to freshen up before the lunch, there's a powder room down and to the left."

"Thank you, Sin." She gave him a kiss on the cheek, shot a scowl in my direction, and strode down the hall, her hips swaying with each step.

The door opened again, and Farns gave a stiffer "welcome" than usual. I'd been so preoccupied with Sin and the woman that I'd forgotten about the other car.

A man strode forward, his hand extended. Sin shook, and my breath caught. It was Cal Oakman. I remained still and forced the surge of hate and rage just seeing him brought to the surface back down inside. It wasn't time yet. Not until Teddy was safe.

"Sophia is freshening up. Shall we go in?" Sin kept his eyes on Cal.

"Sure." He followed Sin down the hall. "I don't believe I've been here in, what is it, ten years or so? Still looks the same."

"We try to keep it up as best we can."

"Well, not everywhere can be the Oakman Estate, especially given your family's late arrival to the game. Still, it could be worse. You seem to have…"

Their voices faded. I was trapped in ice. The joy at Teddy's birthday party had been quickly erased by unease. What was going on? Was this another test?

Lucius came down the stairs and turned toward the dining room.

"Lucius," I hissed.

He changed course and walked to me, his face inscrutable.

"What's happening?"

"A birthday party. You set it up, remember?" He took my elbow and pulled me along with him into the foyer.

"Why is Cal here?"

"The Sovereign can't attend birthday parties?"

I stopped at the foot of the stairs, forcing him to stop with me. "Stop playing games. Tell me."

He lowered his voice. "I just did. Cal wanted to attend Teddy's birthday party."

"The woman?"

He couldn't hide his smirk, not that he would ever try. "That's Sophia, Sin's date for the lunch."

My fingers grew cold, the tips of my ears hot as I digested the information. It was a punch in the gut. It shouldn't have been. I had no claim on Sin. The entire rulebook these people lived by had as its first and foremost tenet that certain people—like me—were nothing more than chattel. Was she the reason he stayed away?

Our last night together was seared in my memory, but perhaps I had mistaken Sin's words, his touch, for more than they really were. The thought rang hollow and false. I knew he meant all of it, that he'd given me everything he had. That knowledge was the only thing that had stopped me from seeking him out during his long absence. I trusted him. But he was here with another woman—one who gave me an unsettling sense of familiarity.

"Why didn't you tell me earlier?" I glared at him and let the hurt ferment into anger.

He shrugged and snaked his arm around my waist. "I figured it was best for you to see for yourself."

"This changes nothing between us." I stepped away from him and eyed the stairs. A retreat seemed like a good idea. Then again, Teddy was more important than any of it.

"We'll see. Come on. Cal will want to get a look at you." He took my hand and pulled me with him down the hallway. "And don't forget what I did to you in the woods."

I closed my eyes and tried to stop the murky thoughts—the ones that lived in my nightmares—from rising up and taking my sanity away. The woods, the cabin, the screams. Brianne's and Gavin's rapes, and my supposed violation by Lucius. He dropped my hand as we entered the room.

"Stella, so nice to see you again." Cal grinned and walked over, embracing me and running his hands down my back. My skin crawled, and I fought the nausea that rolled through me.

Sin was engaged in a conversation with Sophia and didn't even look in my direction.

"I'm still sad I missed out on you at the last trial. Maybe I'll have to arrange a little in-between treat." Cal whispered in my ear before releasing me.

The kitchen door opened and a grinning Teddy walked in, his cheeks rosy, and Laura in step right behind him. The smile died on his lips when he saw Cal.

"Happy birthday, young man." Cal skirted the table and shook Teddy's hand.

Forcing the smile to return to his face, Teddy said, "I didn't know you'd be coming, Sovereign. It's an honor."

"Whoa, look at the manners on this one." Cal laughed and slapped Laura on the ass as she passed with a serving dish.

Teddy balled his fists but did nothing.

"Sophia, how are you doing these days?" Lucius smiled easily and poured himself a drink at the sideboard.

"Same old, same old, really." Her voice was low and husky. I'd heard it before. A memory darted along the edges of my mind, but it was gone before I could grasp it.

"Jet-setting as much as you used to?"

"No." She tossed her hair over her shoulder. It looked effortless enough to be completely calculated. "Daddy didn't like me spending so much time away. So, I've been assigned to the New Orleans office. I still manage to get in a trip to Europe every couple of months, and of course, I spend a great deal of time in New York with Mother."

Lucius sipped his drink. "We're glad to have you here for Teddy's celebration."

"I wouldn't miss it." She scanned my decorations and the cake, her mouth turned down in distaste. "How quaint."

Laura bustled back in with the final dish and backed away from the table to wait.

"Shall we?" Sin motioned for everyone to sit.

Cal took the head of the table as if it were his house. Sophia stood at his side and waited for Farns to pull her chair out before sitting down. Then Sin sat to her right. I followed Lucius and sat between him and Teddy, still trying to get my bearings on what was happening.

"You seem to have recovered well, Stella." Cal lay his napkin in his lap as Laura began serving.

"Have I?"

Lucius gripped my knee.

"Yes, you don't look quite as fresh-faced as you were at the ball, of course, but you are holding up."

I darted my eyes to Sin. He ignored me and whispered something into Sophia's ear. They were close, their body language telling me that they knew each other far better than just as friends—the way their shoulders touched, how he nuzzled into her dark hair, and the way she smiled at his every word.

"She's been a bit more pliant since Christmas, I can tell you that." Lucius slung his arm around the back of my chair.

"What happened at Christmas?" Teddy asked, his voice quiet and his gaze fixed forward.

"You haven't told him about the fun?" Cal tsked and took a drink of wine. "That doesn't seem very fair."

"I tire of Acquisition talk," Sophia said. "And frankly, I'm not certain why this one is allowed to eat with us." She waved her hand at me. "I mean, really, are we going to have the hunting dogs at the table with us next?"

I held my tongue. Not for my sake, but for Teddy's.

Sin laughed, his booming amusement like a knife twisting in my back. "We simply thought the Sovereign might enjoy a look at Stella."

"If you tell a redhead joke, so help me—" She leaned in and kissed Sin, their lips meeting and taking my breath away. It was obvious this wasn't the first time.

They were together. My mouth went dry as she gave him another peck and pulled away.

Cal sighed. "Fine, darling, if it's going to bother you that much, we'll send her out."

"Thank you, Daddy."

Daddy. It all clicked into place. Sophia was Cal's daughter.

"Stella will take lunch in her room. Thank you, Laura." Lucius kicked my foot.

I stood and squeezed Teddy's shoulder before walking from the room. He needed to stay silent, to sit through the meal and pretend to be one of them. Despite his goodness, he had to know that a certain level of acting was necessary just to survive in the world of Sovereigns and Acquisitions.

Just as I reached the door, Sophia called, "How's your arm?"

I turned to her, confusion and déjà vu mixing like a

molotov cocktail in my memory. "What?"

Sin draped his arm across her shoulders and pulled her closer, dropping a kiss in her hair.

She laughed, as if I were behaving like a silly child. "Your arm. Don't you remember?"

"That was you." She'd been disguised by a mask at the Christmas trial, but I recognized her voice and eyes. When I'd tried to dress for the cold and give Brianne my sweater, Sophia had hit me with a black baton. It took a month for the bruise to heal, for the bone to feel strong again.

"That was me. Too bad I didn't break it." She leaned back into Sin, her dark eyes sparkling with malice. "Now get out of here before looking at you puts me off my lunch."

CHAPTER FOUR
SINCLAIR

Three months earlier

"IF HE LOSES THE Acquisition, Sin has to kill Teddy?" Stella's weak voice floated down the hall.

My steady steps turned into a sprint until I was at my mother's open door.

"Teddy dies." Rebecca's voice, wizened and brittle like a fallen leaf, cut through the air.

Panic sliced my heart when I saw Stella standing at the mouth of hell, her skin pale, her eyes wide.

"Stella!" I rushed to her.

"I see no harm in telling the peasant girl the rules." Mother smiled, hate in every wrinkle, every line.

"Tell me. Tell me all of them." Stella stared up at me, her green eyes watering, though not a single tear fell. "I have to know." She gripped my arms, holding me tight and pinning me to the spot with the anguish in her voice.

"Tell her, son. Tell her." My mother's gleeful cackle was too much to bear.

I wrenched myself free of Stella's hold and went to the medicine cabinet. *Locked.* I gripped the handles and yanked, pulling until the wood splintered and the doors flew open. Grabbing a syringe, I turned and approached the demon on the bed.

"Please don't." Renee cried, but didn't rise to stop me.

"No." Mother tried to scoot away, fear darkening her wild eyes.

I grabbed her arm and pulled it straight. She slapped me and scratched my neck. I ignored it, just like I ignored every bit of pain she'd caused since that hellish night in Brazil. Even as she struggled and screamed, I hit her vein and depressed the plunger.

Her motions slowed, her words ceasing, and then she collapsed back into the bed, finally asleep. Finally silent.

Renee shoved me aside and sank down on the bed, stroking Mother's face and crying. "How could you?"

"It needed to be done." I tried to clear my head, to douse the fire of emotions that raged inside. I usually had an easy time of it. Not now. Not when my mother had seen fit to shove Stella into the same razorblade straightjacket I wore.

Renee smoothed Mother's hair, doting on her as if the woman were anything other than a venomous snake. "She was fine. She wasn't hurting anyone."

I threw the syringe in the garbage and looked at Stella, her eyes haunted.

"She's hurt plenty." I took Stella's hand and pulled her from the room. She didn't resist, shock settling on her like a lead weight.

I took her to my room and locked the door behind us. She sat on the bed and leaned over, her head cupped in her hands.

"Stella?" I knelt in front of her.

"Why Teddy? Why? He's the only good thing in this house, in this entire godforsaken family." She shook her head and still wouldn't look at me.

I pulled her hands from her face. They were soft, so easily broken. But nothing about her was in pieces, not shattered the way I was.

"The rules. It's what makes us compete. It turns us against ourselves until the strongest comes out on top." That was the explanation, but not the reason. Was there any reason for this torment other than providing entertainment for the depraved lot of us?

"Why didn't you tell me?" A tear rolled down her cheek and hovered at her jaw line before dropping onto my scarred wrist.

"Power. If you'd known that from the start, you would have had the upper hand. Teddy is the heart of this family. You didn't know that when you arrived. You could have used that information against us."

"But after? When you knew how much I cared for him?"

"I didn't tell you for the same reason I didn't tell Lucius." I grazed my thumb along her cheek, wiping her tears—the ones I'd caused—away. "How do you feel now that you know? Stronger? Better?" I shook my head. "You are weaker. It's meant to be a spear in my side, as the Acquirer, to know what will happen if I lose. By the time you'd come to care for Teddy, I realized telling you would give you the same pain, the same weight, the same fucking dread that's crushing me."

She put her warm palm to my cheek. I pressed into it, needing so much more from her than I could even admit to myself.

"You've had to bear it alone."

The pity in her eyes, pity for me, almost broke what little of a heart I had left. "I've done what I had to do. I've been the man I had to be. I can't lose Teddy. But you... You were the best choice and also the worst for my Acquisition. If I'd only known..."

"What?" She edged off the bed and sank to the floor in front of me, her body pressing against me and her mouth tantalizingly close. "If you'd known what?"

I couldn't help myself. She was my weakness, my

downfall. Everything about her was my undoing. I pulled her to me, her scent of vanilla and lavender filling my nose as her very essence filled my soul.

I stared into her green eyes. Her heart was laid bare, though she'd never spoken the words to me. I'd acquired her, but she owned me. "If I'd known I'd fall in love with you." I kissed her, needing her past all reason.

She opened her mouth, and I slanted over her, punishing her sweet lips with my rough kiss. She was mine. I couldn't give her up. I needed her raw and wild, rough and passionate. Grabbing a fistful of hair, I pulled her head back and bit her neck like a savage leaving his mark.

She clutched at my shirt. I hated the feel of fabric between us. I needed her satin skin, her hot, wet cunt. I needed to bury myself in her and forget everything else except her taste, her breath, her life.

I pulled my shirt off and yanked her to her feet before shoving her down on the bed. "Strip. Now."

I unbuckled my belt and slid the leather between my fingers. It spoke to me, told me to punish her. But I couldn't wait, couldn't stop myself from having her. Not this time.

She bit her lip, her eyes half-lidded. I kicked my jeans and shorts away as she pulled her pants and her panties off.

"On your back, head on the pillow, and spread your legs wide." I gripped my shaft until it almost hurt, and stroked slowly as she lay back and spread. Her pink pussy glistened, wetness there for me.

She was perfect, her skin luminous and her breaths coming in shallow pants. I wanted to hurt her, but not just that. I knew she would take some of my pain and turn it into her own pleasure.

"Touch your pussy."

She kept her eyes on mine as she reached down and slid her fingertips across her slick clit. My cock leaked at the sight and I slowed my strokes, needing to be inside her.

"Tell me who you think about when you touch yourself."

She swirled her fingers around the tight little nub. I wanted to bite it.

"You," she breathed.

"Finger yourself. Two fingers."

She slid her fingers between her folds and sank them inside, her hips rising from the bed as she did it.

I dropped to my knees and moved between her thighs. Her soft moans echoed through my mind until I seethed with need. "What do I do to you?"

She bit her lip and pulsed her fingers in and out. Watching was torture, but I had to feel the sting before the pleasure. She would, too.

"You push me down and take me rough."

The words were like a lash at my back, driving me closer to her. "What else?"

"Y-you hurt me." The words were barely a whisper.

The animal that clawed at the inside of my chest howled at her admission. I gripped her wrist and pulled her fingers away. I licked them, savoring her taste.

"Grip the headboard." I devoured every inch of her skin with my gaze, searing her pale flesh into my memory.

Her hands wrapped around the antique wood, and I ran my palm from her chest to her pussy. I hovered my hand over her heat, never breaking eye contact. Then I drew back and slapped her wet folds.

She moaned and tried to close her legs. I wrenched them apart and slapped her again.

"Sin."

"Fuck, yes. Say it again." I licked her wetness off my palm and sank two fingers inside her.

"Sin!" She writhed, her back arching, her hips pushing down onto my fingers as I roughly pushed in and out. Her tits shook as I leaned over her, bracing myself with one arm while using the other to finger fuck her.

"This? Do I do this to you in your fantasies, Stella?"

"Sin, please. Don't stop."

The heel of my palm slapped into her clit again and again, and I leaned down and pinned one of her hard nipples between my teeth.

She moaned, low and long, and spread her legs even farther. I sped my pace and she froze, her hips seizing as her pussy clamped down on my fingers. I withdrew and slammed my cock into her as she writhed beneath me, her orgasm squeezing me as I started a pounding rhythm.

Her throat; I had to take it. I wrapped my fingers around her neck, her life, and squeezed. I lowered myself to my elbow and gripped her hair so she had nowhere to go, nowhere to look but into my eyes as she rode the wave of her pleasure.

I shoved into her, jarring the bed with how much I needed to mark her as my own. She needed to feel me for days, to wear my bruises on her thighs. She didn't look away, didn't try to move her hands from the headboard. Even as I stole her breath and refused to give it back.

"Sin." A strangled whisper from her lips that turned me into a demon. Because I needed to hear it again. I needed my name always on her mind, on her tongue.

I released the pressure at her neck and she gasped, but I stole her breath again by kissing her hard and biting her bottom lip until I drew blood. She moaned and opened her mouth, the coppery taste mixing with her sweetness as I took everything from her.

Her blood was honey on my tongue, and her pussy heaven on my cock. I was never free, not until I was here with her. Just the two of us. Just her locked in a cage with the beast who lived inside me. She was unafraid. Even from the start, from the moment I'd seen her, she had been a piece of steel that I railed on, beat, and tried to break. She would never break. Instead, I'd shattered against her like glass against a stone.

Her tongue snaked inside my mouth, and I wrapped

my arm under her back. I wanted to feel every bit of her skin I could, to meld her into me until we were one—my darkest elements wrapped in her light.

"Touch me." I growled against her lips and moved to her neck. She obeyed, her nails streaking down my back, the pain heightening the pulse in my cock.

I thrust into her and stayed there, pushing against her deepest parts as I rocked my hips. She clawed my ass as I bit her shoulder, sinking my teeth in until I almost broke the skin. Pushing my hand between us, I stroked her clit with my thumb as I thrust deep.

"Come for me. I need to feel you." I dragged my teeth up her throat and rested my forehead against hers. "Give me all of you."

We panted, our breaths mingling as we surged into each other. Her body tightened and my cock thickened even more.

"I'm there. I-I'm coming."

"Say it, Stella." I shoved harder into her as her walls clamped down. "You know what I want."

"Sin. I'm yours." She repeated my name.

The sound was the richest aphrodisiac, one that sent my hips into a frenzy as I came, my release ripping through me as I shot deep inside her. I grunted as she moaned, her pussy still spasming as I emptied everything I had into her, coating her with me.

Her lips were swollen, the bottom one red and angry from my bite. I grazed my mouth across hers gently, the need to hurt her momentarily extinguished. I let go of her hair and put my palm to her cheek. She answered by wrapping her arms around my neck and pulling me into a possessive kiss. Her tongue sought and took, and I was more than willing to give. I'd already given her everything.

I pulled away so she could take a breath. So much emotion flitted across her eyes, but mostly the one that spoke to my soul. The small flame of something I'd tried to stamp out, to destroy. Somehow, it burned still. For me.

"I love you, Sin."

Her words were a balm and a barb. Just as she had always been both.

I slid out of her, hating the loss of her tight warmth. I dropped onto the bed next to her and pulled her to my chest. She lay her head over my heart. Could she feel my fear in its rapid beat?

I had to stop it all. To bottle my feelings back up and stow them away. Was it even possible anymore? "I have to do things, Stella. I have to hurt you. The spring trial."

"I know." She said it as if it were simple, as if me harming her were as normal as the sun shining or the breeze blowing. "And now I know why."

"I have to win."

"Yes." She nodded against me. "*We* have to win."

I clenched my eyes shut. "You don't understand."

"I do." She craned her head back to look me in the eye. "I will do anything to keep Teddy safe. Just tell me what to do. Tell me about the trial. Give me the rules. All of them."

"They won't help."

"Then what will it hurt? Tell me." She pushed away from me and sat back, pulling the sheet to her neck.

I wanted to yank her back down and cover her body with mine, but I stayed my hand.

Her jaw was set and she cocked her head slightly to the left. I knew the look—it meant she wasn't going to relent, no matter what I said or did. Her stubbornness was beyond even my comprehension.

I took a deep breath and let out a shuddering exhale. "The trial has to do with some sort of physical contest. I believe Cal's year was an obstacle course that turned into a grueling competition for the Acquisitions."

She nodded against me. "I can train for that. I'll start tomorrow. Do we know anything else?"

We. The word was so small, but nothing had ever held more meaning for me. "Red told me at Cal's party that the competition is to be held at Fort LaRoux."

"Hmm, that's familiar." She quirked her lips as she thought. "I think I know which one you mean. I thought it was abandoned to the state as some sort of historical site."

I laughed, the sound hollow. "The governor has no problem allowing use of government lands for this little game. He'll likely be standing at Cal's right hand."

"Does it mean anything? I mean, the location—what does it tell us?"

"Yes, it means something. The terrain isn't made for any sort of obstacle course. It's more suited as an arena, the battlements serving as seating for the open center area."

"You think they'll have us fight each other?" She lay back down and snuggled in closer to my side.

"Maybe. Or it could be some series of tests or feats the audience could watch. I don't have enough information." And wasn't that always the fucking problem? Cal had obscured this year's trials more so than any in the past.

"And why would Red tell you any of this?"

"He thinks I'm the frontrunner." I shook my head. "He thinks if he helps me, I'll save his sister when I become Sovereign."

"Will you?" Her voice quieted even more.

"No. Not if it means I put my family in danger. The rules are quite clear on the penalty for losing, and I won't risk any challengers to my reign. I'll take her life to spare mine, Teddy's, or yours."

"How old is she?"

Eighteen years, six months, and seventeen days. I knew the length of her life as well as that of Eagleton's younger brother, Carl. Counting down the days to their deaths was the only way I knew to accept the inevitable—I would see them dead by their siblings' hands or my own. "It doesn't matter."

"Please, how old?" She rested her hand on my chest, her delicate fingers pulling the information from me bit by bit.

"Eighteen."

"Jesus." She buried her face in my neck, and I pulled her to me. "You can't kill her. She's so young—"

"I will. For Teddy. For you. I will. I'd kill her ten times over."

She pressed her fingers to my lips and looked at me with troubled eyes. "Don't say that. Please don't say that. You can't. We'll think of something, some way out."

Her fingers stilled my lips but not my thoughts. *There is no way out.*

She lay back against me and dropped her hand to my chest. "Now the rules. I need them all."

She already knew the worst. The rest just completed the depraved puzzle. "First rule." I swallowed hard. "Is Teddy. Second rule, you know as well—the Acquisition can choose between first and second born. Third, an Acquirer may not harm an opposing Acquisition except during trials."

She nodded. "That's why Renee told me I would be safe the night we went to the party at Cal's."

"Yes. Fourth is that maiming an Acquisition or permanent loss of limb is not allowed."

"That's comforting."

"Fifth, we can't kill you."

"Even better."

"Sixth, the current Sovereign is the sole vote on who becomes the next Sovereign."

"Renee mentioned that. Cal wields all the power."

"And now that he's brought in your stepmother's family, he's solidified his stranglehold on the power structure. He'll only choose someone he trusts to keep him at the top."

"Makes sense." A shadow fell across her eyes. "He's our target, the one we're trying to convince."

"Yes, but a large part of that is putting on a show for the rest of them. We have to make it look good. Keep them entertained."

She sighed. "So what's the seventh?"

I glanced to the ceiling, as if I could see through it to my mother's suite. I hadn't known the seventh rule until after I'd been chosen. That particular cut of the knife was a master stroke by my mother. As chaotic as her mind was, there were still plenty of sharp edges.

"Sin?" Stella asked again.

"The seventh is that the previous Sovereign, not the current Sovereign, chooses the competitors."

She jolted, as if she'd touched a live wire. "You mean your *mother* chose you to compete?"

The weight of my mother's legacy crushed both of us, leaving nothing but destruction in its wake. "She did."

CHAPTER FIVE
Stella

"Who is woman?" Dmitri sank onto my bed, the antique wood groaning under his weight.

"Sophia."

"Why so rude? I go to party. She say I don't belong."

I reached over and patted him on the back. "Same here."

"*Pizda.*" He shook his head. "And why she with Sinclair?"

I tried to brush away my feelings, like crumbs off the bedspread. "I assume they are together. Like a couple." The crumbs were still there, grinding into my skin no matter which way I turned.

"Foolish man." He glanced at me, his scowl deep. "Now I all dressed up. No party. No nothing." He lay back on my bed and laced his fingers together over his chest. "We should train, eh?"

I lay next to him, and we both stared at the ceiling fan's lazy circle. "Yeah."

Neither of us moved. My body was tired, sore, and losing an afternoon of training was beginning to look like not such a bad thing. My thoughts strayed back to Sophia.

She'd taken such pleasure in hurting me at the last trial, and now seemed to delight even more in rubbing it in my face. She and her father topped my list of people I would seek vengeance on once Teddy was safe.

After a few quiet minutes, Dmitri began to snore, softly at first, and then growing louder over the span of half an hour until I began to fantasize about smothering him with a pillow. A bump at the door had him awake and on his feet in a second.

"Who?"

"Just me." Teddy's voice. "Can you get the door? My hands are full."

Dmitri opened it for him, and Teddy entered carrying a large plate full of cake, another large plate full of sandwiches and some silverware, and a bottle of wine with red cups under his arm.

"This pleases me." Dmitri grinned and closed the door as Teddy laid the food out on the bed.

"This is a feast." I hugged Teddy as soon as his hands were empty and kissed him on the cheek. "Happy birthday."

"Thanks." He squeezed me tightly and then shook Dmitri's hand.

"Happy birthday." Dmitri pulled him in for a bear hug.

Teddy laughed and escaped. Then his face grew somber. "I'm sorry about downstairs."

"Don't worry about it. I know it's not you."

"No." He ran a hand through his unruly blond locks. "It's not, and I really didn't appreciate them showing up here like that. They're not the ones I want to spend time with."

"Have they gone?" I eyed the croissant sandwiches, and Dmitri's stomach rumbled.

"Yes. Well, Sin's still here. He's staying for the weekend." Teddy pulled the loosened cork from the wine bottle and poured us each a cup of red. "Dig in. I'm hungry, too. Cal and Sophia turn my stomach, so I didn't eat much."

We settled around the platters, Dmitri eating two sandwiches in one go.

"Anything important discussed while we were hiding up here?" I tried to make it sound as nonchalant as possible.

Teddy wasn't fooled. "No. I didn't get any information. You're the one who knows things. I'm in the dark." He put his sandwich down. "I wish you'd tell me."

I shot a look to Dmitri and back to Teddy. "You already know I'm training for the triathlon in the spring. I don't know what it will entail, exactly. So, we're on the same page."

"What else?"

"Like what?"

"How many more—" He glanced to Dmitri, who seemed to remain oblivious while munching away. "—*competitions* are there?"

"After this triathlon, only one more in late summer." I took a bite of sandwich despite the tightness in my throat. I wouldn't tell him everything, just enough to keep him even-keeled for the time being.

"That's it? Then you're done? Win or lose?"

I nodded and forced myself to chew. "Right. Win or lose, I'm done."

"That's more than anyone else tells me." He nodded and sat back. "Thank you."

"You're welcome."

I changed the subject to his time at college, and Teddy lapsed into how excited he was to start med school.

"When you doctor, you prescribe medications?" Dmitri asked and forked a chunk of cake into his mouth.

"Yes, that's part of it."

"Hard stuff?"

Teddy cocked his head. "Narcotics, you mean? Yes."

"I have friends. You make good money. All you have to do is—"

I stood and clapped my hands. "Well, I think I'm stuffed. Since they're gone, want to go downstairs? Maybe go outside and let me show you my skills?" I brought my fists up.

"You're kidding, right?" Teddy laughed.

"She no kidding." Dmitri puffed his chest out. "She taught by best fighter in all Russia."

"Well, hell." Teddy downed his wine. "On that note, let's do it."

Dmitri laughed as we walked into the hall and down to the front door.

"Your ass is going to be on the grass, pretty boy." I punched him in the shoulder.

"Ow." He grabbed his arm as we strolled out into the sunny yard, then dropped his hand and rolled his shoulders. "Just kidding. I didn't feel a thing." He grinned and pulled his hands up, palms open. "Come at me, bro."

I rounded up my hair into a ponytail and tied it with an elastic from my pocket. "I didn't realize you wanted an ass-whipping for your birthday."

He smiled bigger, getting into tough-guy character. "I hate to hit a girl, even one with a mouth like yours."

"Don't worry. You won't." I easily moved away from his first swiping grab.

"Can't catch me that way." I circled him, my knees bent and my hands up.

He darted toward me. I ducked and shot my foot out, tripping him. He hit the grass and rolled from his momentum.

"Damn." He laughed and got to his feet, slivers of grass hanging from his otherwise neat button-down shirt and jeans. "Slippery. You come get me instead."

"Okay." I advanced.

He backed away a step and barreled into me, tackling me to the ground. I landed on my back, him on top. He sat on my hips and put a hand on each side of my head, smiling and proud of himself. I held my arms out and he fell into them for a friendly embrace.

"A hug for the victor."

"Don't feel bad. I'm pretty strong." He returned my squeeze.

I slung my right arm over his shoulder, linked my hands, and shoved up from the ground with my left leg. He cried out in surprise as I flipped him and wrapped both hands around his throat.

"Yes! Krasivaya, yes!" Dmitri walked to us and towered overhead. "Now, Teddy. You must get free. Knock her off."

"Well." Teddy grabbed my wrists. "I wouldn't want to hurt her."

"Pussy." I grinned down at him.

He wrenched my hands from his throat and wrapped an arm around my neck, pulling me down into a submission move so my head was trapped between his torso, his arm, and the ground.

"Oh. No, Teddy." Dmitri laughed.

"What? I got her."

"Look down, comrade."

My hand was snugged in his crotch ready to squeeze as hard as I could to get out of the hold.

Teddy let me go. "Oh, fuck no."

"That's why you got a warning." I kissed the tip of his nose and got up, offering him my hand.

Teddy pulled himself to his feet. "You weren't kidding about the training."

"No. She fighter now."

"Let's test that theory, shall we?" Sin's voice whipped around my heart like a lasso, constricting and pulling at the same time. No longer dressed in a suit, he wore jeans and a dark t-shirt.

He studied me as if he were ticking off a list against his memory of how I looked the last time he'd seen me.

I balled my fists. He thought he could parade Sophia Oakman in front of me and treat me like the dirt under his shoe. And now he was taunting me?

"You game?" His eyes challenged me as much as his tone.

I was more than ready to hurt him any way I could. I met his dark gaze.

"Let's do this."

CHAPTER SIX
Stella

"You sure you want to fight me?" I re-tightened my hair in the bun, taking my time as I tried to figure out how to best him.

"I want to take you down." He gave a predatory smile as his gaze raked my body again.

"You no hurt her." Dmitri stabbed a finger at Sin.

"But she likes it when I hurt her." Sin smiled.

Dmitri glowered and stepped toward him.

I put my palm to Dmitri's chest. "I can handle him. Go on inside. This won't take long."

Dmitri mumbled some curses in Russian. "Come, Teddy. Let's eat more cake."

"Go easy on him. He's not as tough as I am." Teddy swiped the rest of the grass off his shirt.

"Come. Come." Dmitri led him away as Sin circled me, sizing me up.

Teddy threw a worried glance over his shoulder as Dmitri herded him into the house.

"Why was Sophia here?" Of so many questions that bounced around my mind, the pettiest one came out first.

"Because she was my date for Teddy's party." He

dashed toward me.

I backed up, trying to time what his moves would be.

"Nice decorations, by the way." He smirked and circled me slowly, like a bird of prey.

I wouldn't wait for him to come to me. I rushed him and gripped his shoulders, throwing my weight forward and swinging my legs up. It would have been the perfect take down if he hadn't seen the move coming and twisted so I couldn't maneuver my legs around his neck.

He held me for a moment before taking me to the ground, his heavy wait crushing me as he knocked the wind from my lungs. The sun was high overhead, and I remembered this. I remembered the first day when I'd run for freedom but found only him.

Not this time. I wrapped him in my arms and did the same move on him as Teddy. Though Sin was bigger, he flipped just the same until I was straddling him, my hands at his throat. I pressed hard, far harder than I'd done with Teddy.

Sin didn't fight back, only slid his hands up my thighs.

"Where have you been?"

"Wooing Ms. Sophia Oakman." His voice was terse, the words barely passing my palms.

"Do you love her?"

His hands roved higher until they were at my waist. He pulled me down onto him, rubbing me back and forth against the hardening length in his pants. "No. Just courting an alliance, something like a business arrangement."

I eased my grip as he kept rocking my hips against him. "Are you dating her to help us win?"

"You're getting smarter the longer you stay with us, Stella. I applaud your love for learning, even at this late juncture."

I slapped him hard across the cheek and he growled before flipping me and pinning my hands next to my head.

"Asshole." Tears stung my eyes as he stared down at

me, his brows drawn together. "You didn't have to stay away. You could have said something. You just left."

"No. I did what you needed me to do. You've been here, training every day and getting stronger and better. I would be a distraction. I already am, and I've only been back for a few hours. My time was better spent away, trying to catch Sophia's eye, and your time was better spent here with that fuckwad Dmitri." His jaw tightened. "Has he touched you?"

I laughed, the sound maniacal. "Yes. Every day. We spar and swim, and he gives me a massage."

"You know what I mean." He leaned closer, his sapphire eyes becoming my whole world. "I will kill him with my bare hands if he's tried anything."

I glared at him. "You show up here with that psychotic bitch on your arm, treat me like I'm beneath you, and then have the nerve to ask me if I'm fucking one of my only friends?"

"I have more nerve than that. I want to fuck you, and I have half a mind to strip you right now, flip you on your stomach, and punish you until you scream. So, answer my question. Has he touched you?"

"You wouldn't dare!" Heat rushed through me at his threat. Because I was fucked up. Because I wanted him to want me. Because he was all I could think about—his face, his body, his scent, his twisted mind.

"Wouldn't I?" He got to his knees and pulled me up before throwing me over his shoulder.

"What the fuck are you doing?" I beat at his back as he got to his feet and headed away from the house and toward the oaks that lined the driveway.

He ran his hand up my thigh and pressed hard against my pussy. "Hot and wet, just like I thought."

"Put me down."

"I will." He strode into the shade of the oaks and pushed me up against one of them. The oak's wide trunk hid us from the house.

I pressed my palm against his chest. "I'm not—"

He kissed me, pinning me between his chest and the tree. His hands roved me, and before long, he had one up my shirt, palming my breast through my bra. I dug my nails into his chest, but he only leaned in harder, as if he wanted my violence.

He ripped up my bra, exposing both breasts, and groaned into my mouth as he squeezed them. My knees went weak at his touch. Every thought of anger or hatred burned away as he consumed me as surely as fire does black powder. Breaking our kiss, he whipped me around to face the tree.

"Pull your pants down or I'll do it myself."

I glanced over my shoulder as he unfastened his belt. He ripped the elastic from my hair and tossed it aside.

"Do it, Stella." He growled and slapped my ass.

I fumbled with my button and unzipped my pants. He did the rest, ripping them down my legs to my knees.

He pressed his palm flat to my back, bending me over as I braced against the trunk. In one harsh movement, he entered me, his cock embedded deep as I moaned.

"Give it to me." He thrusted hard and slapped my ass, the sting mixing with the pleasure until I was panting, my pussy slick and wanting. "This is how you like it, isn't it?" He gripped my hair and pulled me to him, walking me forward until my breasts pressed against the bark as he fucked me in punishing strokes. His lips blazed a hot trail down my neck as he cupped my breast. "Tell me."

"Yes." I craned my head back and kissed him, his tongue darting in and setting the same pace as his cock.

"Touch yourself." He pushed me harder into the tree, the bark scraping against my nipples.

I ran my fingers down my stomach and rubbed them against my clit. He kissed my neck, sucking my skin between his teeth and biting down, his hand still tangled in my hair. I moved lower, brushing my fingertips along his cock as it surged inside me.

"Fuck." He groaned and squeezed my nipple, twisting it between his thumb and index finger and pressing me into the tree. "This is all I could think about. Every day. Every night. Every time I closed my eyes. You." As if the admission made him angry, he bit my shoulder.

My body was drawing into itself, the pressure sweet and tense between my thighs. I stroked my clit to his harsh pace. He maintained the bite on my shoulder, like an animal in heat, a wolf pouncing on its mate.

"Give me your fingers."

I pulled them away and lifted them over my shoulder. He sucked them into his mouth, his tongue licking them clean as he groaned and pounded me harder. My body was strung tight, his tongue on my fingers kicking my heat up a notch.

Once satisfied, he released them. "I want you to come on my cock."

I snaked my fingers back down and rubbed my swollen nub. He sank his teeth into my shoulder again and fucked me roughly as I cried out and scraped against the tree. My pussy constricted and my hips tensed.

The tiny explosions grew inside me until I couldn't stop the cresting wave.

"Sin!" My body shuddered as I came, and my mind went completely blank.

He growled into my skin and slammed inside me, staying deep as his cock kicked and shot in strong spurts. I let my hand fall and leaned my head against the tree. He grunted and thrust one more time before kissing the vicious bite mark that would surely bruise.

"I needed that. You. I needed you." He rested his forehead against my shoulder and steadied his breathing.

I turned to him. "I needed you, too."

He kissed me softly, his lips a gentle melody instead of the crashing crescendo of a few moments earlier.

"Stella?" Dmitri's voice drifted on the warm air.

"Shit." I pushed back against Sin.

He didn't move, just shoved his hips forward, his half-mast cock sending a tingle through me.

"Krasivaya? We train?" His voice sounded closer.

"Sin, he's going to see. Get off."

"I already got off once. I'd like to do it again." He smoothed a hand down my stomach and rubbed my too-sensitive clit.

"No." I jerked at his touch.

"I like it when you fight." His voice was a low rasp.

"You haven't seen me fight. Not yet." I tried to buck him, but it only pushed him in deeper.

He grunted and pulled my hair, still thrusting his cock slowly inside me. "You'll have to do better than that."

"Krasivaya?" Dmitri was close and getting closer.

Panic rose right along with my embarrassment at the thought of getting caught.

"Fight some more. Come on. You know I enjoy it." Sin's voice in my ear was hell, his mastery of my body, heaven.

"You asked for it." I reached over my head and grabbed a fistful of his hair, yanking viciously while I simultaneously threw my elbow back.

He grunted and backed off enough so I could spin to face him. The move dislodged his cock, but I scraped my side on the tree bark as I went.

His eyes were full of amusement, even as he tilted his head to the side because of my grip of his hair. He shoved me back into the tree. "What now?"

"Now she throat punch you." Dmitri walked around the trunk, and I scrambled to pull up my pants. My shirt had thankfully fallen to cover my breasts.

Sin, not caring about his state of undress, glared at Dmitri. "Get the fuck out of here. We're busy."

"She need practice." Dmitri looked everywhere but at me.

"No shit. You've been teaching her to pull hair? That's it?" Sin tucked his cock back in and zipped up. "That's not good enough."

"Not good enough for what?" Dmitri exploded forward until he and Sin were almost nose to nose. "What you do to her? What?"

"Fuck off, Russian. This won't end well for you." A wave of menace rolled off Sin like heat rising from pavement.

"Stop." I pushed at their shoulders. Neither man backed away.

"Stay out of this, Krasivaya. If he will not tell me truth, I beat it from him." Dmitri's scowl would have made even the fiercest fighter balk, but it seemed to only make Sin angrier, more ready to spill blood.

"Let's show him. Come on, Dmitri." I backed away from the shadow beneath the tree and out into the sunny grass. An ache shot between my legs thanks to Sin's attentions, but I had to separate the bristling men before they fought. "Let's spar."

"I rather *spar* with Sinclair."

Shit. "Please?" I tried my best wheedling tone. "Don't you want to help me get better?"

Soft-hearted Dmitri broke his death stare with Sin and glanced at me. "I do."

"Come on then." I brought my fists up. "I need help."

Dmitri snarled at Sin. "This not over."

Sin grinned. "Go on. Show me the tricks you learned in your Russian gutter. Let me see what I've been paying for."

"Sin!" I hissed.

"What?" He shrugged as Dmitri turned and entered the sunlight with me. Crossing his arms over his chest, Sin tilted his chin up. "Show me what you've got besides hair pulling."

"Position one, Krasivaya."

I bent slightly at the knees and kept my hands up, palms open. Dmitri ran at me. I shifted my weight to the side, let him barrel past, and aimed a kicked at the back of his knee. He stumbled and then straightened.

"Good. Position Two."

I straightened, hands still up, as Dmitri approached. He drew back his right fist and aimed it at my face. He jabbed and I dodged, slapping his fist away and shoving hard against his arm to throw him off balance. He took a step and caught himself.

"Attack." He bent at the knees and waved me to him.

I edged to his right and darted in, aiming the tips of my straight fingers at his throat. He swung when I got close. His fist grazed the top of my head as I ducked and stabbed upward with my hand, but he caught my wrist before I made contact.

"Good." He grunted his approval.

"Your greatest strength is surprise. Your greatest skill—speed. Do not forget, Krasivaya. You look weak. You small." He tapped the side of my head. "Use to your advantage."

Sin approached. "She's got a few moves. I can see that. But I think you could have done more to—"

I exploded off the ground and kicked my legs up. Sin wasn't quick enough this time, so I was able to straddle his neck and take him down. Landing on his back, he tried to shove me off. I tightened my legs around his neck as I sat on his chest, pinning him.

I pulled my fist back and smiled in triumph. "I could break your nose if I wanted to."

He glanced between my thighs, his eyes sparkling in the sun, before staring up at me. "I think I like this brand of training."

CHAPTER SEVEN
Sinclair

I RAN MY FINGERS through her hair, sifting the strands while my mind did the same with memories. She slumbered at my side, snuggled up to my darkness as if it gave off some sort of heat. The only warmth I had was a reflection of hers. Nothing more.

Sun streamed through her bedroom windows, lighting the bed and the quilts along the walls. Mother still asked every so often if I would make one to commemorate my Acquisition, as if it were a badge of honor. I enjoyed disappointing her each time she brought it up. If it were up to me, I'd destroy every one of them.

I studied the oldest one, the seams still tight. Its artistry reminded me of what we once were—sharecroppers and seamstresses. When my great-great-grandfather unwittingly saved the life of the reigning Sovereign, he'd damned us to this life. Seeing us now, raised so high amongst our wicked cohorts, would he regret his act of mercy?

I closed my eyes, blocking out my history, and relished every point of contact I had with Stella as her breath tickled my chest.

I'd been back for two weeks, ignoring my work and,

instead, focusing on her. She trained and fought, thriving despite the hellish environs of the Acquisition. I wondered at her strength, where it came from, why I didn't have it. But I also saw her self-destruction—how she pushed herself further to the brink every day. Her torment was mine. It pained me to see her so hell bent on punishing herself for wrongs she never committed. Still, trying to stop her was like trying to stop the Acquisition itself.

She shifted and her breathing quickened. Perhaps my shadowy thoughts had invaded whatever pleasant dream she'd been having.

"Who was Cora?" Her voice was still thick with sleep. "Renee told me she was your aunt, but nothing else."

"What makes you think of that?" I ran my fingers along her smooth side.

"I dreamed of that night. The one with your mother." Her eyelashes fluttered against my chest.

That hellish night. I sighed. I kept nothing from her anymore. She knew me, all of me, and yet she still lay here in my arms as if I weren't a twisted monster. I kissed the crown of her head. "My aunt, yes. She was the youngest in my mother's family. The one my mother fought to save."

"She was Rebecca's Teddy?"

"Yes."

She rolled back so her head was nestled on my shoulder, her green eyes piercing even as she emerged from the cobwebs of her dreams. "But Rebecca won. So, what happened to Cora?"

"Cora witnessed it all. She saw what Rebecca and Renee went through. She knew from the start that it was her life on the line. Years after it was all over, she hung herself in the woods."

Stella clenched her eyes shut. "God. I'm sorry, Sin."

"I don't remember her much." Her red hair and warm smile were almost lost to me, just like my mother—both women erased by the Acquisition. "My mother took it in, ingested the blame like a fine meal, and let it drag her down even further. *It was all for nothing.* My mother screamed those words at Cora's funeral." The memory of her, all in black, sinking to her knees and screeching at the clear blue sky, passed before my eyes before disappearing.

Stella scooted on top of me and cupped my cheek. "You were too young." The unshed tears in her eyes glistened, and I wanted to take them away.

"That's why Teddy can never know." I smoothed my palms down her back. "That's the past. We have plenty to think about without it."

Resting her chin on my chest, she said, "One more week. I just wish we knew what the trial will be."

"So do I." I'd tried to get information from Sophia, but she was almost as cold as her father. I still had my claws in her, I knew—she'd been texting me while she was in New York for the past few weeks. I hadn't failed with her, not yet.

Even if she agreed to an alliance with me, I still had the problem of her lover, Ellis, to deal with. If Cal found out she was seeing him instead of setting her cap at the next Sovereign, his displeasure would be lethal. So, if she wouldn't go along with my plans of her own accord, I could always dangle Ellis in front of her like a tasty lure. I would be the hook.

Still, she'd divulged nothing about her father's plans. The trial was almost here, and I hadn't been able to divine the actual mechanism Cal would use to wreak havoc on Stella. Rage exploded in my chest, and I beat against the cage I was born into like I'd done so many times before. In the end, I was still trapped, still lying here with the woman I'd kill to protect, but harm to save Teddy.

A light knock sounded at my door.

I pulled Stella next to me in the bed and covered her with the blanket. "Yes?"

"I'm sorry, sir. There's a man at the gate demanding to see you." Farns' voice wavered through the wood.

"Who?"

"Red Witherington."

"Fucking hell." I moved to the edge of the bed and stabbed my legs in my jeans. "Farns, let him in."

"Very good, sir."

Stella rose and pulled her tank top over her head.

"You're staying here."

"Like hell I am." She yanked on her panties and jeans.

I turned. "He hates you. If he has even a shred of information that can help us, then I need you out of sight. Understand?"

"What makes you think he came here to help?" She threw her hair over her shoulder and pulled her top down the rest of the way, covering the sight of her mouthwatering breasts.

I strode to her and grabbed her shoulders, holding her gaze. "I don't know why he's here. But if he sees you, it won't matter. It will all go to hell."

She opened her mouth to argue, then closed it.

"Do you trust me?" I asked the question I had no right to even think in her presence. I held my breath, wishing we were different people in a different life. Even as we were, could she give me the trust I didn't deserve but desperately wanted?

She rested her hand against my chest, over my heart. "Yes."

She must have had something in her palm, because warmth spread from it as surely as if she were the sun on a hot day. I kissed her harder than I'd intended. I must have put the weight of everything I felt, everything I was capable of feeling, into it. She wrapped her arms around my neck, pulling me closer, matching me with the same fiery intensity I'd seen in her the very first day we met.

She broke the kiss and stepped back. "Okay. I'll stay away, but I won't promise not to eavesdrop."

I took her hand and kissed her palm. "I would expect nothing less."

I turned and strode out and down the hallway to the

main stairs. I met Lucius on the landing. Dragging his carry-on behind him, his clothes were rumpled and he needed a shave.

I smirked. "You look like hell."

"Thanks. Just got back from Brazil. Rough fucking flight."

"Everything all right?"

He shrugged. "Nothing I can't handle."

"Good." I dropped down the next few steps.

"What are you up to?"

I glanced over my shoulder at his curious expression. "We have a guest."

"Who?"

"Red."

He let go of the handle on his carry-on. "Fuck yeah. I'm dying for a fight."

"We aren't fighting."

"Since when?" He raised an eyebrow and stripped off his jacket.

He had a point. We'd never gotten along with Red, even before the Acquisition.

"I need to see if he has any information about the trial. That comes first."

"So we're just going to take his shit?" Lucius shook his head.

"Of course not. Still, we will listen to what he has to say."

He followed me down the stairs. "I can live with that, but if he pulls anything, I'll knock his goddamn teeth out. Where's Stella?"

"I just left her in her room. She's getting dressed."

His jaw tensed, and I felt a decidedly non-brotherly satisfaction in him knowing I spent the night with her.

Farns waited at the door in the foyer and swung it open before Red had a chance to knock. He barreled inside, his hair mussed, and with dark circles under his eyes.

"What the fuck, Red?" Lucius stepped ahead of me,

already itching for confrontation.

"You." He pointed at me. "I need to talk to you."

I smirked. "It may shock you to know this, but there are phones for that very purpose."

"Fucking prick." Red stepped forward, and Lucius matched his advance until both men stood nose to nose.

"Let him through, Lucius. He can say what he came to say before we come to blows."

I walked down the hall, feeling Red following at my heels as Lucius trapped him between us. "State your business, Red. I assume this isn't a friendly visit."

Turning into my study, I waved Red to a seat as Lucius closed the door behind us.

"Is that bitch here?" He looked around, as if Stella might be hiding in the drapes. My hands itched to crush his voice box, but I remained still and stared him down.

"Cut the shit. What do you want?" Lucius crossed his arms and leaned against the door.

"Evie." Red turned his bloodshot eyes to me.

"What about her?" I sat on the sofa across from him.

"Promise me you won't—you won't—"

"Kill her if I win?" I finished for him. "I can't promise that and you know it."

"But I'll promise I won't kill your brother if I win."

"That's not really an issue for me. You aren't going to win. I am."

He shook. I couldn't tell if it was from fear or rage. I hoped it was the former. "I know what you did at the last trial. I know it was you who caught her and brought her back."

An icy trickle of unease slid down my spine, but I affected an air of nonchalance. "What of it?"

"I'm sure Cal would like to know of the rules violation."

"I'm sure he would, too. Then what? I'd be disqualified?" I steepled my fingers and drew out the logical conclusion that he feared most. "You'd have to go up against Eagleton alone. Eagleton would win, obviously. You're already coming apart, and your Acquisition broke in the first trial. Eagleton won't cut a deal with you, but he will cut your sister's head off and hand it to you by the hair."

Red dry heaved and clapped a hand over his mouth.

"Vomit on this rug and you're buying a new one, asshole." Lucius curled his lip in distaste.

Red swallowed hard and tried to compose himself. "P-please. I have information."

"Why this sudden urge to work together?" Lucius asked. "You've always been a royal fucking prick, and now, out of the blue, you want to be a helpful fucking prick instead? What changed?"

"What you said. Brianne is broken. She's not strong enough. She's not like your bi—"

"Call her a bitch, cunt, or anything other than Stella or Ms. Rousseau, and I can promise you, you will not like the results." My words were calm and even, though my need to do violence increased with every syllable of weakness Red uttered.

"N-not like Stella. I can feel it. You are going to win. I know it. But if you do... I can't close my eyes without seeing Evie dead, and I-I'm the one who..." He ran a shaking hand over his face.

"What's the information?" Lucius walked over to stand behind Red. "What did you want to tell us?"

"Not until you promise. You have to promise me Evie's life. Please." He leaned forward, his hands clasped.

I glanced to Lucius. He shrugged. If Red told me and I won, my promise wouldn't matter. I could kill Evie and kick Red's family out of the aristocracy. Then again, I never broke my word.

"If I promise you that, and I win, they would rip me apart. The rules are clear. If I win, Evie has to die. No losing last born has ever lived past the coronation."

"Fuck the goddamn rules!" He screamed, his voice raw

and explosive.

I studied him as he took a deep breath, torment in every movement from the shake of his hands to the sorrowful look in his eyes.

"Please, Sin. Please. I can't kill her. I can't let you kill her. I'd rather die. I thought I had a chance to win. I thought I could save her myself. I can't. I need you. Please." He slid to his knees. "I'll do anything you ask, give you whatever you want, just please—spare her."

"Fucking pathetic." Lucius slapped the back of the sofa.

Red didn't move from the floor, only stared up at me with watery eyes. I liked him broken and begging. Even so, I needed whatever scraps of information he'd brought me. If it would help Stella and Teddy, I had to have it. I would sort the consequences later.

I leaned forward. "The deal is this. You win, you spare Teddy. I win, I spare Evie. But the upfront price for this bargain is that you tell me everything you know about the remaining trials."

"I know what happened ten years ago. I can give you the details."

"That's it?" Lucius pushed off from the back of Red's chair and walked around to glare at him. "Some shitty intel from ten years ago?"

I held up my hand. "Let him talk." Any shred of information was helpful at this point.

"Okay, okay." Red pushed himself from the floor.

"No. Stay there and tell me." I pointed to the rug beneath him. This brief negotiation had done nothing to wipe away the insults and threats he'd made to Stella. He would pay for each of them in time.

Red slid back down to his knees and glared up at me. "That year, there was this hellacious obstacle course. Crawling through glass, swimming in a leech pit, climbing barbed wire."

"Jesus Christ." Lucius sat next to me.

"The winner was the only Acquisition who made it through."

"I suspected something like what you've described." I would deal with all of the horrors later, when Stella and I were alone. The thought of her suffering through any of it made acid boil in my stomach. "But why does this trial focus on family? I didn't hear any family angle whatsoever."

Red rubbed his eyes, grinding his palms into them as if trying to erase an image. "Because the last-borns were part of the trial. The two losing families had to send their youngest through the same obstacle course as punishment."

CHAPTER EIGHT
Stella

"How will we keep it from Teddy?" I punched Dmitri's palm and ducked as he swung.

"I've called him home from school. He'll stay here with Lucius." Sin walked around us in a wide circle as we sparred.

A courier had arrived earlier in the week carrying a missive with the familiar Oakman seal. The trial was set, and my time was up.

"He hasn't been summoned with us tomorrow?" I dodged Dmitri's hand and smacked him on the back of the head as I dashed past. "For the triathlon?" I added for Dmitri's sake.

"No." Sin stopped as my opponent and I circled each other.

"Isn't that odd?" I lunged at Dmitri. He caught me around the waist. I threw my hip out and tried to pull him over and flip him, but he kept his balance and shoved me to the wet ground. "Fuck!"

"Patience, Krasivaya. Must wait for right opportunity." Dmitri helped me to my feet. "Surprise, remember?"

"I know." I shook it off and backed away to start again.

The clouds overhead threatened another downpour. I wanted to keep practicing. I had to get better.

"It's not odd per se. It means there's still a chance we could spare him from it. We'll leave him here with Lucius who'll get word to me if and when Teddy is sent for. Then Lucius can explain to Teddy as best he can, so he's not walking into it blind."

"Won't that be too much for him?" I tried to grapple Dmitri into an arm bar, but he pushed me away and I sank to my knees. The grass gave way to mud the more we practiced, and large drops of rain began to fall.

"Let's go in. This was supposed to be a light day, anyway." Sin offered his hand. "It's getting dark."

I took it and pulled myself to my feet, my muscles protesting. "No, just a little longer."

"Stella." Sin smoothed some stray hairs from my face as the rain intensified, the oak leaves whispering above us. "You've done all you can. You're as prepared as you're going to get. You need to rest for tomorrow."

He was right. I knew it, but I couldn't stop. I darted past him and launched myself onto Dmitri's back. Taking him down was the one thing I'd never been able to do. And maybe if I could get him on the ground, I could make it through whatever the next Acquisition trial threw at me.

He whirled, and I dug my heels into his sides and constricted my arms around his neck. Reaching back, he gripped my upper arm and yanked. I held on, cutting off his airway even as he pulled at me. A primal grunt ripped through me as I fought to stay on his back.

"Stella! That's enough." Sin's sharp voice cut through the rain, but I held onto Dmitri, refusing to let him go, refusing to fail this time.

I closed my eyes. All I saw was Brianne's frightened face and Gavin's kind smile. I'd let them down, failed them when they needed me most. Squeezing tighter, I put all my strength into my arms. Not again. I wouldn't let Teddy down. I would do whatever I had to do to keep him safe.

Something clicked under my forearm, my enemy's throat on the verge of giving way as I maintained my hold.

He pawed at my arms, his movements slowing. Strong hands gripped my waist and pulled until I was forced to let go, my arms finally giving up. Sin and I fell back into the muddy grass. My heart hammered in my chest, fear and anger washing through me as Dmitri bent over and wheezed breath into his lungs.

Sin wrapped his arms around me, holding me steady as a deluge fell around us. "You could have killed him. Generally, I'd be all for it. Though I think you would have regretted it in this instance."

Shame rose, drowning out the faces and the pain. Dmitri wasn't my enemy. What was I doing? "I-I'm sorry, Dmitri." I tried to get up, but Sin held me fast.

"Is okay, Krasivaya. I fine." He stood tall and took an unsteady step before regaining his balance.

"Sin, please let me help him." At my request, he got to his feet and helped me up.

Dmitri took a few more steps, surer this time, and shook his head as if to clear it. "Is okay."

"Come on. Let's get out of the rain." Sin held my elbow with one hand, and I grabbed Dmitri's with the other.

"I'm sorry." I blinked against the rain, or maybe it was tears. I didn't know. Was I even capable of that act anymore? Crying?

"No, no. It was good move." He patted my hand as we walked to the front porch. "I be fine. I strongest man in Russia."

Sin snorted, and Dmitri glared at him over my head as we entered the house. After removing our shoes, Dmitri headed down the hall to his quarters while Sin and I climbed the stairs.

"Will he be okay?" I wiped the wetness from my cheeks.

"Sure. He's *strongest man in Russia.*" Sin mimicked him

perfectly, and I felt even worse.

"I didn't mean to hurt him, to do that. I was just trying to…" What was I trying to do? Win? Knock him down so I could stop feeling like something was broken inside of me?

"You can't keep blaming yourself for the Christmas trial." Sin pushed through the door to my room and pulled his soaked shirt over his head.

"I-I don't." I stripped, tossing my clothes into the hamper in the bathroom before turning on the warm water in the shower.

He padded in behind me. The vines seemed more alive on his damp skin, the ink even more indelible.

"Come on." He pulled me under the water and into his arms.

Warmth enveloped me and I could breathe again, could think again.

"I know you feel guilty. I know." He smoothed his hands up and down my back as I lay my head against his shoulder. "But you did what you had to. Everything else that happened isn't on you. It's on us. The Acquisition."

"I can't stop thinking about it. About how they looked at me. Brianne and Gavin, the way they screamed." My lip trembled, and I hated my weakness, hated that I had the luxury of falling apart when Brianne and Gavin were the ones who'd suffered.

He wrapped his arms around me. "I know. Time is the only way to soften memories like that. Things you've seen that you can never un-see. They'll still be there, but they won't be able to hurt you anymore."

I pulled away and took his hand, pulling it to my lips. I kissed the criss-cross of scars on the back of his wrist before putting his palm to my cheek. "You're strong. Maybe I can be, too."

He leaned in and kissed me with a gentleness I didn't know he possessed. He rested his forehead against mine. "You are everything. If I could run with you, I would." He closed his eyes, as if thinking through the possibility again. When he opened them, they were stark. "We can't. They'll find us, hurt us, and kill Teddy for spite."

I pulled away and held his gaze. "I'm going to end it. All of it. *We* are. Together."

The water splashed down my back, warming me even as goose bumps rose along my skin from the nearness of him, the heat that lit his gaze at my words.

"It won't be easy. You'll have to kill." He pulled me to him roughly, his hands going to my ass. "You would have their blood on your hands?"

I bit his chest and ran my nails down his back. "Yes."

He groaned, as if my assent pleased him more than he could stand. "This is a dark path. One I'm well acquainted with." He pushed me against the tiles and met my eyes. "Are you sure it's what you want?"

"I want to burn it all down." I pulled him down to me and kissed him with every bit of fierceness I had.

Lifting me, he pinned me against the wall and shoved inside me as I cried out from the pain and pleasure.

"We'll have to destroy every last one of them." He thrust hard, my back slapping against the frigid tiles. "I will never give you up. Nothing can keep me from you."

He plunged deeply again, and I clawed at his shoulders. His eyes were two dark gems, sparkling with intensity. "Because you're mine. You've always been mine, long before any of this." He bit my neck. "And I will always have what's mine."

CHAPTER NINE
STELLA

SIN SQUEEZED MY HAND as we pulled through the gate onto the Fort LaRoux property. Cars formed a line ahead of us as Luke rolled down his window to converse with the guard. All I could think about was the rapid beat of my heart. I kept taking deep breaths, but couldn't seem to stop everything from moving too fast.

"Calm, Stella. Calm." Sin ran the back of his hand down my cheek. "We can do this." The strain in his voice told me he felt the same rush of adrenaline and fear. He was just better at hiding it.

Teddy and Lucius remained at home, no last minute summons disturbing them. All the same, a sense of foreboding took hold in me. Rebecca's sing-song about spring being the time for family played in my mind, sending a shiver through me.

Sin kissed the back of my hand, his face drawn and starkly handsome. "The trial won't last more than a day. It can't. Cal hasn't set up any local accommodations."

"One day. I can do this. One day for Teddy." I took another deep breath and tried to school my features. Even if I was coming apart on the inside, I wouldn't let the circling vultures sense my weakness.

The narrow road to the fort curved through stands of pulpwood on either side, the monotonous pines growing straight and tall for row after row. The rain hadn't let up; a light mist still floated on the air, coating everything with clammy wetness and hiding the early afternoon sun.

We cruised through the pines until the fort rose from the ground ahead of us. I'd studied it for hours, analyzing photos of the layout, trying to determine what Cal had cooked up for the trial. It was circular, built at a time when muskets and gunpowder were the only thing to stop invaders.

The rounded walls were made of large, square stones, but over time they'd become covered with green moss, the surface alive. The field around the structure was all high grass except for some older oaks, gray moss hanging wet and thick from the low branches.

An expansive red tent, bigger than most houses, was set up against the side of the fort. Luke pulled up, and a valet opened my door. Sin squeezed my fingers until they almost hurt before letting me go. I stepped out, my boots solid on the pavement.

I wore dark canvas pants and a long-sleeve sports v-neck, breathable and warm. Despite the pragmatism of my outfit, Renee had done my makeup and curled my hair into flowing ringlets for Cal's benefits. I had elastics in my pocket for when the competition began.

Sin strolled around the car, his mask firmly on as he gave me a derisive glare. "Let's go."

He took my upper arm and pulled me along with him into the tent. Chandeliers hung overhead, and a band played in one corner. Long tables overflowing with food ran down each side, and a bar was set up at the very back beside the fort entrance. The ragged wooden doors were wide open, people steadily making their way into the fort once they'd had their fill in the tent. Overhead lights glowed on the spiral stairs that disappeared upwards beyond my view.

The receiving line was long, Cal shaking hands with everyone who set foot inside. Dread and anger danced inside me as some of the decked out party-goers gawked at me and whispered amongst themselves. Sin shook a few hands and chitchatted as we moved steadily forward.

"I heard Lucius gave it to her good at Christmas." A wizened old man patted Sin on the elbow. "I bet you were sad you missed it."

Sin smiled. "Don't worry, Governor Treadway. I still manage to have plenty of fun with her. She's got a little fight left. Just enough to make it interesting."

Governer Treadway? I didn't recognize him by sight, but I knew him through my history lessons in school. He was one of the staunchest anti-integration governors in the South during the Civil Rights era and was still reviled for that legacy.

The old man eyed me up and down. "Interesting, huh? I can sure see that. I remember back in my day, they strung the bitches up and let us—"

"Barton." Sin clapped the next well-wisher on the back as the former governor gave me one last look before speaking to a man in line behind us.

"You're looking good this year," Barton said. "I may have a side bet on you. But don't tell Cal. He'll want a cut of the action." He winked at me.

I had the urge to knee him. Instead, I stared placidly ahead as we finally reached Cal.

"Welcome." Cal greeted Sin with a handshake. He pulled me into a hug. "And, my goodness, Stella. Glad to see you looking so fetching." Putting me at arm's length, he ran his gaze down my body before grabbing a tendril of my hair and smelling it. "For me?"

I fought my gag reflex but flinched when he rested his hand on my shoulder.

"She still seems to be in fighting form. Well done, Sin." Cal smiled, looking like a toothy shark.

"As whores go, she's not so bad." Sin took a glass from a passing attendant's tray and downed it.

Cal nodded. "Are you a whore, Stella?"

Sin tensed at my elbow and covered it with a laugh. "Answer him."

"No." My voice was barely a whisper, the sound stolen by the rage that constricted my lungs.

"No? Come now. What would it take for me to get one night with you?" Cal tipped my chin up, and I met his eyes. I hoped he could feel every ounce of revulsion that pulsed through me at his touch.

I didn't respond. He wasn't asking me anyway.

"That's something we could negotiate." Sin's fingers dug into my arm despite his words.

"You'd share?" Cal's eyes were still on mine, testing me.

"Hell, if it meant I was the next Sovereign, I wouldn't just share, I'd give her to you." His words rang false to my ears, but I couldn't tell if Cal heard the lie as easily as I did.

"Would you like that? Wouldn't it be nice to be mine? Fancy clothes, big house, warm bed." He grabbed my palm and placed it on his crotch. "This in your mouth, pussy, and ass every night." Cal raised his eyebrows, looking for a response I wouldn't give him. I focused on getting through the trial, not on the foul words falling from his wine-stained lips.

Sin's fingertips pressed deep enough into my arm to hit bone. "Cal—"

"Shh, I'm talking to Stella." He moved my palm up and down his hardening shaft as my stomach churned. "Tell me how tight your pussy is. If I stuck two fingers in there right now, would it hurt? Could I add one more and make it three without you crying? I bet your ass could use a proper fucking. I wouldn't be gentle. A filly like you needs a strong hand. I'd have to break you in. My come mixing with your blood, your tears, your screams—all of it sounds like heaven to me—"

"Daddy, the line." Sophia walked up, a flute of champagne in her hand and a forced smile on her elegant face.

Cal cleared his throat, snapping out of his fantasy of horrors. "Right you are, darling. Can't keep our fabulous guests waiting." He let go of my hand.

Sin eased up on my elbow. "Looking forward to the game as always, Sovereign."

We walked past Cal as he continued greeting newcomers. Sophia joined us and took Sin's arm. She gave me a look so full of venom that the hackles on my neck rose.

"Sin, how are you?" She pulled him away, her short emerald dress and high black boots showing off her hourglass figure and long legs.

Sin glanced at me and continued along at her side. "Fine. Ready for the show. How was New York?"

I wanted to wash my hands, to erase every touch, every word from Cal. Still, I knew it would take more than soap to rid me of his vicious intentions.

Sophia led Sin into the crowd. Left alone for the moment, I kept my head down and walked out of the main aisle toward a bare area against the fort wall. Turning my back against the moss-covered stones gave me some sense of security. It was a ridiculous thought, as if having a centuries-old wall at my back could stop these people. I peered out at the crowd—the rich elite all in one place. I wished for a grenade.

A few moments passed, and I was glad for each second I was left unmolested. I feared my luck was at an end when a man stopped near me. I looked up at him, dreading a confrontation, but he took no notice of me. His eyes were trained on Sin and Sophia several feet away.

He was handsome, his hay-colored hair short and neat. Tall and wiry, he was older, perhaps forty. I wished him dead, just like everyone else here.

"Ellis, my man! How are you?" Another man of about

the same age walked up and shook hands. Even with the distraction, it took Ellis more than a few beats to turn away from Sophia and Sin. They fell into conversation and melded into the mix of people in the center of the tent.

"Ma'am?" A server with black hair and dark brown eyes walked up and offered me a flute of champagne.

I took it with a shaking hand. "Thank you."

He stopped and glanced back at me, his eyebrows raised in surprise. "You're welcome."

I supposed no one ever thanked the servants, never said a kind word. Vultures weren't known for their warmth. And here, where they could be themselves, their worst was on display.

He tilted his head to the side and glanced around before approaching me again. "Are you in some kind of trouble? Do I need to do something?"

"I'm fine." I whispered. "But you shouldn't talk to me. You'll get in trouble."

"It's just, I've heard things. This is my first time working one of these events. Money was too good to pass up. And you look…scared."

"Shh." I shook my head and grabbed another flute from his tray to make it seem like I was keeping him. "Stop talking. You're in danger."

He furrowed his brow. "If you're in trouble, I know people. Something doesn't feel right." He glanced around.

"Go. Now." I wouldn't meet his eye.

He shook his head and backed away. After giving me another long look, he continued his round of offering drinks.

The crowd swelled, overdressed people talking, eating, and drinking to the jazz from the band. I went almost unnoticed, pressed up against the cool stones, until I saw a flash of light red hair and heard Cal greeting, "Red, welcome, my friend."

Red surveyed the crowd, his gaze seizing on me for a second before roving elsewhere. Brianne walked behind him, her head down, her blonde hair hanging in curtains on either side of her face. She was a wreck, even more so than the last time I'd seen her. My stomach sank, and I leaned against the wall for support. The ages-old chill seeped into my bones, and I dreaded Brianne more than Red. Her judgment was far worse than any vitriol Red could spout at me.

Once their introductions were complete, Red dragged Brianne into the mix of people. He glanced at me again, but didn't seem inclined to engage for once. I sagged with relief and edged closer to the bar, toward Sin.

He was in a close conversation with Sophia. He smiled for her as she touched his arm and whispered something in his ear. Jealousy crept along the periphery of my thoughts, but I already had too many emotions competing for my attention. I hid the shake in my fingers by downing the champagne, setting the glass down, and stuffing my hands into my pockets.

The ghouls swirled around me, their vapid conversations focused on either themselves or the trial. I bowed my head to avoid their rude stares, though I could still hear their comments about my "chances," and how much fun the Christmas trial had been.

"Hey, Stella." Gavin approached, the only friendly face I'd seen.

He was like an oasis in a desert of sand and snakes. The warm smile on his gaunt face made tears sting my eyes. His smile faded as he neared.

"What is it?" He smoothed his hands down my upper arms.

"I'm sorry." I finally said the words I'd been wanting to say since that horrible day in December.

"For what?" The concern in his eyes made me want to vomit. I didn't deserve it.

I shook my head, willing the tears away. "For what happened to y-you."

He pulled me into a hug, his arms strong around my

back. "That wasn't you, Stella." He kissed my hair and whispered into my ear, "It was them. Not you."

"I know, but it didn't happen to me. I didn't get..."

He hugged me harder. "How? Wait, it doesn't matter. I'm glad. Don't feel guilty about that. I've got your back, remember?"

"I've got yours, too. I'm so sorry—" My chest shook, and my unspent tears welled up inside me and threatened to overflow.

"Shh, it's over now. I don't talk about it or think about it. It's done." He rubbed my back, and I relaxed into him. Despite his words, I wasn't absolved. But it took some of the weight away to know he didn't blame me.

"I'm going to get them. I swear it. For you, Brianne, and me. They won't get away with it." My voice was a harsh whisper, and I meant every word.

"Let's just get through it. All I want is to get through it."

"We will. All three of us will make it." I nodded against his shoulder.

Letting go, he stepped away and furtively wiped at his eyes. "Have you seen Brianne?"

"Yeah. She came in, but then I lost her. Do you know anything about the trial?"

"Miss Rousseau?" Judge Montagnet moved through the nearest group of people, leaning on his cane as he walked.

Gavin scrubbed a hand down his face and blanched.

"Go. He just wants to torment me," I said quietly.

Gavin gave me a curt nod and walked away toward the band.

"Judge." I crossed my arms over my chest and stared into his faded eyes.

"How are you coming along? Recovered from Christmas?" He grinned, one of his bottom front teeth showing a filthy shade of green.

"Fine." There was no other answer—except the truth.

And if I told him how I really was and what I really thought of him, I'd be putting Teddy in danger. So, "fine" it was.

He reached out and pinched my arm. "You seem thinner. Sin not been feeding you well?"

"He has." Though civil, I kept my words clipped. The sooner he was gone, the better.

"Good. Wouldn't want him starving you out. Not until the trials are done anyway. How's your father?" He was nothing more than a self-satisfied cat playing with its food.

"Fine."

He cocked his head, perhaps unsatisfied with my short replies. But, it didn't matter. The sound system clicked on with a feedback hum. It was show time.

"All right, everyone." Cal's voice boomed over speakers nestled along the metal tent supports. "We have a wonderful show for you today. I can't wait to get started. Make your way up the stairs to the seating along the battlement. Don't worry, we've had special awnings installed as well as heaters, couches, beds—anything you'd want to get comfy on this rainy day."

People began streaming through the door and up the stairs as Cal continued. "I think you'll be pleased at the entertainment. We also have plenty of servants to accommodate your every desire. Even yours, Judge Montagnet."

The crowd laughed, and the judge swiped his hand through the air. "You joker," he called.

"Acquirers and Acquisitions, make your way to me. Announcements are over. Let's get the party started!"

CHAPTER TEN
STELLA

SIN FOUND ME AND took my hand, pulling me from the wall where I'd taken refuge. He squeezed my cold fingers as we made our way back to Cal.

His touch—the same one that once chilled me to the bone—now gave me a slight warmth. I would be the one suffering today. It would likely be my blood spilled, my body broken. The touch of his hand told me that he would be right there with me. Every stab of pain inflicted on me would be mirrored in his mind. I wished I could save him from it even more than myself.

We walked against the flow of people heading to the battlements until we reached Cal. Sin dropped my hand, and I was alone again. Brianne, Red, Gavin, and Bob were already assembled. Gavin gave me a slight nod, but Brianne kept her head lowered.

"We're all here. Excellent." Cal smiled, still in showman mode. "Acquisitions, head into the fort, turn left, and go down the stairs. An attendant is waiting for you. The three of you lucky Acquirers will stay with me. I have a real treat for you." He rubbed his hands together, the machinery in his conniving mind clicking and scraping. "Go on." He jerked his chin toward the door.

Sin gave me one last look, his eyes saying nothing, but I still felt the warmth of his fingers on mine. I followed the crowd through the wooden doors into the fort. They turned right and climbed the curving stairs as Gavin, Brianne, and I turned left and descended. The air was dank, the rain running down the walls and feeding the moss. Naked light bulbs hung in a string along the curving ceiling, and my boots squeaked on the slippery stairs.

Foreboding rose inside me with each step, but I kept going. When we reached the landing, two attendants waited for us. I recognized one of them from the Christmas trial. Mr. Tablet, the one I'd embarrassed in front of Lucius. He didn't have a tablet for me to destroy this time, though he wore the same sense of smug satisfaction.

Gauging by the smirk on his almost-purple lips, he recognized me, too. "Right this way."

I reached for Gavin's hand. He took it as we marched around behind Mr. Tablet, the curving wall obscuring the way ahead of us.

"We'll get through it," Gavin whispered.

I glanced to Brianne. "Are you okay?"

She didn't respond, only darted her eyes up and then back down. She reminded me of a wild animal that had been caught in a trap. One that would gnaw its own leg off just to be free.

"I need to talk to Stella." Dylan's voice cut through the damp air. He leaned inside a dark alcove along the interior wall.

Mr. Tablet stopped our march. Gavin gripped my hand tighter.

"I don't believe we have time. The trial is about to—"

"I didn't ask." Dylan rose to his full height and stepped into the light. He was imposing, a brute with a malicious glint in his eye. "Take the rest of them. She'll be along shortly. Stella, come here." He gave a little smile after the command, as if the power he wielded was some sort of shiny new toy.

I didn't know what his game was, but I knew I didn't want to be alone with him. I edged closer to Gavin.

"I'll come over there and get you. Is that what you want?" Dylan stepped toward us.

"Back the fuck off." Gavin moved in front of me.

"This is going to be fun." Dylan swung his arms over his head, stretching. "Let's go, big guy."

"Wait." I stepped around Gavin. He was strong, but Dylan was a wall of muscle and spite. Gavin wouldn't stand a chance. "I'll talk to him. Just go."

"No." Gavin gripped my elbow. "You don't have to."

"I'll be fine. I'll catch up." I disentangled my arm and walked to Dylan, despite the instinctive desire to run as far from him as I could.

Dylan nodded. "That's right. She'll be just fine with me. Go."

I glanced back to Gavin, his lips pinched and his brows drawn in concern. Then he glared at Dylan. "If you hurt her—"

"You'll what?" Dylan grabbed me around the waist and pulled me back into the shadowy alcove. "Fuck off."

Mr. Tablet pulled a black baton—the same one from the Christmas trial—from his belt. "Come on."

Gavin took another step toward Dylan and me. I shook my head. "I'm fine. Please go."

"I won't tell you again." Mr. Tablet held the baton at the ready.

"If he hurts you, yell. I'll come. I don't care about the consequences." Gavin said the last sentence to Mr. Tablet.

Satisfied he'd won, Mr. Tablet turned and led Brianne and Gavin away.

"Why is it so hard to get to you these days?" Dylan kept one arm around my waist and ran his fingers through my hair. "I couldn't get you at Christmas, though I was so close. And now I still have to fight just for some alone time with my sis."

I tried to push away from him, but he was too big. He may have even been more muscled than the last time I'd seen him. "I'm not your *sis*. Just let me go."

"Why would I do that? You're mine." I couldn't see his eyes in the dimness, and my skin crawled at what I knew I'd find there.

"I'm not."

"You are. I was cheated at the last trial. I still intend to have you, all of you." He gripped my hair and pulled my head back hard enough to hurt.

"Dylan!" I gasped as he bit the side of my neck. When he clamped down hard enough to break the skin, I tried to scream, but he clapped his hand over my mouth.

I struggled, trying to break free. He only bit harder. Tears rose in my eyes at the searing pain. Then he let up and pulled me to him again. My blood coated his lips, and he kissed me, smearing it onto my mouth.

He ran his hands to my ass and squeezed, pulling me forward and rubbing me against his erection. I turned my head and pushed away before he could sink his tongue between my lips.

"There now." He grinned, my blood between his teeth. "I can't wait for the Vinemont boys to see my mark on you. The next time Sin and Lucius are in your cunt, they'll think of me. And then, before long, the Acquisition will be over and you'll belong to me. My little whore to use and abuse. I've already ordered a cage for you. It's custom made. You'll sleep in it every night at the foot of my bed."

"I will never be yours." I couldn't comprehend half of what he'd said. "A cage?"

"I own you." He bent his head to my mouth and pulled my hair again. "Cal gave me a little welcome gift. You. I can't stop the Acquisition. It's too late for that. But once the new Sovereign is chosen, you're mine. You can run. You can try and hide. Don't doubt that I'll find you. Not even the new Sovereign can break this deal. It's done."

Loathing invaded every cell of my body, and my fight kicked in. I balled my hand into a fist and aimed a hard hit at his ear. He howled and shoved me back. I took off down the curving corridor, sprinting toward whatever trial awaited me. I didn't care. I had to get away from Dylan, from the twisted ghost of my former friend.

Voices rose ahead of me, and I ran headlong into Gavin's back. He turned and put his palms on my face, tilting my head as he stared at my neck.

His lips turned up in a snarl. "That motherfucker. Where is he?" He looked over my head, spoiling for Dylan to try and follow me.

"I left him. I d-don't think he followed." The tremor in my voice matched the chaos in my mind. I wiped my sleeve across my mouth.

"Hey, asshole, do you have a first-aid kit or something in this hell hole?" Gavin asked Mr. Tablet.

"Oh, I'm afraid not." Mr. Tablet smiled sweetly and strode to a wide wooden door.

"It's okay." Gavin turned back to me. "It's not that bad." He yanked his sleeve down to cover his hand and pressed it over the wound on my neck.

It stung, but I tried to calm my breathing, calm my mind. Dylan was just an appetizer for the main course of the trial. I couldn't fall apart before the real game even began.

The door had a sliver of space I could see through. It led outside, the low light of the cloudy day filtering through. The ground beyond was grassy, and there was some sort of narrow, circular platform in the very middle. I assumed Cal stood atop it, per his usual.

"Ladies and gentleman! Get your popcorn and take your seats because the entertainment is about to begin." Cal's voice boomed through the door, the speaker system at full volume. "As you all know, the classic theme to the spring trial is family. I've stuck to the theme, but I gave it my own little twist. Are the Acquisitions ready?"

Mr. Tablet swung the door open. "Yes sir!" He called.

"Perfect. Bring them out."

Brianne whined like a dog kicked by its owner.

I tried to grab her hand and squeeze it. She pulled away as if I'd slapped her.

Gavin pressed into my wound one more time and dropped his arm. "I think the bleeding's stopped. Damn. I can tell it hurts."

"I'll live. Thank you."

"You're welcome. We'll get through it." His warm brown eyes still held the same optimism as they had before the Christmas trial. I didn't understand it, but I was comforted by it all the same.

"Go." Mr. Tablet motioned for us to walk through the door.

I took Gavin's hand and stepped into the arena.

CHAPTER ELEVEN
Sinclair

"Right this way." Cal led us up the battlement and around to the side opposite where the spectators lounged.

I scanned the crowd, the ground below, and the central platform for Teddy, but he wasn't there. Relief couldn't take hold in my chest, though. Cal was far too gleeful. Whatever he'd cooked up must have been beyond heinous for him to prance along the stone steps as he did.

There was no point asking questions. He would reveal the game when he felt like it, and in a way that had the most impact. As Sovereigns went, I had no doubt he made an excellent one, despite my constant desire to snap his neck.

"Here we are." He stopped and turned, letting us go ahead of him.

I stepped around him and proceeded forward. I halted in surprise, but then shored up my mask. "Mr. Rousseau. Lovely to see you again."

Stella's father sat on a wooden bench, his hands and feet shackled. A chain ran from the binds to a metal ring affixed to the stone beneath him. Two others—a middle-aged woman and a dark-haired girl of no more than twelve—sat beside him. The girl sniffled quietly and the woman stared, a blank look on her face.

"Where is Stella?" Mr. Rousseau's voice was weak, his skin sallow, and his eyes red and watery. He looked much the worse for wear since the night he had sold me his only child.

"She'll be out shortly. Don't you worry." Cal clapped him on the back, and the old man almost fell forward. I imagined kicking him when he was down, and it warmed me only a little. I was far more concerned with what Cal intended to do with Stella.

Bob walked past the prisoners to a stainless steel cart. Shiny instruments—scalpels, plyers, knives, metal knuckles—were laid out along the top. Rope and other, larger, weapons sat on a bench behind the tray.

"What are these for?" Bob, as usual, asked the dumbest question possible.

"Simple. Annie here is Gavin's little sister. Sin, you already know Stella's father, Mr. Rousseau. And, Red, this is Twila, Brianne's mother." He bent over and patted the woman on her cheek. "Sorry for the less-than-flashy introduction, but you understand, don't you?"

She stared silently, her mind far away from the fort and the cold stone beneath her feet. She and the girl must have been taken while they were sleeping. The girl wore a pair of too-small pajamas and the woman was dressed only in an oversized t-shirt.

Cal grinned and straightened. "I knew you would. We're going to have a round-robin of bouts amongst the Acquisitions. If your Acquisition fails the match, you will have to harm their family member. The more creative the harm the better. So, really, if you think about it." He tapped his finger on his chin. "Your Acquisition could lose, but you could still win if you really go to town. The rest of the rules don't even apply, since their relatives aren't truly Acquisitions. Maim them. Do whatever. Just do it with flair is all I ask."

"Ingenious." I could appreciate his brutality, though I still wanted to grab the closest knife, gut him, and make him chew his own intestines.

"Well, thank you. Means a lot coming from you." Cal grinned and headed back the way we came.

The child shivered and huddled closer to Brianne's mother. Bob ran his hand over the implements, eagerness in his eyes.

"Let me go. Please, I won't tell anyone. Just let me go." Stella's father clasped his hands together, the chains dragging and clinking across the stone.

"Just you? Not the child? Not the woman?" I asked.

He swallowed hard and darted his beady gaze from them to me. "All of us. That's what I meant."

"No it isn't. You chose this far more than they did. Deal with it." I inspected the courtyard two stories below. It was bare. Un-mowed grass covered the ground. The stark walls of the fort rose in a circular barrier, and a wooden platform made to look like a thin oak trunk with a small canopy presided in the center. Nothing to help Stella, but nothing to hurt her, either.

Her father stared up at me. "Stella wouldn't want you to—"

I backhanded him, the slap satisfying on so many levels. "You don't deserve to say her name. Speak again, and I'll use my fists."

The crowd across the way cheered lightly as the old man cowered against the girl, his cheek turning red. I resumed my stance behind him, straightened my shirt sleeve, and twisted my cuff link back to perfection. It was all about the show, after all.

"No head starts now, Counsellor Vinemont." Cal laughed atop the oak platform, his voice booming in all directions.

"Ladies and gentleman! Get your popcorn and take your seats because the entertainment is about to begin. As you all know, the classic theme to the spring trial is family.

I've stuck to the theme, but I gave it my own little twist. Are the Acquisitions ready?"

A door beneath the spectators opened, and a round, balding man yelled, "Yes sir!"

"Perfect. Bring them out," Cal replied.

Gavin and Stella walked out first, their hands clasped as they moved cautiously through the wet grass. Brianne followed behind, her head bowed.

The light rain fell at a steady pace, though we were covered by an awning similar to the one over the crowd. The Acquisitions kept up with the attendant until they stood at the base of the platform, about twenty yards away.

From my vantage point, I saw blood along Stella's neck, red tingeing the fabric of her shirt. I balled my fists. They'd already hurt her. *Fuck*.

"All looking fit and ready. Excellent. Before we get started, I'd like to thank Governor Elliot for allowing us the use of the fort."

The governor stood in the spectator section and waved. A woman knelt in front of him, her blonde head bobbing furiously on his cock. The crowd clapped, and the governor gave Cal a small salute before sitting down and focusing on the woman at his feet.

"Okay, folks, we are going to do a little Louisiana Gladiator. How's that sound?"

The crowd roared, the sound echoing around the fort and up into the cloudy sky.

"Family. Is there anything better?" Cal laughed, the sound hollow, like the man. "No. So, in keeping with our theme, here's the rules. Each Acquisition will fight the others one on one. Bare fists only—"

The crowd broke out in boos and jeers.

Cal held up his hand. "Wait, wait, let me finish. There are rules. We can't very well let them run around with machetes like the Vinemonts back in the day, now can we?"

Laughter erupted, and Cal had them in his palm once

again. "So fist fights are the order of the day. *But,* if an Acquisition loses, then one of their beloved family members will be harmed by one of our competitors." Cal pointed toward us. "We have three new guests with us today. Twila, Brianne's mother, Annie, Gavin's sister, and Leon, Stella's father."

"No!" Gavin turned, seeking and finding his cowering sister. He took two steps before the attendant brought a baton down on his shoulder, sending Gavin to his knees.

Stella gazed up at me, her heart-shaped face set in lines of determination. She dug in her pocket, pulled out a hair tie, and began finger combing her hair into a tight bun. Brianne peeked up and locked eyes with her mother. A litany of "no, no, no" came out of Brianne's mouth, growing stronger with each repetition.

Stella glanced at her father, but kept her face stoic. When she looked at the child, she winced. I shook my head at her. Pity had no place in the trials. Only strength.

"So, first up. Let's go ahead and see what Brianne and Gavin can do, shall we? I want to save the catfight for last." Cal saluted the crowd and motioned to the attendant who shoved Stella inside the hollow oak.

After a few long moments, she stepped onto the top platform. Cal pulled her to his side, their backs to me. I hoped for a second she would shove him off, but that was foolish. I needed Cal alive to win the Acquisition.

He glanced over his shoulder at me before running his hand to her ass and palming it. "Gorgeous redhead, I hope you like to watch as much as I do. Oh! Oh my goodness." He slapped his forehead and guffawed into the microphone. "Oh, dear me. I almost forgot to tell everyone the most important rule of the competition. Can you guess what it is, Stella?"

She squared her shoulders and said nothing.

"If an Acquisition loses both rounds, then their family member dies."

CHAPTER TWELVE
STELLA

THE SPECTATORS SCREAMED, BLOODLUST in their shrieks of approval at Cal's words. Death, misery, ruin—this was their currency. Hate burned in my heart, stripping away everything soft and gentle and turning me into nothing more than a brand of rage.

The child shivered, her eyes wide as she stared at her brother. Her lips moved, but I couldn't hear her words. Maybe they were silent. I knew what she said all the same. The same litany of fear I'd recited until the Acquisition transformed me from fearful to vengeful. Even so, I wanted to weep for her. I wouldn't.

"Mommy?" Brianne yelled up to the woman who sat catatonic.

The sound roused the woman and she leaned over and stared at Brianne. "Bri?"

"Mommy!"

Despite my efforts to avoid it, I glanced at my father. He was a shell of the man I'd seen only a few months before. His hair was faded to white, his cheeks sunken, and his eyes bugged in his too-thin face. Something moved in my heart—sadness or regret, I didn't know which. But I wished he weren't here, for his sake and mine.

"It's going to be okay, Annie. Don't be scared." Gavin called to his little sister, whose terrified eyes darted from him to Bob.

An attendant brought a chair to the top of the small platform, and Cal sat. He pulled me into his lap so I was angled sideways to him. Raising his hand, he pointed to the attendants stationed at the door where we'd entered the arena. They rushed out into the courtyard, batons at their sides.

"KO preferred. Incapacitation acceptable. If you don't fight, we'll hurt you *and* your family members. Red, give them a little taste so they know we aren't just teasing." Cal clicked the microphone off.

Red reared back and sank a fist in Brianne's mother's stomach. Brianne screamed. Bile rose in my throat as Cal dug in my hair and undid my bun, my hair falling messily down my back.

"Isn't that better?" He stroked my hair as Brianne's scream broke when one of the attendants cracked his baton across her back. She fell to her knees.

Cal clicked the microphone back on. "That's enough. I think they're ready."

The attendants hurried back inside the wooden door as Brianne struggled to her feet.

Gavin was still consoling his little sister when Brianne launched herself onto his back.

"That's more like it. Enjoy the show, folks." Cal dropped the microphone and ran his hand along my thigh before peering at my neck. "What's this here? Who bit you?"

I didn't answer, only watched as Gavin yanked Brianne from his back and tossed her to the ground. She scrambled up and rushed him again, her blonde hair flying out behind her. He had at least fifty pounds on her. There was no way she could win. But she fought, screaming and clawing at him as he tried to ward her off.

"Something about you. The more I see you, the more I want you. I *covet* you. I'm not the only one, either. Why is that, do you think?" Cal's voice slithered into my ear.

I kept my mouth clenched shut as Brianne kicked at Gavin's shins. He yelled and shoved her back.

"I find myself wondering if your snatch is covered with the same color hair as this." He twisted a lock between his fingers. "You were bare last time I saw you."

I focused on Brianne and Gavin, analyzing their movements, looking for weaknesses. I could do it. I could fight and win. The only thing I couldn't do was look at Gavin's sister. Her frightened eyes were already etched in my mind, her youth ruined by this foul tournament.

"Hey." He yanked my hair and moved his hand under my shirt. "I need your full attention. Gavin and Brianne can work out their differences without you."

"You have it." I darted my eyes over to Sin. He cut an imposing figure, standing completely still, his eyes on me.

"I don't think I do." He worked his hand up my shirt to my sports bra and pinched my nipple through the fabric. "But I know how to get it."

I froze, humiliation washing over me at Cal's unwanted touch. Even as Brianne screamed below, I met his eyes, the dark pupils wide.

"Was that so hard?" He eased up on my nipple and palmed my breast. "I just wanted to talk to you a little. I feel like I haven't gotten to know you as well as Brianne."

The crowd roared as Gavin let out a shriek, but I kept my eyes on Cal.

"Very good. See? You can be taught." He pulled his hand out of my shirt and rested it on my thigh again.

I fought the urge to watch what was happening on the ground below. *Think*. I had to take this opportunity to learn what I could from Cal. "Dylan told me he owns me."

"Ah." His eyes went to the mark on my neck. "So I assume this is his handiwork?"

I nodded. "Sin owns me. Dylan owns me. You don't.

There's no point coveting something you will never have."

"I wouldn't be so sure. I'm still Sovereign for some time yet. Besides, 'never' is such a broad term, don't you think?" He leaned over and licked along the bite mark. I bit my lip to keep from crying out at the sting.

Brianne's shriek got her mother to her feet as the crowd laughed and jeered. I glanced down. She was on her stomach, crawling toward Gavin. Bloodied and grim, he backed away from her.

Cal took my arm and wrapped it around his neck. "What if I said Sin would win if you'd be mine for the rest of the contract year? Voluntarily agree to do whatever I asked. I don't want to fight you. That's not my kink. I want total and utter obedience."

I stilled and stared into his face, trying to measure the weight of his words. Was he lying? "Why do I care if he wins or not? I wish him dead every morning when I wake up."

He smiled. "You aren't fooling me. I can see you're considering it. Good. Though it's not up to you, really. Sin would have to agree since, technically, he owns you now."

"How do I know you'll keep your word?"

His face hardened, and he slapped me. "Don't ever question my honor, you little cunt."

My ears rung but I tried not to react to the pain along my cheek.

Gavin yelled, the sound throaty and full of rage.

The crowd roared.

Cal's sneer turned into a smile. "I think that's my cue." He scooted me off his lap and stood.

Brianne lay motionless in the grass, her eyes closed. Gavin knelt beside her, tears streaming down his face as he stroked her hair. Her face was bloodied, his knuckles red.

"Looks like we need a medic. Get her revived for her bout with Stella. In the meantime, Red, you're up."

Two attendants rushed out and grabbed Brianne under her arms before dragging her back through the door we'd entered. Gavin sat heavily and stared up at me, his eyes open windows of pain and regret. I kept taking deep breaths, refusing to panic at the rising tide of horror around me.

Red walked to a steel table along the battlement, though I couldn't see what was on the top. I shivered as Cal came up behind me and lay his forearm across my chest above my breasts.

"You're really going to love this part." He held me in place so I was looking right at the chained victims.

Red picked up something that looked like a monkey wrench, the metal dull and heavy.

"Oh, good choice, my man. Let's see what he can do with it." Cal laughed, and the rest of the audience laughed with him.

My blood turned to ice as Red approached the bound woman. She tried to stand and back away, but she was chained to the floor. I glanced to Sin. He shook his head almost imperceptibly. Maybe he was telling me not to watch. It didn't matter. I had to see it, to witness every last disgusting act. It was the only way to keep my fire burning, the same fire that would destroy these animals.

Red pulled the wrench back and swung as Brianne's mother screamed. The sound was cut off as the wrench made contact with a wet thud. Her teeth flew out, like white pearls in the low light of the clouds. Blood poured down her face.

Gavin retched into the grass, and I bit my cheek hard enough to draw blood.

The crowd leapt to its feet and screamed with approval. Brianne's mother screeched and fell to her hands and knees. The child wailed, covered her face, and scooted closer to my father. He didn't comfort her, only stared at Brianne's mother as she moaned and touched her ruined nose and mouth.

"Well, well. Red's been working on his aim." Cal patted my ass. "Good show. Now let's move on to the next round. Gavin and Stella." He pushed me toward the stairs and lowered the mic. "Go on, and don't forget what we talked about. I only hope Gavin doesn't mess up your pretty face too much. I'd like to do the honors on that."

I descended the narrow spiral stair and walked out onto the grass, the turf soft beneath my feet as the light mist continued to drizzle down around me.

Pulling another elastic from my pocket, I wrapped my hair into the same tight bun. Sparring with Dmitri was one thing. Fighting a stranger was something else. But having to fight Gavin when the consequences were torture and death?

Gavin still sat in the grass, head in his hands.

I glanced up to my father. He leaned forward, his eyes imploring me. Sin stood behind him, his arms crossed and his mask inscrutable. The child cried and clung to my father. I'd trained, struggled, and pushed myself so I could win any match. But the more I looked at the child, the more I questioned my desire to win.

I stopped in front of Gavin, my hands at my sides. "Gavin, you need to get up."

"Did you see what he did? Did you see what *I* did?" He turned his hands over and showed me his bloodied knuckles.

"You did what you had to do." Just like I was going to do what I had to do. "Get up or I'll kick you in the face."

"No." He shook his head.

"Bring out the batons, boys." Cal's voice drew the attendants, weapons at the ready.

I let out a breath, steadied myself, and aimed a kick at Gavin's ribs. He clutched the spot and fell to his side.

"Oh, we've got some fireworks."

The attendants retreated as Gavin struggled back to his knees, then his feet. He finally met my eyes. I wanted to hug him. Instead, I raised my hands, ready to fight.

"Are we really going to do this?" His question was more sorrow than anything else.

"We have to." I tilted my chin toward the captives. "For them."

He glanced to his sister and brought up his fists. "I'm sorry."

"Me too." I charged him and darted to the side at the last second, punching him in the side of the head. Pain shot through my fist and radiated up my arm, but I turned to face him again.

He shook his head as if he had water in his ear. "Fuck."

"Come on." I waved him to me.

He looked to his sister again before pounding across the grass. I dodged, letting his weight carry him forward, and jumped on his back. He flailed, grabbing at my arm as I brought my elbow down on his shoulder again and again.

He slapped my face and finally got hold of my arm, then threw me over his head. I hit the ground with a thunk. The wind rushed out of my body as the crowd tittered. I rolled before his foot came down where my stomach had been. Climbing to my feet, I backed away, breathing hard and looking for an opening.

Then I glanced up at my father. The girl sat next to him, frightened and alone. My father ignored her and watched as I fought to keep him from harm.

Gavin leapt toward me, but I backed away, curving around the platform as he followed. He sprinted at me, and I feinted right before kicking his shin as hard as I could. He fell to his knees, and his sister screamed. The sound was piercing, far too powerful for her small body. My father smiled down at me, triumph in the tilt of his head.

And then I knew what to do. My father had made his mistakes, committed his sins. Gavin's sister hadn't. I wouldn't let her suffer. I could lose this battle, but win the war by giving in to Cal's demand.

Gavin clambered to his feet and I kicked him in the stomach. He stumbled back as I launched myself onto him, wrapping my legs around him as he staggered back into the unforgiving wall. I took his head between my hands and knocked it against the stones.

"Fuck!" He grabbed my waist and tried to pull me off.

"You have to win this." I hissed in his ear.

He stopped struggling against me, so I punched the side of his head. "Don't stop. Make it look good. But win. For your sister."

He punched me in the ribs. I gasped and fell back, landing on my feet. I brought my hands up.

The wails of Brianne's mother carried down to our ears as we circled each other again. The crowd went silent, and the rain began to intensify.

He lunged at me, but I sidestepped easily and swung around, landing the back side of my fist into his kidney. Stumbling forward, he doubled over. I kicked his legs out from under him and jumped on top. The crowd roared as I rained blows down on his face. He threw his arms up and tried to block me.

"Fight back." I said through clenched teeth.

He rolled to his right, throwing me onto my back and climbing on top of me. His palms slid against my wet skin as he wrapped his hands around my throat.

"Squeeze harder. Leave marks." I gasped, and he obeyed.

I clawed at his hands as the cold rain soaked into my clothes. When my vision began to dim, I pushed one arm between his and wrenched his elbow out to the side. It gave me the opening I needed to flip him and climb off. I backed away, my neck burning from his pressure.

"We still have a live one down there, my friends." Cal laughed.

I bent over and put my hands on my knees, taking deep breaths as Gavin scrambled to his feet and approached me. We were both wet and muddy as the rain began to pour. "Just give up now. You've put on a good enough show."

I shook my head. "More. We need more. We can't risk it." I exploded off my back foot and nailed him in the jaw with my right fist. Pain burst along my knuckles as he stumbled backwards.

Aiming a kick at his side, I struck him squarely with the tip of my boot. He howled and tightened up, pulling his arm in close to the injured spot. I darted away, adrenaline making my movements even faster.

Tracking my arc, he tackled me and we rolled until I was able to crawl away. He grabbed my ankle and hauled me back. I rolled onto my back and kicked at him, but he grabbed my knees and pinned me between his thighs. His fist came as a blur, and pain radiated from my eye and across my face.

I screamed and fought as he tried to get his hands around my throat again. Another burst of pain at my temple and my vision went dark for a moment before brightening almost unbearably.

"I'm sorry." He hit me again, this time lighting my ribs on fire. Another blow on my other side had me writhing and trying to dig my elbows into the soft ground and slide away from him. Rain pelted my face as he loomed over me, his fist drawn back. I covered my face, but he connected with the back of my forearm. Crying out, I scratched deep gouges in his neck. He slapped me, the sound like a shot, the pain bringing tears to my eyes.

I bucked hard and pushed with my right foot. He toppled sideways, and I scooted back from him. Turning to get on all fours, I tried to crawl away. His weight landed on my back, crushing me as his forearm went around my throat.

"Pass out." He hissed in my ear. "I can't hurt you anymore. I won't. Please don't make me."

I struggled, digging my nails into his arm and trying to roll him off me. He was too big. My breathing became labored simply from his weight on my back.

"That's enough. They'll buy it. Please. It's enough." He squeezed a little. "Just stop."

I slowed my movements and let my head loll to the

ground.

"Thank you," he whispered as the crowd roared.

CHAPTER THIRTEEN
Sinclair

STELLA STOPPED MOVING, AND the crowd erupted in cheers. Her pain had me stretched tight, every fiber I possessed pulled to its breaking point.

"Well done, Gavin! You've made Bob proud. Head on back inside while they attend to Stella. She needs to get ready for the bitch fight."

The crowd chuckled.

"It will be a fun one. I saved the best for last." Cal turned toward me. "Sin, my fellow redhead lover, you're up."

Stella's father cowered as I strolled to the tray of implements. Some of them were far too coarse for my tastes, tools made for rough trades when I was more of an artist. I played my fingers along the handles and blades until I came to a particularly sharp set of pruning sheers. They would have been appropriate, given the vines that snaked their way around me, caging me even as I was out in the open air, but I needed to go bigger.

"Please…" Mr. Rousseau shook and stared at me, his eyes wide and his chains jingling with each shudder.

I ignored him and continued down the row of tools. A

particularly sharp cleaver glinted in the low light, the blade covered with tiny droplets of mist. I gripped it and pulled it from the tray. Heavy in my hand, the blade would do well for what I had in mind. Red sat on the bench in front of me, Brianne's bloodied mother lying at his feet, her eyes open and glassy. The child cowered as I walked past, but Red sat still, eyes forward. Crimson marred his white button-down and a few splatters had crusted on his face.

I stopped in front of Stella's father. He grimaced and leaned away from me. His lip trembled and a line of spit oozed from one side of his mouth.

"Mr. Rousseau, hold out your hand."

"N-no." He shook his head. "Please don't."

"If you make me tell you again, I'll take two hands instead of one." I turned the blade this way and that, watching the light play along the razor sharp edge.

The girl whimpered and tried to scoot away. It was futile. Her chains kept her close.

I glanced at her. "Look at your feet and cover your ears."

Her chin trembled, but she did as instructed.

"Good girl. See? Mr. Rousseau? It's not hard to comply. Do you want me to tell you again, or would you like to lose just the one hand?"

A high-pitched strangled sound came from his throat, and he locked his terrified eyes on mine.

"Tense." Cal's hiss oozed through the speakers.

A tear rolled down his paper-thin cheek and he held out his shaking left hand. "Stella wouldn't want you to—"

I slapped him hard enough to split his lip. The crowd tittered at my back. "I told you never to say her name. And another thing—" I wrenched his hand to the side and pinned it to the bench next to him. "—Stella may as well have told me to do this."

I lowered my voice. "She lost on purpose. She wanted this for you. She knows you deserve it instead of the child. She knows doing this to you doesn't pain me at all. She's saved me. Again. Choosing you to suffer means that neither the child nor I have to suffer. Don't you see?" I pressed the cleaver to his wrist. He tried to hit me with his free hand, but I pushed back, my full weight crushing him as I lined up my stroke on his age-spotted skin.

"No, no, please. I'm sorry. I'm sorry. Please don't—"

I held the blade up high so everyone would see. The crowd gasped, anxious for the severing stroke.

"She's chosen me over you." I brought the cleaver down hard. His scream of pain pierced the air and rent the darkening sky. Cheers went up from the spectators.

The hand pulled away cleanly. I rose and grabbed it by the fingers, lifting it above my head as his agonized screams fed the bloodthirsty crowd. Then I tossed it down into the grass like a piece of garbage.

"Oh ho-ho, Sinclair came to play." Cal gave me an elaborate bow from his platform. "Well done."

Stella's father screamed again before huddling over his maimed limb and rocking back and forth. Satisfaction welled inside me, though I knew Stella wouldn't approve.

"Amazing. Ladies and gents, give Stella's father a hand!" Cal laughed, practically screaming at his own joke.

I leaned down so only her father could hear me. "That was a small price to pay for betraying her. I almost hope she loses again so I can finish the job."

CHAPTER FOURTEEN
Stella

Rough hands dragged me back into the stone walls of the fort. I kept my eyes closed even as they dropped me on the hard floor. Footsteps clacked along the stones, and then I was doused with freezing water. I opened my eyes and sputtered, no acting necessary.

Sophia stood above me, hands on her hips. "Sit up."

I struggled to a sitting position, my body aching, my face especially.

She knelt and wrinkled her nose in distaste before waving the attendants away. "You will win this."

I stared at her, unsure of what sort of pep talk this was.

She grabbed my chin, her nails digging into me. "You will win this." Her voice was a threatening whisper, her eyes malevolent. "Sinclair will be the next Sovereign with me at his side. If you fail me, the consequences will be beyond your worst nightmares."

I laughed and spit in her face. "Get the fuck out of here."

"You little bitch!" She screamed as if I'd burned her, and wiped my bloody spit from her cheek. "Sinclair will hear about this."

I shrugged, the simple movement sending shooting pains down my spine. "Yeah, go ahead and tell him I think you're a cunt while you're at it."

She raised her hand to strike me, but paused as I stared her down. She was beautiful, her face a perfect oval, her eyes dark and sultry, her lips an indulgent red pout. My hands itched to destroy all of it.

She seemed to rethink the idea of hitting me, and dropped her hand. "I'll make sure you regret that."

"Put it on my fucking tab." I would fight to the death to keep Teddy safe, but this bitch would never be a part of that calculus. She was just a grasping climber, trying to hang on to the man she saw as the next Sovereign.

I looked past her and saw Brianne leaning against the wall by the door, her eyes closed. Sophia rose and stormed away, her heels echoing on the cold stone.

"Brianne?" I crawled over to her.

We would have to fight. One of us would lose. I clenched my eyes shut. The knowledge that more blood would be on my hands made the room spin. My actions to protect Gavin's sister had led to this, but was I strong enough to follow through and let my father meet his fate?

A scream sounded, followed by the roar from the crowd overhead, loud enough to make it through the heavy doors and thick walls.

She mumbled and didn't open her eyes.

"Brianne?" I got to my knees in front of her and stroked her hair from her face.

Mr. Tablet walked up behind me. "Let's go. It's time."

"She can't go again. Look at her."

A shooting pain in my ribs took my breath away. I fell to my hip. Mr. Tablet had kicked me.

He tried to grab my hair, but he was slow. I shot my legs out and sent him toppling over. Wrath coated every one of my senses as I climbed on top of him, pinning his arms to his sides with my knees. I nailed him with a right, breaking his nose as he screamed. I hit him again and again, my aching fists making fleshy sounds against his pudgy face.

Two other attendants grabbed my arms and ripped me off him, though I got in a good kick to his ribs before they threw me to the floor next to Brianne. My ass hit the ground hard, and a shooting pain tore up my back.

One of the attendants opened the door.

"Bring them out. We're ready for the bitches to go at it." Cal's irritated voice filled the air.

I got to my feet again as an attendant yanked Brianne up by her arm.

She flailed for a moment and opened her eyes. She looked everywhere, but seemed to see nothing. Despite her reticence, she fell into step with her attendant, and we walked out onto the muddy grass.

"Ah, here we are. Two beauties ready to fight it out. May the best bitch win." Scattered applause rang out as the attendants retreated through the doors and closed them.

"Brianne. We have to do this, okay?" I hadn't formed a plan for her. The knowledge of what would happen if I lost blinded me too much to think.

My father was doubled over, his face hidden. Sin stood behind him, his eyes on me. He lifted his chin toward Brianne, silently telling me to attack her.

"Bri, we have to. Come on."

"Do you need the attendants to beat you into it, ladies? Get to it." Cal's voice was a harsh bark, as if he were worried he was losing the crowd.

A high pitched whine came from above. Red grabbed Brianne's mother and shook her. "Fight, bitch, or I kill her right here, right now."

Brianne raised her face toward her mother, and her eyes widened. "Mommy."

Red threw her bloodied mother onto a bench, and Brianne lowered her gaze to mine. "I'll kill you." She took a step toward me, her knees wobbling and her eyes focused.

"I always love encouragement, Red. Works for me." Cal laughed. "I can't help but notice poor Brianne isn't doing so well. I don't think this is a fair fight. Do you?"

The crowd booed.

"I know. Let's make this more interesting. Give Brianne a baton and one of those shocker things. You know what I mean."

The doors opened, Mr. Tablet hurried over to Brianne. He gave her his black baton and drew a hand-sized device from his belt. She took the weapons but kept her eyes on me. Her face was blank. I could feel her resolve. There was no other way this could end. Either her blood would die, or mine.

"I have to do it." She pressed the button and an electrical current shot through the tines on the end of the taser.

I backed up, trying to buy time. "Briann—"

"I have to." She rushed me and swung hard with the baton.

"And we're off to the races!" Cal cried.

I ducked and threw my shoulder into her stomach. She grunted and fell back, but held the taser out so I couldn't get close. Getting to her feet, she squared herself and followed me as I backed away. She was thin and weak. Even so, her love for her mother fueled her forward on unsteady legs.

Keeping my hands up, I waited for her swing. When it came, I darted close to her body and punched her in the back. She screamed and fell to her knees, but recovered before I could attack again.

"I won't let you kill my mother. I won't." She swung the baton in front of her, as if she were warming up.

The accusation was a deep wound, a slow bleed. "I'm not killing her. They are."

"No!" She screamed. "If you win, it's *you*. You did it." Her voice broke as she advanced.

I'd backed halfway around the courtyard when she

sprinted at me. The baton was a dark blur as it struck the side of my neck, and I narrowly dodged her extended hand holding the stun gun. I tried to grab her as she shot past, but she was already out of range by the time I'd recovered from the hit.

She came again as a close bolt of lightning blinded me. I tried to grab for the baton as she swung, but it connected with my fingers. I didn't know I'd screamed until I pulled my hand back, my index and middle fingers bent at unnatural angles, both numb and yet excruciating at the same time. Clutching my injured hand to my chest, I turned and ran, the soggy ground sucking at my boots. There was no escape, just the circle that endlessly led me back to suffering.

I spun, and Brianne collided with me, both of us falling in a tangle. Crawling away, I got to my feet. She was still on all fours, trying to get up, her breaths labored. I kicked her in the side, and she flipped onto her back. It was my chance to end it.

Dropping on top of her, I pressed my forearm against her windpipe and tried to hold her stun-gun-hand with the other. The baton cracked across the back of my head and the world went dark for a moment. Then a burning sensation rushed up my side and I fell over, my entire body sizzling like a steak in a pan.

Brianne let up with the stun gun and beat me with the baton, her blows raining down on my side and my head as I tried to cover myself. She shrieked with each swing, primal fury rolling off her as agony bloomed everywhere the baton struck. I curled into a ball, and the distinct cracking sound and burst of misery as she nailed my ribs made me scream.

I had to get up. If I didn't, my father would die at Sin's hand. I couldn't let it happen. I took a pained breath and shot my foot out, striking Brianne in the knee. It caved inward and she fell, still flailing with the baton. Darkness crept in at the edges of my vision, and everything was hazed in red. I crawled on top of her as she swung again with the baton. Something snapped in my upper arm on the impact. She'd dropped the stun gun when she fell.

Lightning blasted nearby, and the deep roll of thunder shook the earth beneath us. She swung again, slower this time, and I grabbed the baton and ripped it from her grip.

Tossing it away, I leaned over her and ignored her clawing fingers. I gripped her throat with my good hand and pressed as she scratched at my face. She was too weak, the fight leaving her as surely as the oxygen left her bloodstream. I bore down on her throat with my weight as she stared up at me.

Her movements grew more and more sluggish until the crazed light finally left her eyes. They closed, and she was at peace, as if I'd soothed her to sleep with a caress instead of the bleakest violence.

The crowd erupted in cheers as I collapsed onto the wet ground beside Brianne. Rain poured down my face, but I would never be washed clean of what I'd done.

"It looks like Sin's feisty redhead has won this round. Team Vinemont sure knows how to pick 'em." I could hear the leer in Cal's voice, his words snaking down my body like the rivulets of rain.

"Red, get to it. Give us a grand sendoff for this riveting trial."

I turned to where my father sat in a huddle. The child rocked with her hand over her eyes. Red was bent over, and he bobbed up and down, working on something. He rose, yanked Brianne's mother to her feet, and pushed her over the side of the battlement. But she didn't hit the ground. The rope around her neck stopped her halfway down.

My mind seized.

She clawed at her neck and kicked. It was no use. Red had tied her tight. Her face was a ruined crimson mask, everything obliterated but her eyes. She stared down at her daughter as she gave a few more futile kicks.

The crowd sat in silence—her strangled noises the only sound other than the thud of her feet against the stone wall.

When she quieted, her dead eyes still stared at Brianne. Or was it me? I couldn't tell. I couldn't exist there anymore. The spectators roared with approval, and I screamed until my chest burned and the attendants dragged me away.

CHAPTER FIFTEEN
Stella

"I told you Christmas was the worst." Renee pressed cold compresses to my face. "It was. For me. But you, I think—no, I *hope*—this was the worst of it."

I could barely see her. One of my eyes was swollen shut, and the other gave me only a sliver of vision. Everything ached, especially my arm. I couldn't lift it. Reaching across my body with my left hand, I ran my fingers down the rough material of a cast.

Sin drugged me the second I got into the car after the trial. I should have been livid. Instead, I was thankful for the brief reprieve from reality. Had my dreams been happy? I didn't know. All I knew was that I was awake now, thrown back into the hell of Acquisitions and trials.

"Sin?" My voice was a rasp, sandpaper scraping rough wood.

"He's gone to town. Work."

I tried to shake my head clear, but shooting pains rushed up my neck at the movement. "How long?"

Renee moved the compress so it was against the eye that wouldn't open. "Two days. The doctor came and set your arm and your fingers."

Right. Brianne's eyes, the swing of the baton, and the sharp crack of bone that I could still hear. She was always there now—crying in the woods or screaming at me that it was my fault. Was it?

"Brianne has her mother's eyes." My words slurred and fuzzed, my tongue too thick and my lips too swollen.

"Shh, don't talk about that now. You're here safe. The worst is over."

I wanted to believe her. I didn't. Cal's proposition floated through my mind like a bloated body on a bayou.

A knock at the door sounded. I tried to look, but my neck muscles wouldn't cooperate. Instead, they ached and burned.

"It's me." Teddy's voice was like a burst of sunlight through the vapors of hell.

"No." I couldn't let him see me like this.

"Not now, Teddy." Renee rose to go to the door. "Stella isn't dressed."

"Get dressed. I want to see you. I came all the way home for the weekend just to check on you. The trial was a few days ago, wasn't it?" His voice fell.

"Don't come in." Renee grabbed the door handle right as it turned.

Teddy peeked through.

"No!" My vision blurred even more, my eyes swimming with tears. He couldn't see me broken and bruised.

He shoved the door open, knocking Renee back, and came rushing into my room. "Oh my god. What did they do to you?"

He dropped onto the bed next to me, his kind eyes surveying my face, neck, and arms. Tears flowed down my cheeks even as I tried to stop them, to stop the anguish from infecting him.

"Please go." I couldn't see any more, my eyes useless.

"God, Stella." His voice broke as he put a gentle hand to my cheek. "They did this. Why?"

"It doesn't matter why. It's done." Renee spoke from my side. "You need to go, Teddy. She needs to rest so she can recover."

"No shit!" The ire in his voice reminded me of Sin. He took my hand, his palm warm and soft. "You won't tell me, will you?"

I stayed mute, unwilling to give him any scrap of information he could use to blame himself.

"It doesn't matter. I'll get them for you. I don't know how, but they'll pay for this. Sin will pay for letting this happen to you."

"No." I squeezed his hand. "Not his fault."

"Bullshit. He dragged you here. I saw how he treated you. I know he's making you do these things. He didn't have to pick you." His grip on my good hand tightened until it ached. "He probably volunteered. He wants to be Sovereign so bad that he doesn't care who gets hurt."

"It's not true. Not his fault." I pushed to get the words out, the pain in my throat growing worse.

"Don't defend him. He doesn't regret a thing. I passed him on the way here. He was in the convertible with Sophia Oakman, both of them smiling. Makes me sick."

"Teddy, that's enough." Renee's voice rang out strong, but I heard the tremble. "She's had enough. Please, go."

He let my hand go and patted it. "I'll be back soon to check on you." He rose from the bed, his steps retreating to the door. "I'm sorry about this."

I couldn't respond. I couldn't say it was okay or explain it. The door clicked shut, and Renee took her seat on the bed beside me.

"Is it true? He's with Sophia?"

She sighed and smoothed the blanket over my legs. "Yes."

Her reticence told me she knew more. Renee always knew more.

I wouldn't stay in the dark on this, not when what little was left of me started to quake and shatter. "Tell me."

"I think you should rest—"

"Tell me!" I tasted copper, and my throat scorched.

"I-I overheard them talking. They're on their way to the airport." She brushed a hair out my face and put the compress on my cheek. "They'll be gone for two months. She's attending to some Oakman family business in Paris for two weeks, and they intend to spend the rest of the time in Cannes."

A laugh tried to loft from my lungs. It couldn't make it. Instead, it turned into a strangled sound that seemed more like a sob. He'd put me through a house of horrors, and then left for a vacation with the daughter of its architect.

"I'm sure he's only doing what's best."

"What's best? Right." I was glad I couldn't see her face, because I may have tried to claw her eyes.

"You have to understand. They have their own customs, their own ways. I have no doubt Sophia is making a power play. That's the way of it. Think of what it could mean for the family if they—"

"Get out." I couldn't hear it from her, too. Strategy, lies, and deceit were Sin's specialties, not Renee's.

"I'm not finished with your—"

"Go!"

"Please." She let her hand fall. "I didn't mean to hurt you. Only to explain. I just want to help."

There was no help for me, for anyone caught up in this damned competition. But there was information, and Renee had it. I would twist whatever screw I had to if it meant she'd open up to me.

"Tell me…" I swallowed, my throat clicking and burning with the effort. "…what the final trial is. Or get out."

She remained silent and still for what seemed like minutes. Finally, she spoke. "It's different every year. It's always different."

"Leave." My voice receded to a whisper.

She stood, but hesitated next to the bed. I could sense

her wringing her hands. "There's a theme. It's always the same. Love."

"Love?" The word had no place amongst these people. It was meaningless.

"Yes."

"What happened your year?"

"My year." She cleared her throat. "My year, I was forced to choose between hurting two things I loved. That's all I'll say. I can't relive it, not even for you."

"Renee, please."

"No. It won't help you. It will only hurt me. I've already given you what you need to know. What do you love? It's what they will take from you." Her skirt whispered as she walked around my bed and to the door. It shut softly behind her.

They'd already taken so much. What was left? What did I love?

CHAPTER SIXTEEN
Stella

My recovery happened slowly. First, my bruises healed, and then my fingers. My cracked rib and my arm would take more time, though I was no longer stuck in a cast. The aches faded the further I got from the trial, but not the nightmares.

Teddy visited every weekend, bringing me treats from Baton Rouge. He didn't mention Sin again, but his ire bubbled under the surface. I couldn't explain it to him, no matter how much I wanted to. The truth would destroy him the same way it had the rest of his family.

Dmitri was gone, having caught a flight out on the same day as the trial, but I fell into our old routine. A relaxed version of it—light exercise and easy swims to help my body heal.

I often walked around the property, the sun growing hotter with each passing day as spring turned to summer. Every time I passed the levy or the house hidden in the woods, I felt a pull on my heart. But Sin was gone.

He hadn't called, and he hadn't even spoken to Teddy. He was on the beach with Sophia. Did she warm his bed at night? It would be foolish of me to think otherwise. The pain the realization caused just layered on the rest, like sand falling in an hourglass. I was buried beneath it, time weighing down on me as each second ticked closer to the final trial.

After one of my walks, I climbed the stairs to find Lucius waiting for me on the front porch, a glass of Scotch in hand.

"What?" I wiped the sweat off my brow with the back of my forearm.

"I have some news." He stared ahead at the row of oaks. "Sit down."

A stab of worry cut through me. "Teddy?"

"No, he's fine." He patted the seat next to him on the swing.

After considering for a few seconds, I sat, my feet dangling above the floor as he rocked us gently.

"Sin called." He took a long draw from his glass.

I tried not to spend my days wondering what Sin was doing or imaging him with Sophia. I still wanted to believe that his courting of her was done out of the desire to win. It hurt, even if it was a charade. Every day that passed without a call or even a letter made my hopeful fire burn lower.

"What is it?" I kept my tone even.

"He and Sophia are coming back in three days."

I pressed the tip of my toe to the floor, stopping the sway. "Cutting their trip short?"

"Yes."

"Why?"

"I'm not sure. He said they'll be returning and to have the house ready for guests." He didn't look at me, his gaze still on the oaks.

Foreboding swirled in my stomach. "So?"

"So, he'll be bringing her back here with him. He wants to have a get-together with the Oakmans and a few other families. Something to impress everyone."

"What aren't you telling me?"

The distant rumble of thunder foretold a storm brewing. Afternoons in the early summer always progressed too quickly, the volatile air mimicking the tumult inside me. Clear and sunny turned into dark and stormy in a matter of moments. Lucius swirled his drink around in his glass instead of answering me.

"Lucius?"

"Nothing. That's it." He downed the rest of his drink, his brown hair lifting in the warm breeze. "I just wanted you to know she'll be here with Sin. Together. And he wants a welcome party and for you to look like a million bucks." The corner of his mouth lifted in a small smile. "Shouldn't be hard."

He turned to look at me, finally giving me a glimpse of his sky blue eyes. "How are you?"

I studied him, his square jaw and full lips. "Why?"

He set his glass on the small side table and slung his arm across the back of the swing. "Can't I ask how you're doing without some ulterior motive?"

"No." I moved to get up.

"Wait. I'm not going to do anything. I just want to talk."

I arched an eyebrow at him. "Talk?"

"Yeah."

"You sure?"

"Of course." He smiled.

Though I knew he wasn't capable of such an innocent motive, I didn't care. Some sort of contact that didn't involve Renee's subterfuge or Teddy's pity was more than welcome. I eased back down and let him push us back and forth. The cicadas sang in the trees along the edge of the grass that was freshly mowed in a diamond pattern. Despite his desire to talk, we sat silently for a while, the rhythmic creak of the swing the only sound between us.

Relaxing back into the cushion, I pulled my feet up under me and let him do the work. The movement was soothing, and despite our past, his presence was, too. I lay my head back on his arm and closed my eyes. We rocked as the sun fell behind the treetops and the rumbles of thunder grew louder. Rain scented the wind as flashes of distant lightning lit the sky.

"I feel like we should be drinking mint juleps or something."

I snorted. "What even is that?"

The swing stopped as the wind picked up, whistling along the high eaves. "Are you kidding?"

"About what?"

"Are you sitting here telling me you've never had a mint julep?" His eyes rounded, as if it was the most preposterous thing he'd ever heard.

"No. I'm not from here." I shrugged. "I don't drink mint juleps and play the banjo on the front porch."

He rose and stretched, his muscled body fitting perfectly in his button-down and dress slacks. "Get up. Time to drink."

"We haven't even eaten dinner yet."

"So what?" He held his hand out for me.

Would drinking be so terrible? Maybe it would take my mind off the news of Sin and Sophia. I took his hand and rose. The rain began to fall as I followed him into the house.

"The key to a mint julep, as you may have guessed, is good mint."

"So what's a julep?"

"You'll see."

We walked down the hallway and entered the kitchen. Pots and pans hung above a wide, wooden island, and a gas range, two large refrigerators, and a freezer lined the walls. It was tidy, Laura always keeping it in top shape, and some sort of beef stew simmered on the stove top.

"Mint, mint, mint." Lucius mumbled and opened the nearest stainless steel fridge. "Must be in here somewhere." He dug through one drawer and then another.

"Can I help?" Laura walked through the door from the dining room.

"Thank god." Lucius tossed some celery back into a drawer and turned to her. "Mint?"

"Oh." Laura smiled, her rosy cheeks giving her a youthful glow I feared I would never have again. "Here." She walked to the farmhouse sink and reached up to the window sill lined with small pots. "How much do you need?"

"This is going to be an all-nighter." He began to roll up his sleeves, his movements methodical and sharp. "So, give me all you got."

"No all-nighter." I crossed my arms over my chest. "One drink."

"Right." He smirked. "Just one."

Laura tore off the tops of the mint, the earthy smell permeating the air. He took the bunch from her and rummaged around in a drawer. "Glasses and ice." He pulled out a small mortar and pestle as Laura fetched me two highball glasses with ice. "Go ahead and take an ice bucket to the library for me, would you?"

"Yes sir." Laura turned to a cabinet and plucked out a silver pail.

"Stella, come with me." He pushed through to the dining room and opened the sideboard. "Where's the good bourbon?" After leaning over and inspecting each bottle, he shook his head and grinned. "I know where it is. I'll meet you in the library. Put on some music."

Usually, I would have snapped back at orders from him, but the fact that he seemed intent on actually making something for me had me complying and strolling, glasses in hand, to the library. Laura had already placed the ice on the table beside the sofa, and I set the glasses next to it.

The library had a small music console, the speakers hidden in the bookshelves. I flipped through several internet stations before settling on something I figured Lucius would like. Classic rock.

He walked in with a large bottle under one arm, and the mortar, pestle, and mint in his hands. I sank onto the sofa and watched him with interest.

"I didn't know you were a Boston fan." He smirked and got to work on the mint. "Some people think that crushing the mint ruins the drink. They're idiots." He dropped pieces of mint into the small bowl, his long fingers tearing the leaves. Then he grabbed the pestle and began to twist it. "You want the mint to infuse the bourbon, not just serve as a garnish." The mint crunched under his attack until it was wilted and the library smelled like an herb garden.

Lightning struck close by, the windows rattling from the ensuing boom. He gave the pestle a few more turns before he scooped the crushed mint into the glasses. Then he poured the bourbon over the tops and swirled them.

"Garnish is for pussies. Let's drink." He handed me a glass and held his out.

I clinked with him and took a sip. The mint was strong, the bourbon stronger. "Whew." I took another drink and let the heat race into my stomach and expand from there.

He plopped down next to me. "This is the good shit. No joke." He took a large swig and settled into the couch, his warmth radiating along my side as the wind howled outside. "Sin's going to kill me when he gets home and goes looking for his hidden bourbon stash."

"It's good. Minty. Definitely strong." I took another sip. "And I think you enjoy pissing him off."

"Indeed I do. I had to do a little lock picking to get ahold of this bourbon, so enjoy it." His tone turned dark even as he smiled at the taste of his drink. "I intend to make sure the bottle is done for by the time Sin gets back."

Just hearing his name set off a reaction inside me—longing and something akin to being stung. But then my thoughts turned to Sophia. He was with her, maybe fucking her right this moment. I took another pull on the mint julep, the taste less bitter this time than the first.

Lucius got up and went to the fireplace. The muscles in his back pressed against the soft material of his shirt as he leaned over and reached for some wood. Before long he had a fire going and had finished his drink.

He claimed my glass and fixed two more mint juleps. After killing the lights, he sat even closer to me as the fire blazed orange, keeping the clammy air at bay. My head swam, but I enjoyed the lessening ache in my heart. Dulling my senses seemed to be the only way to look at Sin's conquest of Sophia objectively. It was a ruse. It had to be. He loved me. I'd seen it in his eyes, felt it in his touch.

Before long, Lucius made me another drink and put his arm around me. We didn't speak, just watched the fire and listened to another storm roll past with a rock tune thumping in the background. I was as content as I could be under the circumstances.

Uncertainty still ruled my future, but I had a trump card—Cal's proposal.

"You know." I snuggled into his side, enjoying his familiar sandalwood scent. "Cal made me an offer."

He tensed. "What sort of offer?"

I giggled, the sound foreign to my ears, especially because what I was about to say didn't strike me as humorous in the least. I blinked my eyes to clear my swimming head, but it didn't work, only made it worse.

"Stella." He gripped my injured upper arm and I yelped.

He eased up. "Fuck, sorry. I forgot. What did Cal say?"

"He said all I have to do is give myself to him for the rest of the contract year and Sin will win."

He finished his drink and slammed the glass onto the side table. "Drink up."

My glass was half full, and my eyelids were heavy. "I don't think I should."

"Drink it, Stella." His voice was an insistent whir when I wanted silence.

"Fine." I drained my glass, the taste barely registering. He took it, set it next to his, and turned to face me.

"Tell me *exactly* what Cal said. Don't leave anything out." His light eyes were close, his brow wrinkled as he focused on me.

"I did. He said he wanted complete obedience. Said Sin would have to agree to give me to him and then Sin would win." I tried to make my mouth stop moving, to stop giving away my secrets, but the gates were open and I was gone. Why did telling someone make it easier?

"Complete obedience?"

"He wants to hurt me." I shuddered, my body quaking as if another peal of thunder had sounded overhead. "And it'll save Teddy."

His jaw tightened, and he put his hand to my cheek. "It won't come to that."

I leaned into it, suddenly desperate for a touch that was gentle instead of cruel. "I was going to tell Sin, but he ran away from me. Went to *her*." I loathed the sorrow in my heart that leeched into my voice.

He put his palm on my other cheek and kissed me. I tried to lean away. He held me steady. His lips were soft, his kiss gentle. It felt like a caress, not him trying to take something from me. He licked my lips, asking instead of forcing. I opened my mouth as he deepened the kiss, his tongue sinking into my mouth as he wrapped one arm around me and pressed me close.

I ran my hands along his shoulders and then trailed my fingers through his hair. He groaned into my mouth when I tugged lightly. His tongue flicked against mine as he lifted me so that I straddled him. Emotions flashed through me—desire, guilt, and anger chief among them. I didn't love Lucius. My heart belonged to his brother, and there was nothing either of us could do to change it.

I pulled back, breaking the kiss and breathing deeply as he moved to my neck. "I can't."

He gripped my ass and ground me against his cock, the

movement sending tingles and heat through me. "You can." He ran his teeth along my throat. Gripping the hem of my shirt, he tugged it until I lifted my arms. He pulled it over my head and tossed it to the floor.

"No." I protested as he wrapped his arms around me and turned, laying me on my back.

"Yes. Stop fighting it." Settling between my thighs, he shoved my bra over my breasts and sucked a nipple into his mouth. I moaned and arched off the couch, clawing at his scalp as he bit and licked.

He worked his way back to my mouth, his kiss no longer gentle as he ground his hips into me. My skin crackled like the heat from the fire, and I gave in, letting his hands rove me as his mouth slanted over mine.

As if he sensed my defeat, he gripped my wrists and pinned them over my head. His kiss intoxicated me more than the mint juleps, and I craved the contact, the closeness, the heat he offered. But I didn't crave it from him. Could I take it anyway? The same way Sin was taking it from Sophia?

His tongue swirled in my mouth as he kissed me with more passion than I'd ever seen from him. His movements became rougher, rawer. I knew he could give me pleasure, make me forget, if only for a few fleeting moments. It was right in front of me, mine if I would have it. But even as he set me alight, my mind whispered another name and my heart spoke of someone else.

"I don't love you." The words flew out as he kissed to my ear.

"You don't have to." He nipped at my earlobe and palmed my breast. I made an *mmm* sound as he ghosted over the healed bite on my neck. Reaching between me and the couch, he crushed me to him, as if he wanted every bit of closeness he could get. Even as Lucius promised me a respite from reality, Sin was there in my memory, his eyes open, and his soul bare. I had to stop.

I embraced Lucius and buried my face in the crook of

his neck. "Please don't. I can't say no. I need you, but please don't make me do this."

He stilled and nuzzled into my hair. My chest constricted, because I needed him more than I desired him. More than that, I was asking for something he'd never offered. Comfort.

He thrust his hips against me, and I bit my lip to stifle my moan at the naked want the friction created.

"You don't want this?" He nipped at my throat. "You sure? I can feel how hot you are."

"I want..." I swallowed hard. "I want you, but not like this."

He stilled. "You've got to be fucking kidding me. Again, Stella?" He groaned. "You're going to cock block me again?"

I nodded and clung to him even harder. "I'm sorry. I just can't."

"Fucking hell." He pried my arms off him and sat back, eyeing me with open irritation.

I yanked my shirt down as he let out a large exhale. I expected him to storm out or start destroying things. Instead, he stared, his face unreadable in the flickering firelight.

After several uncomfortable seconds, he shook his head. "Goddammit." He pressed the heels of his palms to his temples. "I can't believe I'm doing this. Go upstairs. Get in bed. I'll be there in a little while. I have some fucking blue ball business to take care of first. I'll be there when I'm done."

He stood, his erection noticeable in his pants, before helping me to my feet. I walked past, relieved that my freedom was so easily won.

"Wait." His strained voice stopped me. "One more kiss. That's the price."

I could say no and sleep alone like I'd done so many times already. The nightmares were always there, as if they fed on my loneliness. Paying for a night of solace with a single kiss wasn't too much to ask, especially not after what almost happened on the sofa. Mind made up, I turned and walked back to him.

He put his palms on my cheeks and stroked my hair behind my ears. "Why do I feel like this is the last time? The last chance I'll get to keep you for myself?"

I gazed up at his thoughtful expression, but I had no answer. He brought his lips to mine and kissed me with a surprising reverence. His touch stayed gentle, and his eyes remained closed. It lasted only a moment. When he pulled away, I could sense he wanted so much more. I couldn't give it to him. My heart was long since gone, grudgingly given to another. I wanted to take it back. Especially when the thought of him with Sophia hurt like someone was searing my insides over a spit. Still, it was too late.

"Go." He dropped his hands and kicked his chin up.

I turned, and he smacked my ass. I yelped at the sting.

He held his hands up, his signature smirk back in place. "Sorry. I deserved at least a little something for my troubles."

I made my way up the stairs, though they seemed far more uneven than usual. Once in my room, I stripped off everything but my panties and donned a tank top and shorts. I crawled into bed and waited.

Then I realized I'd invited a viper into my bed during a haze of drunken lust and sorrow. I rolled over and sank to the floor. Pulling out the bottom drawer, I felt around for my knife, wanting the cold comfort it provided by just being there. Sin had returned it to me after the Christmas trial, his blood dried on the blade.

It was tucked against the bottom of the drawer. Next to the familiar metal, I felt something else. A piece of paper. I gripped it between my thumb and forefinger and pulled it loose. Clicking on the lamp, I winced away from the glare and stared at the paper until Sin's dark, slanting handwriting materialized.

Trust me. Everything I do is for you and Teddy.

I stared at the letters, trying to ascribe every meaning possible to them in the hopes I'd land on the right one. Was this about Sophia? About how he was with her to solidify his future as Sovereign? I shook my head. If he'd only spoken to me instead of running off with her, I could have told him about Cal's proposition, about how I already had the key to winning.

The words blurred again as my eyes began to close of their own accord. Alcohol and fatigue warred inside me, but I would sleep no matter which was victorious. I stuffed the piece of paper into my nightstand and crawled back into bed, the knife forgotten. Trusting Sin was all I could do. I had no choice. I'd already decided to trust him the moment I left my father's house. This was just more of the same self-inflicted torment.

The minutes ticked by, and I dozed off. I woke as the bed shifted. Cool air wafted over me as Lucius climbed into bed beside me. He pulled the blanket back up and ran his forearm under my neck, pulling me to him.

"You're not wearing a shirt." I rested my head on his shoulder and threw my arm across his stomach anyway. I was too tired to care about what he'd done to alleviate his blue balls, or worry about the fact he was shirtless. Maybe just having a warm body next to me could keep the nightmares at bay.

"You are an astute observer. I sleep naked."

I tried to pull back.

"Calm down. I kept my boxers on for you."

"Oh." I settled against him again and inched my fingers down to check. They met fabric at his waist.

He ran his hand through my hair. "I think you were hoping I was lying."

I snorted. "No. I just assumed the worst."

"Maybe you shouldn't do that about me anymore. I'm in your bed after all. Dick dry as a bone. All because you asked and looked up at me with those goddamn green eyes. I feel like I'm pussy whipped, but I don't even get the pussy."

I was already drifting back to sleep as he complained. "I'm sorry."

"Don't be. I'm betting you'll let me fuck you in the morning."

I passed out mid-laugh.

CHAPTER SEVENTEEN
SINCLAIR

I SPED DOWN THE narrow lane, pleased to have control once again. The time spent with Sophia had been full of appointments, duties, and requirements that chafed even the deep-seated decorum I'd been taught.

More than the freedom, I wanted Stella. Not on the phone. Not across a table from me. Not in a fucking first class seat next to me. I wanted her beneath me, crying my name in pleasure and pain. My moods grew darker each day I was away until Sophia declared me "insufferable" and demanded I return home and wait for her arrival.

I was more than happy to oblige, leaving for the airport that night and returning even earlier than expected. My tires hummed on the pavement as a warm summer sun began to heat the muggy air. Impatience stalked back and forth through my mind, and I sped even faster, desperate to hold what was mine.

The gate swung open too slowly for my tastes, but before long I was cruising under the familiar Vinemont oaks. I parked in front and took the steps at a run. The house was quiet, everyone just waking up for the day. I couldn't stop the smile that quirked my lips as I approached Stella's door. I slowed my steps, creeping along the runner, not making a sound.

Turning her door handle, I pushed the door open and peered through.

My stomach sank, and every bit of anticipation running through my blood turned to ice. She lay on her side, face angelic in sleep, as Lucius slept beside her, his arm slung across her waist, his face buried in her hair.

They were beautiful together in the morning light. A stunning pair who encompassed so much—pure and corrupt, light and dark. My hand tightened on the doorknob until my bones pressed into the glass. Something this lovely needed to be destroyed. I followed the line of Stella's body, the curve of her breast through her top, the blanket pulled just to her hip. Lucius's tan arm stood in contrast to her fair skin. My fingertips remembered her smoothness. I'd traced her face every night in my dreams.

My palm grew warm, blood coating the door handle as I took in every breath, every curve, and every hair on her head.

I had two options. I could kill them both as they slept and bring the entire Vinemont line to ruin. Or I could walk away. I stood for long minutes, just listening to them breathing deep and even, no doubt exhausted from a long night of fucking.

Lucius had finally won out, taking her from me while I was busy solidifying our family's safety. She'd chosen him over me yet again, and I was the fool who hadn't seen it coming. I studied the back of my hand, the scars there visible, but not as deep as the ones that remained hidden inside me.

Of course she'd turned her back on me. I was a demon. She'd said it in her sleep on dark nights when she would cry out and awake in tears. I'd cradled her in my arms, fighting off the nightmare version of myself. But as I watched her and Lucius, I realized there was only one me.

I was the nightmare version, the one who terrified her, haunted her—who took everything from her and left her broken.

My head pounded, and each beat of my heart was an individual torment. A maelstrom of dark thoughts rained down and swirled in my mind, each one worse than the last. Pity was that I couldn't make good on any of them. Even as she lay in another man's arms, I still wanted her.

Long minutes slipped by as I weighed my need for retribution against the lives of my two brothers and Stella. Could I destroy it all, killing what little was left of me in the process?

Murder whispered to me. After a few more moments, I shoved the dark thoughts down. Molten lead poured over my heart, charring it and sealing it in an impenetrable tomb. When it cooled, I would finally be the man I needed to be to win the Acquisition.

I closed the door.

CHAPTER EIGHTEEN
Stella

"So, about that morning fuck we discussed." Lucius ran his fingers down to the small of my back and tucked them into the waistband of my shorts.

I groaned and rolled away from him. It was too early, though bright rays of sun streamed through the window. My head pounded along with my pulse, a hangover already setting in.

"Nuh uh." I buried my face in my pillow and stretched my legs all the way down to my toes before relaxing again.

"Come on." He propped on his elbow next to me and squeezed my ass. "It'll be fun. I don't even care if you just lay there. Go back to sleep. I'll handle the rest."

I snorted and reached back to slap his hand away. "Asshole."

"I've never met a girl who jumps right to anal, but sure." He smoothed his hand down farther.

"That's my cue." I slid out of bed and stretched, my arm aching where the break had been. My stomach churned—the bourbon had transformed to acid. He lay back in a huff, his erection noticeably tenting the sheet. Climbing back into bed and sleeping in was preferable, but there was no way I was going anywhere near him.

He sat and pulled his knees up. "How did you sleep?"

"Good, actually. Better than when I'm alone."

"You cried a little." He glanced away. "I woke up and you were talking about leaves and then rope. I said something to you, and you quieted down."

I should have been embarrassed about it, but I wasn't. He knew what I'd gone through at the last two trials. Besides, there was no way I could control what I did in my sleep.

"What did you say to me that helped?" I asked and walked to the bathroom.

"I don't know. I was half asleep. I guess my voice or something made you feel better."

"Maybe. Hey, I'm going to shower." I turned and pinned him with a glare as he smirked. "*Without* you. Your sleeping buddy services, while very much appreciated, are no longer needed."

"Don't get used to it. The next time I'm in this bed, I'll be between those legs." He licked his lips. "Also, I'm about to be out the country for a week or two."

I peered at myself in the mirror, the circles under my eyes still apparent though not as dark. "You'll miss Sin coming home."

"Yeah, I'm real bummed about that. I'll cry into my mojitos over it." His voice receded, and I heard my door click shut.

"Thank you."

He didn't hear me, but I meant it all the same. Somehow, I'd spent the night with Lucius Vinemont and made it through unscathed.

I laughed at the thought as I stripped and stepped into the shower. Halfway through soaping up I heard a knock at the bathroom door.

"It's me," Renee called.

"Hey. What's up?" I rinsed off and stepped out, taking the towel she proffered.

"Nothing. Just wanted to come by and see you." She smiled. Her warmth had dimmed as of late, but it was still welcome.

I glanced to the ceiling. "How is she?"

She lowered her head. "Worse, I think. Lucid less and less."

"Did you know she chose Sin to compete this year?" I toweled off and snagged some lotion from the counter.

"What?" She canted her head at me. "No, she didn't."

"Yes." I walked into my bedroom. "She did."

Renee followed and sat on my bed, her mouth drawn into a frown. "That can't be true."

"Sin said so. The previous Sovereign chooses who will compete."

She shook her head slowly as I dressed. "Cal Oakman visited last summer. It was odd. He only came to see Rebecca. The boys weren't even home." She lifted her wide eyes to me. "She did this? How could she do this to her own blood?"

I'd never seen a good side to Sin's mother. When Renee described Rebecca talking and laughing about the boys when they were little, I couldn't picture it. The cruel old crone on the third floor was the boogie man to me, but Renee still believed there was some good left inside her.

"This is what she does. What she's become." I sat next to her and took her hand. "Rebecca set this in motion. I don't know if it was to keep the Vinemonts in power or what, but she chose him. I'm sorry she kept it from you."

She stayed silent, though her thoughts were loud enough I could almost hear them.

I squeezed her hand. "Let's go down to breakfast. Maybe Lucius can shed more light?"

"No. I'm going upstairs. I need to hear it from her." She set her lips in a thin line.

I knew the look. There was no arguing with it. We stood and walked into the hall. She took the steps to the third floor as I descended to the first. The scent of bacon drew me toward the kitchen, but I stopped as I passed the dining room. Sin sat at the head of the table, his eyes already focused on me as I rounded the corner.

I couldn't stop the happiness that swelled in my heart, but he regarded me with a cold stare. My joy at seeing him faded like leaves in the winter. Had he fallen for Sophia after all?

"When did you get here?" I strode toward him, wanting to touch him. Instead, I stopped and sat at my usual place. I couldn't gauge him. The look on his face was stony, but the fire in his eyes was hot enough to burn.

"This morning."

"Why didn't you tell me?" I lay my napkin across my lap and met his glare.

"Why would I have to tell you anything?"

"What?" I stopped what I was doing as anger overtook my earlier happiness. "You watch me get beaten to within an inch of my life, watch me choose between killing my father or Brianne's mother, and then you leave for a European vacation with that Oakman bitch? And now you're back and don't feel the need to even mention it to me?" My voice rose to almost a yell.

He stood and towered over me, hell in his eyes. "Don't you *ever* refer to Sophia in that manner. You aren't fit to speak her name, much less stand in her presence. In fact, get the fuck out of here. You can eat with the dogs where you belong." He swiped my table setting onto the floor. My plate shattered at our feet.

I rose and stood toe to toe with him, craning my head back so I could look him in the eye. "You asked for my trust. I gave it. I believed this entire time that you were cozying up to Sophia to save Teddy. To save *me*."

He gripped my throat, his palm clammy. "I *said* do not speak her name."

I couldn't see him anymore, not the real him. The devil who'd come to my house and offered me the contract was back, his mask firmly in place.

"What is wrong with you?"

He leaned down until we were nose to nose. "What is wrong is that I ever thought you were anything more than the whore daughter of a petty criminal." The hand at my throat tightened. "Now get out of my sight."

He shoved me back, and I stumbled into the sideboard. Lucius walked into the dining room and looked from me to Sin.

He bristled. "What did you do?"

Sin calmly returned to his seat at the head of the table. "Get your whore out of here before I do something she'll regret."

"What?" Lucius took my elbow and steadied me. "What the fuck are you talking about?"

"You heard me." Sin leaned back and gave me a withering glance. "I'd do it quickly, if I were you. Otherwise, there will be a bloody mess to clean, and that just wouldn't do."

"Wait just a fucking minute. You need to explain—"

"No." I pulled away from Lucius's grip. The room spun, but not from my hangover. "I'll go. I don't want to be in here anymore. I don't want to be here at all." I turned and ran as my heart hammered, my ears burning.

Bounding up the stairs, I almost bowled Teddy over. I'd forgotten school was out for a few weeks before summer term.

He put a hand on my shoulder. "You okay?"

I couldn't look at him, couldn't bear his kindness right after Sin had treated me so horribly. I refused to cry, especially in front of Teddy. Explaining it wasn't an option.

"I'm fine. Hungover is all." I side-stepped him and continued climbing the stairs. "I'll catch you later today. Promise."

"Okay." His voice remained uncertain, but once I reached the second floor landing, I heard his steps retreating downward.

I turned toward my room and hesitated. Raised voices from the third floor caught my ear. Throwing another glance toward the sanctuary of my room, I took a hesitant step up the stairs.

"Why?" Renee's yell had my feet moving faster.

Was she asking about why Rebecca had chosen Sin to compete? I wanted to hear that answer. I hurried up the stairs and down the hall, the yelling covering any noise I made.

"Because he's strong." Rebecca's screech raised the hairs on the back of my neck.

"You've doomed him. You've killed Teddy."

"No, no, no. Don't cry. Come here. Let me hold you." Rebecca's voice switched to something soothing. The sweet timbre drew me closer and I peeked between the hinges as Renee sat on the bed. Rebecca pulled her into a hug and rocked her back and forth.

"Why?" Renee's question was thick with anguish.

"I had to. It's the only way." Rebecca smoothed Renee's hair. "Do you know I've always thought your hair is the most beautiful I've ever seen? The softest I've ever touched?" Tenderness suffused every word.

I blinked hard, trying to reconcile the calm, attentive woman before me with the raving lunatic of a few months ago.

"You've told me, yes."

"I'll tell you again and again, because it's true. You're the best thing in my life. You and my boys." Rebecca continued rocking Renee, the two women locked in a loving embrace.

"But Sin, he could break. The same thing that happened to us could happen to him."

"No." Rebecca shook her head. "He's strong. He can end it."

"End it?" Renee pushed back and stared into Rebecca's face. "What do you mean?"

"I mean he's strong enough and smart enough to win.

And once he does, he will bring it crashing down."

"How?"

"He already has what he needs to do it. Stella. He loves her." Rebecca cupped Renee's cheek. "My love for you broke me. His love for her will save him. I know it. He's stronger. You'll see."

Renee shook her head. "But what do you mean by—"

Rebecca's kind face twisted in disgust, and she slapped Renee hard across the face. "Goddamn bitch. Who let you in here? Why are you in my room?"

"Rebecca, please."

She slapped Renee again, and I was about to walk in and restrain her, but Renee rose.

Rebecca wielded her harsh words like a bludgeon. "You're a curse. I wish I'd never laid eyes on you. I wish I'd left you where I found you so you could die in the gutter where you belong. You shouldn't be here."

Renee calmly walked to the repaired cupboard, unlocked it, and pulled out a syringe.

Spit flew from Rebecca's lips. "Answer me! Where are my boys? Where's Cora? What have you done to Cora? It's all your fault. All of it. You did this."

Renee returned to the bed, and before long, the screaming stopped as Rebecca drifted off to sleep.

Renee pulled the blanket to Rebecca's chin and smoothed the hair from her face. She kissed her on the forehead and curled up in the bed next to her, holding her hand. "I hope you're right about Sin and Stella, my love. For all our sakes, I hope you're right."

CHAPTER NINETEEN
Stella

Sin left that morning. I pressed my fingertips to the window pane as his sports car retreated down the long drive.

"He thinks we fucked." Lucius walked up behind me. "Wouldn't listen to a word I said, but that's nothing unusual."

"He didn't even ask. Just assumed." I bounced my forehead on the glass. "And he's been fucking Sophia this whole time so he has no right—" I bit my cheek to stop the waterfall of bitter words.

Lucius squeezed my shoulders and turned me around to face him. "I know, but I also know that when he gets like this, there's no talking to him, no explaining, no nothing."

"I've gathered." I let him pull me into a hug. "Why are you being so nice to me?"

He smoothed his palms up and down my back. "I figure if he already thinks we fucked then we may as well do it, right?"

"Lucius—"

"Or look at it as getting back at him." He gripped my

ass and pulled me up his body until I was eye level with him. "Don't you want to?"

Yes. I wanted to punish Sin for assuming the worst, for being with Sophia while expecting me to stay behind, pining for his return. *Trust me.* His note asked for something he wouldn't give me—trust.

I wanted to hurt him. But I wasn't like him. I couldn't turn off one emotion and turn on another like water from a spigot. He could exchange one mask for another as easily as changing clothes. I'd never had the luxury of a disguise. I was always out in the open, my heart on my sleeve. The foolish thing was, I didn't want to change. I wanted to remain the same. At the end of the year, when I walked away from this cabal of vultures, I still wanted to be me.

I answered Lucius's questioning look with a shake of my head. "Put me down."

"Fuck, Stella." He set me on my feet and scowled.

"I thought you were leaving on business."

He sighed. "I am."

I lay my hand over his heart and got to my tiptoes to kiss his rough cheek. "Thank you for last night."

He peered down at me. "Nothing to thank me for."

"It's okay to be a decent person every so often, you know?"

"Keep talking like that and I'll throw you on the bed and show you just how decent I'm not." His eyes flickered to my lips in his usual, wolfish way.

"Stella?" Teddy pushed through my half-open door. "Oh, hey. Sorry. I didn't know you two were—"

Lucius gave me one more long look before turning and walking away. He clapped Teddy on the back as he walked past. "No, it's cool. I've got a plane to catch."

"Where you headed?"

"Cuba for a little while."

"Is everything okay there?" Teddy sat on my bed.

"Nothing me and a .45 can't fix." Lucius strolled out the door and down the hall.

"Is he kidding?" Teddy raised his eyebrows.

Definitely not. "Yeah. I think so. He's just in a mood."

Teddy lay back and ground the heels of his palms into his eyes. "Seems like everyone is. Sin bit my head off about talking to Laura before tearing out of here. What's going on?"

I plopped next to him. "Sin thinks I slept with Lucius."

He stopped rubbing his eyes. "Oh, well then that makes more sense. Wait, did you?"

"Yes. I slept with Lucius as in he literally slept in my bed with me last night because I needed someone. No, we did not have sex."

"Thank god. I was beginning to question your judgment."

"Shut up." I swatted his leg.

"What about Lucius? What's his problem?"

"Naturally, he's mad that he got to spend the night but didn't get any."

He laughed. "He's such an ass sometimes."

"He isn't as bad as he seems." I lay back so we were shoulder to shoulder.

"Huh. I thought I was the only one who knew that."

"Nope. I know it now, too."

"Neither of them are bad. Not really. Sin can be sort of…"

"Psychotic?"

"Yeah, something like that. But it's because he's had a lot of pressure, I think. Dad died when we were little, and then Sin became the man of the house. And then there was the Brazil thing that we don't talk about." He drummed his fingers on his chest. "And Mom. And now the Acquisition. He's just really strong, and it makes him sort of, I don't know, focused and driven to the point of seeming cold and, like you said, psychotic."

"Not to bring up old wounds, but you seem to have changed your mind since our last conversation about him."

He shrugged. "I'm doing what he didn't do for you. I'm giving him the benefit of the doubt. There *has* to be a reason, some really good reason, for the things he's done to you. Right?"

"There is." That was the closest I'd ever come to telling him the stakes. I couldn't say more.

"I *knew* it. If you think it's worth it, then it has to be."

I took his hand and squeezed it. "It is."

"And the thing with Lucius... We'll get it straightened out."

"Sin didn't even ask me. He just assumed the worst and stormed off."

"Give him a minute to cool off. He'll come back. And then you can explain it to him and see if he'll, I don't know, grovel or something to get back in your good graces."

I laughed. "I don't think Sin has ever groveled in his life."

"He'd do it for you. I know he would. He loves you. He may be too caught up in this Acquisition bullshit to see it clearly, but I know he does."

"You try to see the best in everyone. Sometimes it isn't there. You know?" I sighed and shifted, my arm beginning to ache.

"It is."

I had my doubts. But then I remembered the conversation I'd overheard between Rebecca and Renee. Maybe Teddy was right. Rebecca wanted Sin to bring the Acquisition down. There was light left in her despite the dark roads she'd travelled. I wanted to tell Sin what I'd heard, to let him know what his mother intended. Would it change anything?

"Maybe you're right about seeing the best in people. Though, I must say, I've seen some pretty horrible human beings over the last few months."

"I know. But maybe some of them could change?"

"What about Cal Oakman?"

He stopped drumming his fingers. "Okay, yes. I'll give you that one. He is, without a doubt, an evil person. When Sin wins Sovereign, maybe he can clean house or something?"

My thoughts turned murkier as my mind clicked and whirred about how to end the Acquisition. I hadn't seized on any solution yet, though I'd contemplated contacting authorities in Washington. Sin's warnings that some of the most powerful people in the South, and the country as a whole, attended the trials tempered the idea. Maybe the only way to dismantle it was from the inside.

Farns cleared his throat in the doorway.

"What's up?" Teddy asked.

"I've just received a phone call from Mr. Sinclair. He gave me instructions on how he would like the house prepared for the luncheon on Saturday. And…" He scrubbed a hand down his face in a move that was utterly un-Farnsian. He was always so put-together and stoic. "Mr. Sinclair also gave me specific instructions on how you are to be prepared, Stella."

"What luncheon?" Teddy sat up. "What do you mean 'prepared'?"

Dread settled in the pit of my stomach.

Farns continued, "Mr. Oakman wishes to celebrate his daughter's return from Europe. The families and a few close friends will be here for the party Saturday afternoon."

"Party?" Renee's voice sounded from the hallway. She scooted past Farns and came to stand beside me.

"Yes." Farns nodded. "But there's more." His eyes watered. "He asked me to-to tell you…" He sagged against the door frame and Renee rushed over and took his elbow.

"Are you all right?"

"Fine." He straightened. "I'm fine. Mr. Sinclair instructed that you are no longer to have this room. Instead, you will stay in the barn, beginning today. He also said that you are to wear servant's attire for the party and that you will wait on Ms. Oakman exclusively."

Not only would Sin not speak to me, he also set out to humiliate me in front of the very people who saw me as nothing more than a plaything. I was stunned into silence, disbelieving what I was hearing.

"No. She stays here." Teddy put his arm around my shoulders.

"Teddy, it's best you don't get involved. Mr. Sinclair's word goes." Renee knit her brows together, as if she disagreed with her own statement.

"I don't give a shit. He can't just order her around like this. She's a person."

"He can." I found my voice, a thin, fragile thing. To disobey would make Sin look weak, lessen his stature in the running for Sovereign. I was caught between wanting to fight him and wanting to keep Teddy safe. I would always choose the latter. "I'll go."

"No." Teddy tightened his hold. "This is yours."

"It never was." I disentangled myself from him. "I don't belong here."

Farns clutched his hands in front of him. "We are going to have several people in and out doing cleaning and such for the next three days. So the barn will be quieter." Then he bowed his head. "I truly am sorry. I tried to talk him out of it, but that has never worked."

"It's all right. I appreciate it." I scanned the room, trying to decide what to take with me.

"You know what?" Teddy walked to the door. "If you're sleeping in the barn, so am I. I hope you're cool with a roommate. I'm going to pack."

"Teddy, you'll just piss him off—"

"I don't care! He's being a dick. I won't let you stay out there alone. No one is going to change my mind. So don't bother trying to talk me out of it. I can make my own decisions." He stormed down the hallway as Renee and Farns watched me grab a few items from my drawers.

"At least come down and eat before you go." Farns

squared his shoulders. "I know you missed breakfast. I had Laura keep a plate on the stove for you."

I threw some painting supplies into the same piece of luggage I'd brought when I first came to the house. "I'll take it with me. Thanks."

"Very good." He left.

Renee wrung her hands. "This isn't what I was hoping for. I hoped he would—"

"Fall in love with me?" I zipped up my bag and pulled out the handle.

She nodded.

"I think he did in his own way. But he's made up his mind. I can't change it. He won't even speak to me. And now…" I looked around at the room I'd come to call home that he'd so easily taken from me. "I don't know if I want him to. Maybe it's better this way." I lowered my voice. "I'll do what I have to do to keep Teddy safe. And when it's done, it's done. I'll leave here. There's nothing to keep me."

I only hoped Dylan wouldn't come after me, but even if he did, I'd handle it. Fearing him wasn't high on my list of concerns, not when Teddy's life still hung in the balance. And, no matter what, I could still give myself to Cal. Sin wouldn't object. Not anymore.

I would suffer, Teddy would live, and then I would escape and never look back.

CHAPTER TWENTY
Stella

TEDDY'S BLONDE HEAD APPEARED at the top of the ladder. "Hey, the guests are arriving."

"Great." I smoothed down the plain maid outfit Sin had sent out to the barn for me. It was an ill-fitting white button down shirt and a black skirt.

"You don't have to do this."

"You keep telling me that. If you're awake, you're saying that. If you're asleep, you're snoring the words out and waking me up." I glanced to our cots. The barn loft had turned out to be not so bad. My easel and paints were set up next to the wide barn window. I left it slung open to let in sunlight and fresh air. Teddy would play on his laptop while I sketched his profile. His face was plastered all along the wall around the window.

As far as punishments went, this was one I could bear. The lack of air conditioning could be a problem, but it wasn't full on summer yet and the barn stayed relatively cool. Teddy treated it like a tree house more than anything else, as if we'd run away from home and were hiding out until the grown-ups found us.

The afternoon storms made the straw smell sweet,

and the chickens pecking around below kept things interesting. The roosters crowing at daybreak, though, I could have done without.

"I don't snore," Teddy said.

"Ask Laura. I'm sure she can independently verify."

He grinned. "She may have mentioned it in passing. I'm sure she thinks it's cute."

"She's mentioned it. She says the only way to stop it is to poke you in the ribs until you sputter and wake up a little." I smirked at him. "Not that I've done that at least once every night or anything."

"Jerks." His smiled faded. "Come on. Let's get it over with. I hope it only lasts for an hour or so, but who knows?"

"Remember what we talked about." I clambered down the ladder, my heels hooking on each rung. "It's not going to be fun for me, but you have to play along like it's cool with you. No matter what they do to me, just act natural."

He took my hand and helped me off the last step. "I'll do my best."

"Do better than even that. Put on a show. That's all I'm doing." My show would consist of feigning obedience and pretending my insides hadn't been shattered by Sin. I'd broken so many times in the past few months—I feared my pieces had become too small to put back together.

We piled onto his ATV and sped up the winding drive to the house. Cars were lined up out front near the oaks, their polished metal glinting.

I took a deep breath as we entered the back door. He squeezed my hand and walked down the hall toward the dining room while I went into the kitchen. Several hired workers bustled about, their attire the same as mine. Laura directed all of them, the kitchen running smoothly under her guidance.

"Stella!" She stopped mid-order and gave me a hug.

"What can I do to help?"

"Nothing. But Mr. Sinclair has already asked for you. Best if you go on in." She shook her head at a man who was ladling soup. "Hey, not yet. That won't be ready to go out until after the salad course. It'll be cold by then. Put it back."

I threw my shoulders back and pushed through the doors leading to the dining room. The guests chattered amongst themselves as I entered. Every seat at the table was filled. Four servers, two on each side, stood against the walls, staring straight ahead.

"Stella!" Cal sat at the head of the table, a wide grin firmly in place. Sophia sat at his right already glaring at me.

Sin sat directly across from her, his eyes boring into me, disgust writ large in the tilt of his head and the slight wrinkle of his nose. My fingers went cold, and I could hear my blood pumping over the sounds of talk and clinking glasses.

"About time." Sophia tossed her raven hair over her shoulder and held out her empty drink. A diamond the size of a marble graced her ring finger, and she tapped the band on the glass.

It wasn't an ordinary ring.

My body chilled. I closed my eyes, letting the pain rip through me as my heart struggled to beat. This was an engagement party, not a welcome home lunch.

Sin's betrayal was complete. Sophia wasn't simply a ruse to solidify his position. He'd chosen her to be his wife.

"Stella, Sophia needs a refill." Sin's voice struck me like a shard of ice. "Get to it."

I glanced from her to Sin before taking the glass to the sideboard and refilling it. My hand shook as I poured her tea. I needed to hold it together. I would mourn later, once I was hidden from Sin's cruel stare.

Taking a deep breath, I set the pitcher back down. I spied Teddy sitting halfway down the table, watching me as an attractive young woman spoke in his ear.

After placing the glass on the table next to Sophia, I backed away.

"You seem to have trained her well." Cal smiled.

"She doesn't listen worth a damn, and takes direction even worse, but when put in a situation befitting her station, she reverts to true form." Sin sipped his coffee. I had the brief mental image of taking his cup and dousing him with the steaming liquid.

The kitchen door swung open, and servers poured out with salad plates, waking me from my fantasy. Once the servers placed the dishes, they disappeared back into the kitchen.

"Stella, where is Sophia's salad?" Sin's voice was hollow, cold.

"I-I—" I rushed into the kitchen. "Laura? Sophia's salad?"

"There." She pointed to a plate on the island.

I snagged it and hurried back into the dining room, placing it in front of her. Before I could back away, she grabbed my hair and yanked, the burn at my scalp forcing a yelp from my lungs.

"Make me wait again and I'll have you whipped." She pulled me closer so only I could hear. "I'm nowhere close to repaying you for what you did at the trial." She let me go, and I backed away until I bumped into the wall.

Sin made no move, though his eyes narrowed as he stared at Sophia.

They began to eat, the conversation picking back up. I glanced down the table and gave Teddy a reassuring nod. His face was pinched, but he picked at his salad and tried to continue the conversation with the pretty girls at each elbow. Looking farther, I recognized some faces from the trials, and one in particular caught my eye—the blond man from the tent outside the fort. His gaze was glued to Sophia again. Who was he? I continued along the row. My eyes stopped when they met Dylan's. He sat next to Red, both of them staring me down. Loathing slithered through my stomach, and I forced myself to look away.

Cal stood, and the table went silent. "I'm afraid I've invited you here under false pretenses." He gave a grin.

Some of the guests shifted uncomfortably in their seats.

"Don't worry, the actual reason is to celebrate the engagement of two people who are very dear to my heart. I confess I was a bit surprised at how quickly love bloomed between these two, but if you've seen them together, you just know it's right. No point in stalling. I couldn't be more pleased to announce that Sophia and Sinclair will be wed next spring."

A smattering of polite applause sounded and then died out.

He raised his glass along with everyone else at the table. "To my beloved Sophia and my soon to be son-in-law Sinclair."

"Sophia and Sinclair." They echoed in unison before drinking to the couple of the hour.

I hid my hurt as best I could, standing still and keeping my eyes up like the men along the sides of the room. I wouldn't let them see me suffer.

After the salad course, the servers brought out a shrimp appetizer. I retrieved Sophia's from the kitchen and set it before her.

"There's something on this plate." She pointed to a stray grain of rice along the lip of the plate.

"It's rice."

"I didn't ask what it was. Take it back." She picked it up and shoved it against my stomach, some of the broth staining my oversized shirt.

I bit my cheek and took the dish back to the kitchen. Laura whipped up another one and made sure to wipe the rim of the plate before sending it out. "Chin up. You're doing fine."

"Thanks." I took it and set it in front of Sophia again. She found no fault with the food, but turned her sights on me. "You look disgusting. Go change. Now." She waved me away with a flick of her wrist.

Pushing back through to the kitchen, I found a rack with white shirts for the staff. I chose one in my size and darted into the powder room off the main hall. As I stripped off the stained shirt, the door opened.

"I'm in here." I tried to push against it, but the intruder shoved harder. I shrank back when Dylan appeared and closed the door behind him, clicking the lock like I should have done.

I held my hands out in front of me as my bare back hit the wall. "Don't."

He slapped my hands away, a cruel smirk on his face, and grabbed me by the throat. "You do well as a servant."

"Stop. I have to go." My voice came out as a hushed croak. Fear controlled my thoughts, and all I wanted was to run.

He worked his fingers between my bra and my skin and yanked, the material stinging across my back as it pulled away. Palming a breast, he squeezed my throat and lifted until my feet dangled from the floor.

"Stop," I squeaked and tried to scratch him, but I couldn't get a grip on him.

"Fuck, I've been waiting for this. And here you are, right place, right time." He hiked my skirt up and slipped his fingers in my panties. I jerked as he pushed lower, seeking my entrance. "Not even wet for me? That's okay. Your blood will work just as well."

He dropped me and I gasped for breath. He bent me over, my hands on the toilet as he pushed my skirt up.

"No!" When I tried to stand up, he punched me in the back. I cried out and fell forward, hitting my head on the back of the toilet. He took the opportunity to rip my panties off. I tried to turn and fight, but I wasn't used to close quarters, and he was too big.

"Shut up." He clapped a hand over my mouth. "Get loud again and I'll knock you out. Either way, this pussy is mine. Maybe your ass, too, you filthy slut."

His belt buckle rattled and my gorge rose.

"Stella?" Teddy knocked.

"She's not in here." Dylan pressed his hand harder to my mouth. I flailed my hands out and knocked the soap dispenser from the sink. Anything to make noise.

"Stella, are you in there?" Teddy knocked harder.

Dylan inched his hand up so his palm covered my nose and mouth. I tried to pull in air, but his large hand blocked any breathing.

"Go the fuck away, man. I'm trying to take a shit." Dylan pulled his dick out and rubbed the wet tip down my ass.

I bucked forward, shaking the toilet, but not breaking his grip.

"Teddy, what are you doing? Get back in the dining room." Sin's voice wafted through the door as Dylan tried to push his cock down to my entrance again.

My vision faded and I could feel myself going limp.

"No. I think some guy has Stella in there."

"What?" The question was sharp, but not as loud as the splintering sound of wood as the door burst inward.

Dylan was ripped away from me and I fell against the sink, trying to get air into my burning lungs.

"Stella!" Teddy yanked my skirt down and turned me to his chest, wrapping his arms around me. "Jesus, what did he do to you?"

Thuds and yells erupted from the hallway, and the wall shook, plaster dusting from the ceiling. My throat ached, and I buried my face in Teddy's shoulder.

"It's okay. Shh." He shook his blazer off his shoulders and wrapped it around me, drawing it tight at my front before pulling me to his chest again.

"Don't you fucking touch her!" Sin's rage-filled roar shot to every corner of the house as the servers rushed past in the hallway.

"Boys, boys! This is why we can't have nice things."

Cal's laugh rang out and was followed by cackles from the dining room.

After the servers were gone, Teddy peeked out the door toward the foyer. He scooped me into his arms and ran for the back stairway. I held onto his neck as he took the steps two at a time.

"What happened?" Renee hovered at the top step.

"Some guy attacked her in the bathroom." Teddy rushed down the hall and carried me to my room, sitting me on the bed as I clutched his jacket to me.

I couldn't stop shaking. He sat next to me and pulled me close again, rubbing my back and shushing me as I trembled. Renee knelt in front of me, and tilted my chin up. She gasped when she saw my neck.

"He could have killed her." Her voice was unforgiving. "Who was it?"

"I don't know, but he was big."

"Dylan." My voice croaked through my teeth.

"Your stepbrother?"

I nodded. Renee and Teddy exchanged a look as raucous cries erupted from downstairs.

"We have a victor!" Cal's showman voice lofted to our ears. "Congratulations, Sinclair. Well done. Somebody get Dylan cleaned up. He gave a good showing. Now, let's finish our lunch."

CHAPTER TWENTY-ONE
SINCLAIR

I TOOK ANOTHER SWIG of brandy as Farns did his best to patch up my busted knuckles. I barely felt it.

The party was at an end, and the last guest had left hours ago. I glanced at the stairs. Teddy still hadn't come out of Stella's room.

"I heard what that nasty fellow tried to do. I am proud of you, Mr. Sinclair."

I shook my head. "I'm the last person in this house for you to be proud of. I can promise you that."

"Don't be so hard on yourself. You didn't choose this." He glanced up at me, his blue eyes faded while the man inside was still sharp. "You are doing well."

Steps on the stairs had my heart speeding up. But it was only Renee. Stella remained above, hidden from me.

"Did you kill him?" The steel in Renee's voice sent a chill through me.

My memory flickered alive like a beast needing to be fed. When my mother and I returned from Brazil, Renee met us at the airport. She rushed up and kissed me on the forehead before taking Rebecca in her arms.

"*Did you kill them all?*" She'd whispered. I'd barely

heard her, but the timbre was the same as what she'd just asked me.

"No." I finished my glass and slammed it on the table. "I damn well would have if Red hadn't pulled me off."

Renee gripped my chin and pulled my face up to her scrutiny. All pretense of being anything other than my second mother fell away as she perused my black eye and bloody nose. "You'll heal."

"How is she?" I knew I shouldn't care, that I should keep up the charade that I was only angry with Dylan for trying to take what was mine or for tampering with my Acquisition. Instead, the thought of him harming her churned my stomach and fueled my fury. I wanted his blood, all of it, on my hands.

"She's been better. Her throat is swollen and bruised. Teddy is comforting her."

A stab of jealousy punctured the careful cocoon that wrapped my heart. "The same way Lucius comforted her?"

"Yes, as a matter of fact." She frowned and dropped her hand.

I stood so fast that Farns would have fallen if I hadn't caught him. Murder roiled in my breast, emotions spilling into my heart through the cracks of jealousy etched into my armor.

"Calm down. You've misjudged her *and* your brother, for that matter."

"What, by seeing them in bed together?" I forced myself to stay put even as I imagined Teddy on top of her.

"That's all you saw. Maybe if you'd asked her instead of going off half-cocked, or maybe if you'd listened to your brother—"

"Lucius was telling the truth?" The ice water running through my veins grew colder. "They never—"

"No. And now you've punished her, nearly got her violated, and driven her away. And all the while you were courting that fork-tongued Oakman girl. How do you think she felt? You need to fix this." She pinned me with a fierce gaze. "For all of us, but for yourself most of all."

She took Farns' elbow and helped him through the dining room and out the door. He walked with slow steps, his age creeping up on him like a masked assassin.

I lolled my head back and stared at the coffered ceiling. Had I misjudged her? I tried to put myself in her shoes—not something I'd ever even thought of before, much less attempted. Maybe Renee was right. But surely, Stella knew I only dated Sophia for show, a business arrangement, nothing more.

Sophia treaded a fine line as it was. Her lover Ellis stayed with us the entire time we travelled Europe, the two of them dining together and spending the night in a tangled heap as I smoked, drank, and thought of nothing except Stella.

During the day, Sophia and I made a handsome pair, and the deal had been struck. I would marry Sophia, set her up with a trust fund flush with Sovereign cash, and we would go our separate ways for the majority of the time, or at least until we were needed for events. She could live happily ever after with that ponce Ellis, and I would keep Stella.

I'd left Stella a note telling her to trust me. I didn't dare call or write any other way. Ears were everywhere, and I had to keep Sophia—and by extension, Cal—happy by acting the perfect son-in-law. I knew my trust was broken the second I'd seen Stella in bed with Lucius. But maybe she'd trusted me after all.

I was no longer content to wait for answers. I stalked into the hall and up the stairs. Her door was closed, but I heard voices. I huddled close and listened.

"Just tell me what it is. Why do you stay? We could run away. I can take Laura. What keeps you here?"

I couldn't hear her response. My fists tightened at the thought of her voice being taken by Dylan's rough hands.

"Fine." He sighed. "I just wish you would share it

with me. I could help, you know?"

Another pause.

"Yes, I'll stay the night. Let me go to my room and get out of these stuffy clothes. Renee already laid some PJs out next to you. Do you need help changing?"

After a moment, Teddy laughed. "Busted. Okay, I'll be right back."

I stepped aside as the door opened. Teddy closed it softly and gave me an unforgiving glare. "What do you want?"

"I want to see her."

"No." He crossed his arms over his chest and blocked the door.

"What are you doing?"

"I'll stand out here for as long as it takes. You aren't seeing her. You don't get to see her after what you did." His temper reminded me of my own.

"If I have to go through you, I will."

"Fuck off, Sin. You leave her here beaten and broken. You take off to Europe with Sophia fucking Oakman while Stella has to heal from whatever torture you put her through. Then, you never give her a chance to explain what happened with Lucius." His brows lowered, actual rage coloring his face. "And then you force her to sleep in the barn and wait on that cunt Sophia hand and foot." His voice turned into a hiss. "She was almost raped because of *you.*"

He'd only told a fraction of my actual sins against Stella. I was heartened that he didn't know the rest.

"All that may be true. Even so, I *will* get through that door." I'd never hit Teddy, and I didn't want to start, but the roaring need inside me to be with Stella drowned everything else out.

Teddy huffed his breath out through his nose. "Are you going to hurt her?"

Not today. "No."

"Are you going to apologize?"

I tasted the word, bitter and rotten. Still, if it would get me past Teddy without violence, I'd do it. "Yes."

"For everything?" He leaned closer.

"Yes."

"I have your word?"

I nodded. "Yes."

"Then you can go in. Just know that if I hear from Stella that you even *said* something to upset her, I am going to do my best to kick your ass. I know I won't win, but I will give it all I've got. Understand?"

How did this fucked up family ever turn out a beautiful soul like Teddy?

"I understand."

"Good. Give her a minute to change clothes." He shuffled away from the door and gave me one more pointed scowl before heading to our wing of the house.

I waited for a few moments, the anticipation pacing in my chest like a lion on a leash. The bed creaked, and then silence. I waited a while longer to be sure before wrapping my palm around the door handle.

I turned it and eased inside. She lay curled up in a ball, her back to me. Her soft breaths were deep and slow.

Her resting form was beyond tempting, and I'd thought of nothing except her for so long—either with longing or hatred—that all I could do was stare. She was all mine now. No one else's prying eyes watched her. I grew hard in my pants, but chided myself for already treading too harshly on Teddy's rules.

Quietly, I removed my shirt and pants. Sliding into her bed felt like coming home, and for the first time in months, the hellfire that leapt in my heart quieted to embers. I moved my arm under her head and pressed into her back. I wanted to groan from the feel of her. My skin was numb until it touched hers, and then it was alive with every sensation.

She mumbled something and snuggled back into me, her hair tickling my nose as I pulled her close. I didn't care that she thought I was Teddy. All I wanted was her in my arms. Everything quieted inside me, the sections of my mind that were always calculating or planning finally clicking off.

Her breathing changed, and she stirred. "Teddy. You're um, you're sort of poking me." Her voice was a scratchy whisper, and I wished all over again that I'd killed Dylan.

She turned to face me and shrank back with a gasp. "What are you doing here?" She pushed at my chest, but I trapped her in my arms. I was never letting her go again.

"Stop, please. You'll only hurt yourself more."

She didn't stop, only struggled harder, like a wildcat in my arms.

I nuzzled into her hair. "Stella, please. I'm sorry. I'm so sorry."

"Sorry?" She froze. "That doesn't even begin..." She swallowed hard. "To cover what you've done."

"I know. But I will make it up to you somehow. All of it."

"You can't make it up to me." Her voice broke, the pain in her piercing me more deeply than I thought possible.

"I can." I stroked her cheek. "I will. You'll see."

She pulled away from my touch. "By marrying Sophia?"

"I'll never marry her."

"But you've been with her this whole time." Her eyes shimmered in the low light.

"I've never touched her. I swear. She's with someone else. I've only been with her to please Cal. They think I'll marry her, of course, after I become Sovereign. I won't." Spending time with Sophia had been my personal ninth level of hell. Vapid, selfish, and cruel—we were a perfect match. I already wanted her dead for harming Stella, and having to spend time with her only made me come up with various gruesome ways for her to meet her end.

"I didn't sleep with Lucius." She shook her head. "I mean, I slept with him, but we never—"

"I know." I kissed her forehead. "I'm sorry."

"I believe you." She relaxed into my arms more, though she still held back. "So what will happen when you don't marry Sophia?"

"I don't care. Cal will try to retaliate. I'm not sure what he'll do. It won't be pretty. Nothing approaching all-out war between our families, but things will be strained."

"He's promised me to Dylan."

I froze. "What?"

"Cal is going to give me to Dylan once the Acquisition is over." She shuddered.

"You're not his to give." I clutched her tighter and wished, once again, that I'd killed Dylan downstairs.

"They've made some sort of deal. I don't know the details."

"You don't have to. It isn't going to happen. I don't care if it results in all out war with Cal after I become Sovereign."

"Could you boot Cal's family? Stop the infighting that way?"

"Yes, but playing that card early could lead to trouble later. I'd prefer to keep that in my back pocket. The very threat of it will help keep him in line." Or so I hoped. Cal had consolidated power during his reign. He would be a particularly vicious adversary.

"There will be fighting. You and Lucius will be in danger, like in Cuba?"

I brushed my hand down her hair. "Yes."

"Then no."

"What?"

"I don't agree to this plan at all." She chewed her bottom lip.

I arched an eyebrow. "Are you saying you *want* me to marry Sophia?"

"Of course not. But you simply winning isn't going to

be enough. Not for me, anyway."

I took her hand and pulled it to my heart. Her palm was warm and small, but she held me in it. "Anything you want me to do, I'll do it." I inhaled a deep, shuddering breath. "I'm yours. I've been a fool and treated you worse than you deserved—"

"Sin—"

"Let me finish. Even if what I'd thought was true—that you'd slept with Lucius—I should never have punished you like that. I'm sorry. And when Dylan…" My jaw tightened, and I struggled to continue. "When Dylan tried to hurt you, I realized I didn't care anymore if you had or hadn't slept with Lucius. You are mine to protect, to cherish, and to love." The last word was one I said with the same care I would use in handling a live grenade.

I cleared my throat as her expression softened, and she stroked my cheek. That feeling welled up inside me, the one I only had when I thought of her. It was my drug, far more intoxicating than anything else I'd found. "After I had a moment to calm down, I decided that I would only have killed Lucius. Not you."

She tilted her head. "I think that's one of the nicest things you've ever said to me."

I covered her hand with mine. "I don't know what else to say or do to prove it, but I love you. All of you. I will gladly kill for you, buy you whatever your heart desires, and show you the world. Anything. If I have it or I can get it, it's yours." My heart constricted. Is this what love felt like? Like you were on fire, and instead of turning to ash, your mate only made you burn brighter?

"I love you, too." She kissed me, soft and chaste. "But I need something from you before I can forgive you."

"Anything. It's yours. Just name it."

Her eyes narrowed. "Promise me that we will burn it all down. Every last piece of the Acquisition. Or we will die trying."

I couldn't look away from her, my vengeful queen. "How did I never know when I first set eyes on you that you were the strongest person in the room?" I kissed her, not chaste, not gentle. She moaned in my mouth and tangled her fingers in my hair. I needed her taste on my tongue, every inch of her body beneath my fingertips, but she pulled away.

"Promise me." She dotted kisses on my cheek and bit my ear. "Promise, because you never break your word."

I slid my hand down her body and into her panties. She was wet, and I needed to be inside her.

She grabbed my wrist. "Promise me first."

I got to my knees and yanked her panties off before shucking my shorts away. Lining up at her entrance, I stared down at her, the warmth in her flowing to me and making me more than I ever thought possible.

"I promise." With one hard thrust, I seated myself deep inside her. Leaning down and claiming her mouth was the sweetest reward I'd ever tasted.

I pushed harder, needing to give her every bit of raw aggression I'd felt for anyone who thought to hurt her or take her from me. She clawed my back and I kissed to her collarbone, careful on her neck. It was too dark to see, but I knew she was bruised there. I would have Dylan's head for it.

"Sin." She clung to me as I slowed my pace and wrapped my arms around her.

"Do you trust me?" I teased at her lips.

"Yes."

I rested my forehead against hers and kept my thrusts smooth and even. I wanted it to last, to stay inside her for as long as I could.

She was my home, where I belonged. And I would never doubt her again.

CHAPTER TWENTY-TWO
Stella

THE SUMMER ARRIVED WITH full force, the hottest on record. I spent the days with Sin, except on the odd times when he was called to make an appearance with Sophia. He always came back irritable, but after some particularly enjoyable attention from me, he was back to his usual dark and brooding self.

Sin showed me more of the estate and even took me to see his office in town. He barked at his staff to get to work as they gawked at the "mystery woman" on his arm. He hid me away in his private office. I ran my fingers over his many diplomas and reveled in his plush domain.

"Not bad for government work."

He sat in his desk chair and pulled me into his lap. "Have you ever played a game called naughty secretary?"

"No." I laughed. "Have you?"

"Of course not." He ran his hands to my hips. "Though I'm quite disappointed to hear you're unfamiliar."

I rubbed my ass back and forth over his growing erection. "I've never heard of it, but that doesn't mean I wouldn't be good at it."

"I like it when you're up to a challenge."

"Always." I stroked his dark hair, the strands soft on my fingertips.

He pulled me in for a kiss, his hands roving my body as he bit my bottom lip. The singular sensation of tingles and warmth, one that only he could draw from me, ricocheted around my stomach.

"Mr. Vinemont." A woman chirped through his phone.

He growled into my mouth before reaching over and pressing a button. "What, Kim?"

"You have a visitor."

"I don't have any appointments today." His tone turned cold, displeasure coating each syllable. "I checked."

"He's a walk-in. He believes you'd want to speak with him."

"Who the fuck is it?" He clicked off the speaker and kissed me again, his impatience growing by the second.

"Leon Rousseau. He specifically asked to speak to the young lady you're with."

My heart fell at my father's name. I hadn't seen him since the trial, though Sin told me what he'd done to him. It had been gruesome, but I understood why it had to be.

Sin leaned back and looked up at me, his lips pressing into a thin line. "Fuck. He must have seen us arrive. I'll send him away."

"No. He can see me if he wants to. Both of us, I mean." I took his hand and laced our fingers together. "He can see both of us."

"Are you sure?"

"Yes. I think I'll be fine. And maybe it will be a good thing, to finally see him face to face on equal footing. No more pretending." The certainty in my tone wasn't matched inside my heart. My love for my father had grown stale and brittle, but something remained. Would it always be there?

"Send him in." Sin shoved the phone away.

I tried to stand.

He held me in place. "He can see you here with me, where you belong."

"Claiming your turf?" I leaned my shoulder into his chest.

"If you'd rather I piss on you to mark you as mine, I will." He dug his fingers into my sides and I squirmed, trying not to laugh. "Is that a yes?"

"No." I grabbed his hands as the door opened.

My short-lived amusement died away as my father hobbled in, his back hunched and his face sorrowful. So many emotions rushed through me that I thought I might burst at the onslaught. Of all of them, pity won out.

He sank down into a chair across the desk as the secretary closed the door.

His bloodshot eyes found mine, and he held out his left arm, the end covered in graying gauze.

"Look at me. Ruined."

Sin spoke through gritted teeth. "You got what—"

"Let me, okay?" I squeezed his forearm and he quieted, though he wrapped his hands around my waist. Meeting my father's eyes again, I said, "Go on."

"I need you, Stella. I need someone to take care of me. The money..." He shook his head, unshed tears wobbling in his eyes. "It's all gone. No one cares about me. Dylan hasn't spoken to me in months. I need you to come home. Please."

"To the home you burned to the ground?"

His eyebrows rose, but he shook his head. "Who told you that? Him?" He shot a glance to Sin. "It was lightning. The damned insurance people wouldn't pay up." His tone turned bitter and his top lip curled into a sneer. "Only gave me half what it was worth."

I saw right through him as if he were a pane of glass on a sunny day. "Can you still not tell me the truth, even now?"

"What lies has he told you? He poisoned you against

me. You're sitting in his goddamn lap like a pet!" As his voice rose, Sin tensed beneath me. I smoothed my hand up and down his arm, trying to tamp down the beast I could feel raging beneath his surface.

"Sin told me the truth. He showed me your signature. Stop lying to me." The brittle love I had for him was breaking into pieces, disintegrating into the wind of his lies.

"That stuff can be forged. You know that. Why do you believe him? He's the one who framed me, hounded me, convicted me based on lies. Don't you remember?"

"I remember believing in you so much that I sacrificed myself to save you. I remember accepting my fate if it meant you would be safe." I rose and stared him down. "And then I was told the truth. You brought all of this on us. Your lies, your schemes." I flattened my palms on the desk. "How long until the million ran out?"

"What? No. There was no million." He glared at Sin. "What have you told her?"

"Look at me. He told me the truth. How. Long?"

He sputtered and shook his head. "N-no. It wasn't like that. I was—"

I slapped my hand on the desk. "How long!"

He covered his face with his hand. "Just a few months. I-I thought I could get you back somehow. Keep the money and get you back, but he took you and told you lies about me."

"Do you even hear yourself?" Realization hit me, and I straightened. "You believe your own lies, don't you? You actually think you were innocent, that you could somehow sell me and keep me at the same time."

"I just need you. My hand. He took it, and it's all his fault. He caused every last bit of it." He vacillated between crying and yelling, and pointed a shaking finger at Sin. "He wanted you all along, from the first moment he saw you."

"That's the only true thing you've said." Sin stood behind me and put his hands on my shoulders. "I think it's time for you to leave, Mr. Rousseau."

"She's mine." My father snarled, more animal than man. "You can't keep her from me. Her mother tried to take her from me once. That didn't work out very well for her."

"Take me from you? She never tried…" My knees went weak and I leaned against the desk for support. "Did you—was it you? What did you do to her?" My mother's face flitted across my vision. "What did you do?"

He changed yet again, the vehemence gone and weakness in its place. "Please, Stella. I need you. Please."

My head spun, the room flickering light to dark. "You said it was suicide. It was ruled a suicide."

He nodded. "Yes, suicide. Come with me."

"Liar!" I screamed and tried to get around the desk. I wanted to rip him open until the truth finally spilled out. Sin wrapped his arms around me and held me in place.

"I suggest you leave now, Mr. Rousseau. I'd love to watch her destroy you, but it may cause her pain, and I can't have that."

"I need you. Please, come with me. Please." His teary plea made bile rise in my throat, and all I could see was my mother, her warm smile and sad eyes.

"I'm warning you, Mr. Rousseau." Sin spoke quietly, hatred infusing every word.

"You killed her. You killed her, didn't you." It wasn't a question, but the answer was in his bowed head. The lies were finally at an end.

"I thought we'd get more money to live. Stage it like a break-in. It didn't work. Insurance wouldn't pay because it was deemed a suicide, and I had debts. I'm sorry. I would never hurt you. Please—"

"I warned you." Sin released me.

I tore around the desk and shoved my father to the ground. Dropping to my knees, I hit him as tears blurred my vision and rage lit me up like a house on fire.

"How could you? I loved you!" I hit him as he

covered his face, cowering beneath my onslaught. My movements slowed as sobs rose in my chest. I kept swinging even as my arms tired and my knuckles burned. And then, after I'd worn myself out, I was done. Finished with him.

Sin lifted me to my feet and picked me up, cradling me in his arms as I cried into his chest.

"Get out." He turned to the door and yelled. "Kim!"

She hurried through as if she'd been waiting just outside. "Have Burt or Clancy escort Mr. Rousseau to his car. Call the sheriff and make sure he is escorted to the parish line."

"Yes, okay." She bustled out of the room.

"The next moment I set eyes on you will be your last." Sin backed away, holding me close.

"M-Mom." I sobbed.

"Shh, it's all going to be all right."

A man walked in and helped my father to his feet. His cheeks glowed red from my fists and one eye was already starting to swell shut. The man asked no questions and hustled my father out the door and closed it behind them.

I clung to Sin, the world ripping to shreds around me as he stood firm.

"I'm sorry." He kissed my hair. "I'm so sorry. If you want me to have him killed—"

"No. There's been enough blood. Too much." I calmed my breathing, taking gulps of air to stop the tremors.

"I'll do anything to make you happy. Anything." He was a wild, tormented creature, but everything about him soothed me, lulled me.

"I know."

Another knock and then Kim's voice. "He's out of the office, sir, and the sheriff is on his way to escort him away."

"Good."

The door closed and another round of sobs shook

me. "He took her from me. She loved me, Sin. I remember her. Her smile, her hair, the way she would sing while I played with my finger paints." Her yellow dress with the blue checks, the time I got into her makeup and painted my lips and cheeks with her red lipstick, choosing my dress for my first school dance, playing in her garden—so many memories welled up inside me. How many more had my father stolen from me? "She'd still be alive. She'd be with me. H-he took her."

Sin rocked me back and forth, trying to ease the ache that could never fully be erased. "Shh, I've got you."

I cried for the parents I'd lost as he held me close, his strong arms cradling me until my tears finally subsided. He kissed my hair.

I leaned back to look up at him. "Thank you."

"I'm sorry." His face softened, and his tenderness made my tears threaten again.

I cleared my throat to try and stave off another crying fit. "Is all this going to be a p-problem with your staff or anything?"

He laughed, a deep rumble in his chest. "After what they've heard about Judge Montagnet, my eccentricities seem rather run-of-the-mill, I'm afraid."

"I hate that man."

"We'll get him." He dropped a reassuring kiss on my lips. "We'll get them all."

One stormy afternoon, Sin, Lucius, and I climbed the stairs to the third floor. Renee had interrupted our strategy session with Lucius to let us know that Rebecca was back—the real Rebecca.

I followed Renee, both Sin and Lucius on my heels. We moved quickly. Catching Rebecca lucid was like trying to see a shooting star. Spotted rarely, and only briefly before burning out.

Though I'd witnessed her change for Renee briefly, I couldn't imagine her as anything other than spiteful toward me. My trepidation grew as we approached. But when I walked in with Sin and Lucius, she smiled without a hint of malice.

"Boys." Rebecca motioned them over, her joy like a mirror to her past when she was young and full of life.

I hid my surprise and stepped aside so Sin and Lucius could go to her bedside.

"Mom?" Sin hurried to her, Lucius on his heels.

"Sit. Let's talk before I go back under. Hurry. We don't have much time." Rebecca patted the bed.

They sat as I hovered at the door.

"Stella? Come here. Let me look at you." I walked over, Renee at my elbow.

"See? It's her. It's my Rebecca." Renee dabbed at her eyes.

"Rebecca." I nodded in greeting, still unsure if I was going to get a kind word or a kick in the teeth.

"You are beautiful. Almost the spitting image of my sister, Cora. And I hear you have her spirit, as well." The woman in front of me wasn't the same one who'd run into the dead of night screaming, or who had told me with glee about the trials. She was warm, friendly—a total stranger.

"Thank you." I didn't know what else to say.

"Renee, leave us for this part. I know how it upsets you." She reached out and squeezed Renee's hand before letting it go.

"I'll be just down the hall." Tears rolled down Renee's cheeks, joy mixing with sorrow.

Once Renee was gone, Rebecca turned back to me. "The final trial is more of a mental test than anything else. Stella—"

"Is it true?" Sin asked. "That you want me to end the Acquisition?"

She took his hand. "Yes. I've never wanted anything more in my life. If I had any strength left, I'd do it myself. We don't belong. The Vinemonts were never meant to be a part of this." She shook her head, her white hair flowing around her shoulders. "We were poor sharecroppers. Your great-great-great grandfather unknowingly saved the life of the Sovereign, who repaid him by adding us to this disgraceful club. Don't you see? It's not in our blood. We don't belong here."

"But you always said we were better, that we were above everyone else—"

"Forget what I said." Her tone turned desperate, and her bottom lip shook. "Forget everything I ever told you. Forget everything I've done to you." She ran her fingers over the scars she'd cut into the back of his hand. "But remember what I tell you now. The final trial will force Stella to sacrifice something she loves." She turned to me again. "Child, what do you love? Tell us."

"I-I love Teddy and Sin and Lucius. I love Renee, Farns, and Laura."

"Is there anyone else they could try and take from you?"

"Dmitri." Lucius glanced at me. "And the rest of them. The flaming hair guy and the blonde."

"Yes, them too."

Lightning crackled through the sky, and the boom of thunder shook the house.

Rebecca leaned back, her eyes beginning to dim. "So many to choose from. So many. I'm afraid I'll be no help. But Cal is the worst of them all. He will make it hurt. He will try to turn you into something you're not." She held her hand out to me.

I took it, the skin thin, and the bones frail.

"Don't let it happen to him. Please. Don't let him turn into this." She looked down at her withered body beneath the covers. "I couldn't bear it if I'd doomed him to live this way. He's a good boy. They're all good boys.

Please help them."

"I'll try. I promise. I don't want anyone else to suffer ever again in the Acquisition. We have plans. We—"

She snatched her hand away. "What are you doing in here?"

Sin's face fell, and Lucius stood.

"You two just let anyone in my room?" Her voice cut through the air, shrill and poisonous. "Servants and riffraff from the street?"

"Mother, please."

"Get out!" She turned her face away, staring out the window as the rain hammered against the glass.

Sin sighed and rose. We trudged back down the stairs, silence enveloping us like a too-warm blanket.

"After that exciting interlude, I'm calling it a night." Lucius gave us a two-finger salute and strode toward his side of the house.

I stroked Sin's cheek, but his gaze was far away, likely in the past. "Hey. It's going to be okay."

He blinked and kissed my palm. "I know. As long as I have you, it will be." Striding off toward his room, he pulled me behind him.

When we got there, he shut the door and locked it. Pushing me down onto the bed, he went for my neck, his teeth sliding over my pulse.

I stared up at the canvas I'd done of the first trial, the dark vines swallowing me whole. "You never told me what you did with the North Star. My painting."

"I know what the North Star is, and I sold it. Why do you insist on wearing so many clothes?" He yanked my top over my head.

I laughed as he kissed my chest. "I'm wearing a t-shirt and jeans."

"That's the problem. Nothing is preferable."

"You want me to walk around the house naked for Teddy and Lucius to see?"

He bit my breast, and I yelped. "No. But in my room,

or your room, or any room with just the two of us, is nude really too much to ask?" His tongue grazed my nipple.

"Stop trying to distract me. What about the North Star? Why did you sell it?"

He sucked my nipple into his mouth and swirled his tongue around the hard tip. I raked my fingers across his scalp as he kneaded my other breast.

He switched to the other nipple, licking and sucking until I was panting.

Kissing to my lips, he continued, "I sold it to a very high end collector. It's on prominent display in his Manhattan home. I hated to part with it, but I had to sell it to launch your career. Last I checked…" He nipped at my lower lip. "You were still the talk of the art scene, your mystery only enhancing your reputation."

"You did that for me?" I stroked my fingers through his hair, wondering at the softness that lived at the very heart of him.

He kissed me, hard and possessive, before gazing down at me with an intensity that belonged only to him. "I would do anything for you."

I laced my fingers behind his neck. "Do you think we can do it?" Doubt flittered around my mind, worry as well. "All of it, like we planned?"

"Of course. Lucius has already moved our money." He got to his knees and yanked my pants down before tossing them to the floor. He stripped his shirt and pants off, his muscles rippling. "We've stockpiled everything we need for the coronation ceremony. Teddy will be safely stashed at our compound in Brazil. All we have to do—"

"Is win the final trial." I finished for him, the words far easier than the deed.

"And we will." He sank back on top of me, his weight keeping me grounded.

"What if we don't? What if—"

"Shh." He stroked my hair. "Everything will fall into place. If anyone so much as talks to Dmitri, or Teddy, or

Alex, or anyone you love, we'll know."

"Knowing won't stop me from having to hurt them." The whispered truth roared in my ears.

"I could win it. I could give myself to Cal—"

"No." He gritted his teeth. "We'll win without it. I won't give you away. Not to anyone, but especially not to him. There's no point discussing it."

"I'd do it. To save Teddy, I would."

"I know you would. I can't let you. I couldn't stand it. He would do horrible things, and I would know. Every night, I would know you were being tormented because I wasn't strong enough to save you."

"Even so, I'd do it."

He peered down at me, disbelief in his eyes. "How did I ever manage to catch you?"

"If I remember correctly, you didn't play fair."

He smirked.

"Just tell me we'll be okay, that Teddy will be okay." I pulled him closer and rubbed my cheek against his stubble.

"We'll get through it. Together. The same way we've done each trial." He kissed to my mouth.

"I'm scared."

"I know." He kissed my forehead. "But they're the ones who should be afraid."

CHAPTER TWENTY-THREE
STELLA

"STELLA!" SIN'S VOICE HISSED in my ear, and I shot up from his bed. "They've sent a car. The trial's today. Fucking Cal surprised us." He dropped a kiss on my lips. "This changes nothing."

"They're coming." Lucius stood in the doorway, peering down the hall.

"Hurry to your room. Get ready. I'll meet you downstairs." He kissed me again quickly and pulled his sheet free, wrapping it around me.

I rose, clutched the sheet closed at my chest, and hurried away with Lucius.

"What's going on?"

"Just more fucking dickishness by Cal." Lucius' back was tight, his pace hellish as we turned the corners toward my room.

"Get in your bed, quick. Cal wants to surprise you himself. I held him off with coffee. Go." Lucius pushed my bedroom door open. I slipped through and jumped into my bed as he closed the door. The sheet slipped off and I kicked it down beneath my blankets.

My heart raced, and I glanced to the dresser. I hated

the thought of Cal catching me naked. The hall was quiet, so I slipped out of bed and pulled my drawer open. Then I heard footsteps.

Fuck. I crept back to my bed empty-handed and slid under the sheets. Feigning sleep with my eyes barely open, I turned my head toward the door and lay on my back.

I breathed long and steadily, completely at odds with the frantic beat of my heart. When the door handle turned, I clutched my pillow. It opened farther and Cal peeked in, a large grin spreading across his face as he "caught" me sleeping.

Lucius peered at me over Cal's shoulder, his face pinched. Cal opened the door the rest of the way and eased toward my bed. Chill bumps broke out across my skin, and I wanted to curl up into a defensive ball. Instead, I closed my eyes so he wouldn't realize I was awake.

The bed shifted, and his hand brushed the hair from my face.

"Stella." His voice was soft, with a hint of merriment.

I opened my eyes and tried to shrink away from him, but he closed his fist in my hair.

"That's no way to greet the day." He tsked and let his gaze slither down my neck to my bare shoulders. "Sleeping nude?"

I pulled the blanket to my chin. "Why are you here?"

"Today's your big day. The final trial. Excited?" He rested his hand at my throat.

I didn't answer, silently willing him away.

It didn't work. He leaned closer. "I thought you'd at least try and convince Sin to let me have you." He wrapped his fingers around the blanket and pulled it down.

I resisted, trying to keep myself covered. When he pulled my hair so hard I thought it might rip out, I let go. He shoved the blanket away and surveyed my body. I crossed my arms over my breasts. He pulled them away and pinned my hands to my sides. I was helpless, the same way I'd been so many times at the hands of these people. I wouldn't let my fear win. Hatred burned brighter.

"It doesn't matter now. It's too late. The last trial is here." His malicious eyes took in all of me. "Still, I have a few tricks up my sleeve." He let one hand go, and I moved to cover myself.

He slapped me, my cheek stinging as the crack shocked the still air. "Don't fucking move."

I lowered my hand back to my side, humiliation burning and rising to the surface, painting my skin red.

"Better." He trailed his hands around my breasts and down to my waist and then lower. He smirked and ran his fingers across my pussy as I clenched my legs shut. "Red like I thought." He met my eyes again. "As I was saying, I have a trick or two left. Your stepbrother has been kind enough to let me have you for a week before he takes delivery."

I fought the instinct to hit him as he took my nipple in his mouth. He groaned and bit down on it as I tried to keep breathing.

"Lucius?" Sophia's voice carried down the hallway.

Cal popped his head up and winked at me. "I'll taste the rest soon enough."

He stood, and I wrenched the blankets back in place.

Sophia and Lucius air kissed in the hallway as Cal strode out. "Get ready, we're leaving in ten minutes," he called over his shoulder.

I rolled into the fetal position, holding onto myself because there was nothing else. I wanted to scrub every square inch where Cal had touched me with steel wool. Instead, I gathered my wits and got out of bed. Considering the hot weather, I would have dressed light in a tank top and shorts. Given the twists of the trials, I dressed in layers—tank top, light jacket, jeans, and boots.

Once I'd tucked my knife into my boot, I whipped my hair up into a ponytail. My stark refection in the mirror barely resembled me. What little curves I possessed had turned to muscle, my eyes had grown colder, and my cheeks were almost gaunt. But it was the woman inside who'd changed most of all, to the point where I felt I was looking at a stranger. Would I ever get myself back?

"Stella." Sin stood in the hall, his medium gray suit hitting in all the right places. He didn't even throw me a glance. "Let's go."

I followed him down the stairs and into the breakfast room. Cal held sway over the table, ordering Laura around and discussing the sugar business with Teddy. Sophia met Sin's eyes as we entered and gave him a chilly smile.

I sat, trying to keep calm despite my growing sense of dread. Laura poured me an orange juice and set down a plate of my favorite breakfast—bacon, two eggs over-easy, and fresh fruit. My hand shook so badly I almost knocked my glass over.

Cal smiled. "Calm down, Stella. My goodness. Would you like to sit on my lap? See if that makes you feel any better?"

"Oh Daddy, you're the worst sometimes." Sophia tittered what I assumed was a laugh.

"I was just trying to be nice. Comfort her a bit." He watched me over his coffee cup as I sipped my orange juice.

"What's the plan?" Lucius leaned back in his chair, giving off an air of relaxation.

"We'll be taking the lovely Ms. Rousseau and Sin to an undisclosed location for a little fun. They may be back by nightfall. They may not." Cal shrugged. "So, what wedding plans have we settled on?"

My stomach turned. I forced myself to eat. I couldn't be certain what was in store, but keeping my energy up was key.

Sophia sighed as if shouldering a heavy burden. "We'll have the wedding at our chateau of course. I haven't decided on much else."

"You'll need to get to work as soon as the Acquisition is over. I want some grandsons sooner rather than later."

"Daddy, there will be plenty of time for that." She turned to me. "I hear you'll belong to your stepbrother after the coronation." She simpered. "I hope he treats you as you deserve."

"I hope you choke on your coffee."

"Stella!" Sin slammed his hand on the table. "Apologize."

"And there it is. The fire that's never been snuffed out. Will today be the day?" Cal laughed before turning icy again. "Apologize to my daughter."

I clutched my napkin in my fist and stared at her, hoping she'd fall over dead as I'd said.

Lucius squeezed my knee, and I knew I had to do it.

"I apologize."

"More punishment is needed, to be honest, but we simply don't have the time. I think it's best we be on our way. The guests will be waiting for us." Cal rose, as did the rest at the table.

Lucius waited for me to walk past and fell into step behind me. "You can do this," he whispered as we entered the foyer. I glanced over my shoulder. His light eyes weren't fearful, but they weren't colored with his usual mischief, either.

I gave him a small nod as Sin strode past, Sophia on his arm, and walked onto the front porch.

"Go on, now." Cal shooed me out to the waiting limos. "Stella, honey, ride with me."

"Actually, I apologize, Cal." Sin helped Sophia into the car, her lemon yellow sheath dress perfectly accentuated with narrow floral pumps. "But I did have some business I'd like to discuss. The Cuba conflict brought up some information you'd likely find of interest."

Cal wrinkled his nose and stared at me, as if trying to decide if hurting me was more important than Cuban business deals.

"Fine, fine. Business before pleasure. Besides, I'm

sure Sophia would enjoy Stella's company just as much as me." He laughed and slid into the back seat.

Sin shot me a look, his face hard but his eyes warm. *Together.* We would get through this together.

I walked around and sank into the backseat next to Sophia. She was speaking fluent French into her phone and paused, craning her head to watch as Sin got into her father's car.

"*Merde!*" She swiped her phone off as the car started moving. "Why?"

"I guess Sin got tired of your sparkling personality." I grinned as she balled up her fists. "Daddy's not here to make me behave, so do me a favor and shut the fuck up for the ride. Sound good? Good." I leaned back and turned my head, watching the oaks recede and the woods encroach.

She fumed beside me and finally found her voice. "I will tell them both that you spoke to me like this. You *will* be punished."

"Then I'll tell your father you've been fucking Ellis. So go ahead, be a bitch. See where that gets you." I raised my voice as she sputtered. "Hey, can we get some music back here? I don't think I can even stand listening to her breathe."

The chauffeur raised his eyebrows at Sophia and she stammered out "f-fine."

The music rose, classical and airy, as we hit the main highway. Sophia didn't speak for the rest of the trip. It was only a small victory, but it was mine.

CHAPTER TWENTY-FOUR
Stella

The journey ended at a sprawling Tudor mansion surrounded by a lush lawn dotted with shade trees. No gate stopped entry from the main road, but a guard stood at the ready to check our credentials. Several cars hemmed us in as we approached the mansion.

We pulled through the roundabout and stopped in front of the massive dark wood doors as people climbed the shallow front steps. I opened my door, happy to be away from Sophia's presence. Sin and Cal walked up behind us, Cal greeting everyone in his usual jovial manner. He stationed himself outside the doors and waved us through.

"Whose house is this?" The interior was dark. Heavy curtains and old, faded paintings gave it an 18th century feel.

"Judge Montagnet's." Sin took my arm as Ellis walked up to Sophia. The two of them slipped into a side room.

Sin led me toward a bar set up in a stuffy sitting area. The room wasn't large enough to hold the number of people, and we had to wade past several well-wishers and gawkers before making it to the bar.

"How was your car ride?" Sin pointed to a bottle and held two fingers up. It should have come off as rude, but seemed more authoritative than anything else.

"Blissfully quiet."

He snorted. "What did you do?"

"Nothing." I snagged a strawberry from the nearest serving platter and bit into it, the cold, sweet juice running down my throat.

The barman poured two reds and handed them over.

"What's this?" I sniffed, the odor strong and almost bitter.

"Port." He tipped his glass, and I took a sip, the flavor overpowering.

"That's kind of intense." I shook my head and set my glass down.

He smiled and drained his.

Was it always like this? Us talking like two normal people in a normal house surrounded by normal guests? We couldn't be further from reality.

Sin set his glass on the bar and leaned close. "Have you found him?"

"No." I scanned the crowd, looking for a particular server.

"Let's mingle. Maybe you'll see him."

I pulled the card with Sin's cell number and instructions from my pocket and lodged it in my palm. Following him through the throng of people, I kept an eye out for the server who'd spoken to me at Fort LaRoux. My hope faded each time a server passed and it wasn't him.

Sin stopped and talked with different groups of people, laughing and joking about the trials. It gave me the opportunity to continue my search. I tried not to meet anyone's eyes, but the occasional guest leered at me or tried to touch me. Sin moved us along to prevent any scenes and to keep the too-eager at bay.

We'd made the circuit through the room with no

luck.

"He's not here."

"He has to be. Let's keep looking." Sin pulled me along behind him through the crush of bodies.

My name whipped through the surrounding crowd as the guests voiced their ugly thoughts. I ignored them and focused on finding the one friendly face.

We wound around through another sitting area, a library, and past the door to the kitchen.

"Stop. Let me look in there."

Sin glanced around at the almost-empty back hall. "Make it quick."

I pushed through the door and darted to the side as a server with a tray full of crawfish barreled past. The kitchen was all sound and smells—too many people cooking, chopping, and layering food onto trays. Everything was stainless steel, and the room was almost unbearably hot. I peered at the workers, hoping to see him.

There. He was busy adding garnish to a platter full of bacon-wrapped scallops. I bypassed someone flaming up a pan on a wide range and several servers carrying trays. A man in a high chef's hat stood toward the rear of the kitchen barking orders. Something told me I didn't want to be noticed by him.

I stood at the server's elbow. "Hi."

His brown eyes met mine and his fingers stilled. "I remember you. You okay?"

"Yes. I think the guests said they wanted more of the bruschetta." I pressed the card into his hand and turned.

"O-okay. I'll get right on that." I didn't look back as I slipped out the door.

"Success," I whispered as Sin took my hand and led me back to the foyer. He glanced to the sweeping stairs to the second floor, wider at the bottom than the top, as people climbed.

I took the lead and joined the steady stream, approaching my destiny step-by-step and surrounded on all sides.

The second floor gave way to a series of rooms down the hall on the left and a walkway overlooking the foyer to the right. I followed the crowd to the right until the tight corridor opened into a ballroom almost as big as the one at the Oakman Estate. Wide, sunny windows looked out on the swath of green lawn, and chandeliers glowed warmly overhead.

Plush couches and chairs were situated around a raised platform only a few feet off the ground. A single metal chair sat atop it, open shackles attached the arms and legs. My knees tried to give way and my heart faltered, but Sin pushed me farther along until we stood in front of one of the windows. Other guests walked past and chose their seats.

"Keep it together." He lifted my shirt and pressed his palm to my lower back.

The contact helped, and just knowing we were a team made it more bearable somehow. I lowered my head to focus on breathing, and also to keep the chair from my view. Would I go first? Would my skin feel the initial bite of the metal as the crowd roared and salivated for my blood?

He rubbed my back slowly enough that no one would notice. He even shook hands with a few people, all the while soothing me. I focused on thoughts of Teddy. The pain would keep him alive. His fate was in my hands, and I couldn't break now.

"Ms. Rousseau?" Judge Montagnet's bony fingers wrapped around my elbow. "Welcome to my home. I hope you enjoy your stay." He smiled, his face striated with each year of his horrible existence. "Sin. Doing well, I heard. Just one more task. Cal told me his plans for the day. Exciting." He scratched his ear. "It should make for one hell of a show. Best of luck. I've got my money on you, young lady."

I forced my mouth to stay shut, but every vile curse

I'd ever learned swirled on the tip of my tongue. Control was imperative if I were to succeed, and I couldn't let this ghoul shake mine.

Sin gripped his shoulder. "Thanks, Judge. I'm glad for your support."

He smiled, and then moved into the rows to sit next to a young man in servant's attire. He couldn't have been more than twenty. The judge's hand darted between his legs, and the man stared at the ceiling, as if he switched himself off. I turned away and caught Gavin staring at me from across the room.

His lips creased, a fraction of a smile for me. I did the same, letting him know I was here and that we would get through this. Guilt pounded in my veins as I scanned the crowd for Brianne. I spotted her sitting in Red's lap as he chatted with some people. Her face was blank. No words passed her lips, and her skin hung from her bones.

"Don't look at her. It wasn't your fault." Sin kept easing his hand back and forth.

"She blames me."

"She's foolish. She should blame everyone in this room except you and Gavin."

"Even you?"

He nodded. "Even me."

I wanted to pull him close and tell him he wasn't bad, that he didn't suffer from the same evil that infected these people. He wouldn't believe me. The scars on the back of his hand and the ones in his heart were too old, too thick for me to break through completely. But I would keep working until he saw his own light, his own goodness.

A too-loud laugh crackled through the room, and Cal bounded up to the platform.

"Ladies and gents—this thing on?" He tapped the microphone until feedback kicked in. "Ladies—ah that's better—and gents, welcome to the final Acquisition trial!"

Whoops and yells went up from the crowd as Cal smiled and turned in an appraising circle.

"We've had some *stiff* competition this year—looking at you, Judge." He pointed to Montagnet, and the room erupted in laughter as my blood turned to acid.

"I don't think I've ever seen a stronger slate of competitors. The highlights—Stella's whipping, Gavin's time in the woods, and Brianne's mother. Could we have wished for a better year?"

"No!" The crowd roared.

"That's right. *So* right. On to the delights of the day. The theme for this trial, as we all know, is love. This is my favorite one, because I love all of you." He kissed his palm and spun around to blow it to the entire audience as they laughed. "I do. Same faces I grew up with, here supporting me as my reign slowly comes to a glorious end. I appreciate you all and look forward to many, many more fabulous years."

More applause and yells erupted before Cal put his hand out to quiet them down.

"But you know, love is a two-sided coin." He pulled a quarter from his pocket and flipped it into the air, catching it with ease. "And on the other side—" He held the coin up. "—is hate. Now, without further ado, let's get started! Sin, Red, Bob—come on up with your Acquisitions."

Sin dropped his hand and straightened my shirt. I lurched forward, the floor seeming to give way under my feet. Dizziness swirled through me as he took my elbow and led me through the seating area and to the platform. To the chair.

"That's it. Come on, come on." Cal waved us up to stand beside him.

I edged closer to Sin who stood rigid and still. Brianne was already crying, her sunken eyes clenched shut and her nose running. Gavin stared at me, his eyes warm but tired. His clothes fit loosely now, the Acquisition taking a toll on him just like Brianne and me.

"You three—Sin, Red, Bob—have pleased me beyond my wildest dreams. You made excellent choices of whom to acquire. You've put them through their paces. I couldn't be prouder. Show them some *love*." Cal held his hand out as if he were displaying a prize on a game show as the audience responded with thunderous clapping and crowing.

"Perfect. Now, perhaps I'm getting a bit old fashioned, but I believe that if you truly love something, you will suffer for it. You will do what you must to keep it safe. Nurture it. Never harm it—well, unless she asks for it. Am I right?" Chuckles rose from the crowd as he went on. "So I've created a special task for this final trial. It's going to be a surprise for our competitors."

He snapped his fingers. Three attendants rushed to the stage. "Go with them. All three of you have separate rooms. Wait there until I send for you. And no peeking. I don't want anything ruining the surprise."

Sin and I dropped off the platform and followed an attendant out of the ballroom. The doors to the ballroom closed once Brianne, Gavin, Red, and Bob stood in the hallway with us. The attendants herded us back across the walkway over the foyer and down to the end of the far hall. We were divided among three rooms, and an attendant took position outside our door as it swung shut.

"That chair." I rushed into Sin's arms. "Oh, god." My voice caught, and I fought away tears. Not here. I wouldn't cry here. Not until the pain was too great and I couldn't take it anymore.

"Stella." He put his palm to my face, and I realized it was trembling. "The chair. They'll make me hurt you."

"I know." I looked into his wild eyes as he scanned the room, like an animal seeking escape through the bars of a cage. But we were in a bedroom, high on the second floor. "Hey." I got on my tiptoes. "We can do this."

"I don't think I can bear it." He scooped me into his arms and sat on the bed.

"We can."

He rocked me and rested his lips in my hair. It was as

if I could feel him coming apart beneath me, the layers of armor he usually wore stripping away until a broken boy stood there, begging me to save him.

"You don't understand. I can't hurt you again."

"Shh." I scooted so I sat upright in his lap and pressed my lips to his. "When this is over, I will still love you. Nothing will ever keep me from loving you."

"Don't say that." He glanced to the window again. "You don't know what's going to happen."

"I know they won't make you kill me or maim me. It's against the rules to do it to an Acquisition, right? And anything else, I'll heal from it. Sin, please just look at me."

He brought his tortured gaze back to mine.

"I'll be alive on the other side. I'll be with you. Do it for Teddy."

He didn't respond, only pulled me to him. We sat in silence for over an hour. I thought I heard footsteps and the doors close from the adjoining rooms, but I couldn't be certain.

Random bits of noise filtered down from the ballroom, but not enough for us to have an inkling of what was going on. After another two hours had passed, our door opened. Sin set me on my feet as the attendant motioned for us to follow him back to the ballroom.

We entered, and the coppery scent of blood surrounded us.

"Our final competitor at last. Come on up."

My feet didn't want to move, but Sin pushed me forward roughly. He was back in character, which was a good sign, though I feared how he'd react when he had to hurt me.

"Oh, Stella." Cal pulled me into his side. "Have I mentioned that I have a thing for redheads?"

The crowd laughed as I stared at the blood on the platform, red streaks on the chair, and what looked like a tooth on the smooth ballroom floor. My stomach heaved, and I vomited. Cal backed up as it splashed onto the floor, and the ladies in the front row all broke out their fans.

"Clean this up." Cal motioned over some attendants who used dirty, bloody towels to mop up my mess. He slapped my ass. "Feeling better? Where was I? Right. The final show. Bring the goodies over."

An attendant wheeled a small cart to the edge of the platform. It was littered with various tools—some bloody, some untouched, and none of them pleasant. Sin's eyes were wide, terror written there like I'd never seen before.

Cal continued talking, the speakers booming his voice across the crowd. "You can do this," I whispered to Sin.

He met my eyes and calmed as I held his gaze, his face returning to its cold mask. To show him I could take it, I stepped to the chair and sat down, resting my wrists in the shackles.

Cal turned around. "Oh, no, no darling Stella. The chair is for Sin."

CHAPTER TWENTY-FIVE
Stella

I SHOOK MY HEAD, my ears ringing as if a bomb had gone off.

"Look, she doesn't believe me." Cal laughed and took my hand, ripping me up from the chair. "See? Not you, gorgeous." He turned to Sin. "You."

The room fell silent as Sin looked down his nose at Cal. Then he smirked and whipped off his jacket.

The crowd cheered as Sin sat down with dramatic flair and placed his wrists and ankles in the restraints.

"Could you at least tell her to go easy on my face? A, it's a handsome face, and B, I want to look good enough to marry your daughter."

Cal roared with laughter as an attendant snapped Sin's shackles closed. "You are one cheeky asshole, you know that?"

I rested my hand on the back of his chair. Maybe it would stop the room from spinning. Sin tilted his head back and met my eyes. A quick nod, and then he was facing forward again, smiling.

"You amaze me, Counsellor. You really do. Do you have any idea how Bob quaked and cried? How much Red begged Brianne to go easy on him? Did she go easy on him, y'all?"

The crowd laughed, and several cries of "no" rang out.

"Indeed, she did not. It seems Red underestimated her. But here's the rules. Stella can visit any harm upon you she sees fit, with any of these tools I have at her disposal. Like I said, love and hate, same coin. You understand, right Sin?"

"I understand that you better have lunch ready when I get out of these restraints. I'm going to work up a real appetite." Sin's voice, confidence dripping from the words, boomed over the crowd without the benefit of a microphone.

"Damn. That's my man. I'd like to shake your hand right now." He glanced to the shackles at Sin's wrists. "Too bad on that one, my friend." Cal smiled. "Rules are simple, Stella. You can't kill him. He can't lose parts."

"The same rules." I gripped the back of the chair harder.

"Exactly, the same rules. It's up to you. Have your revenge. All I ask is that you make it good enough for our entertainment. Brianne and Gavin sure did." With that, he hopped off the platform and took a seat between two redheads, throwing an arm around each of them.

The room quieted until I could hear my breath, the steady pump of blood in my ears. I walked around to Sin's front.

"Do your fucking worst, cunt." He flashed his eyes at me. No fear. Instead, relief sat in the crease of his mouth, the turn of his chin.

"Damn. I love this guy." Cal stage-whispered.

So do I. I stepped down to the cart of tools. I clasped my hands in front of me, my fingers shaking and frozen.

"Pssst."

I turned toward the sound. Dylan sat two rows back, leering at me. I ignored him and went back to perusing the weapons. A scalpel was coated with blood, and a larger pocket knife was, too. The claw hammer had bloody fingerprints along the handle, and a vicious-looking set of needles sat neatly to the side.

"Come on, Stella." Cal's tone lost some of its showman quality, impatience seeping through. "I'm beginning to feel a bit peckish. It's after lunch. Get to work."

I glanced up to Sin. His face was calm, his body relaxed. This felt right to him. He was used to someone he loved bringing him pain. Not just the back of his hand, but the wounds that went so much deeper. He was calm in the face of what he knew, that love was pain. Would I be that to him? Someone he trusted who ultimately made him suffer because of the Acquisition?

I backed away from the cart. "No. I won't."

"Stella." Sin leaned forward. "Do it."

"No."

Cal stood. "Why on earth not?"

"I can't." I lowered my head.

"Stella!" Sin barked. "Do it now!"

I stared at the bloody floor.

"Oh, dear me. This is a problem. Stella, doll, look at me." Cal put his finger under my chin and brought my face up to his. "If you don't do this, you'll take his place. Is that what you want?"

I shook, my teeth chattering as my body trembled.

"Stella. Stop this prideful refusal or I swear that I will beat you again as soon as we leave here!"

"Sin, she just doesn't have the stomach for it. Totally understandable." He turned back to me. "Now, it's up to you. Either you take your revenge on Sin—the one who stole you, who whipped you, who let his brother rape you—or you let me take my aggressions out on you."

Sin growled and his shackles rattled. "Stella. Do as I say." It was a harsh command, but I felt the fear in it.

I wouldn't hurt him. Showing him that love didn't

always end that way—with pain and torment—was more important to me than an hour of suffering. I took a deep breath, and exhaled only one word.

"No."

"You heard the lady. Unlock Sin and put her in his place." Cal began to roll up the sleeves of his dress shirt.

"Goddammit, Stella. Do it!"

"Too late now. I appreciate your efforts to make a good showing, Sin. I sure do. But I suspect Stella and I will make the best showing of all." He plucked at my jacket. "Go ahead and take your top off. I want more canvas to work with."

"No!" Sin pushed the attendant away and dropped down to the floor. "Stella, don't."

"I have to." I couldn't meet his eyes.

"No, I can take it."

"I know you can." I looked up at him, his brow furrowed. "But you shouldn't have to," I whispered.

"Enough chit chat. Let's get going." Cal ripped me away and pushed me up onto the stand.

Sin grabbed Cal's arm and whipped him around. He pulled his fist back.

"Sin!" I cried.

He turned to me, his fist still cocked, and I shook my head. *Teddy*, I mouthed.

"What do you think you're doing?" Cal recovered from his defensive posture and shoved Sin away.

"Sorry Sovereign. I guess I just hoped I'd get to do it myself is all." Sin opened his fist and dropped his arms to his side.

Cal considered him for a moment, the room tense. Then he rolled his shoulders and smiled. "All worked up, eh? Good man." He motioned to the redheads on the couch. "Sit with the girls and enjoy yourself, but not too much. He's taken, ladies. Stella, why's your shirt still on?"

He climbed to the platform and yanked my jacket off my shoulders. Gripping my tank top at my chest, he ripped it apart in one harsh movement and threw the tatters to the ground. I couldn't stop the squeak of fear that caught in my throat. He didn't stop, only slid my bra straps off my shoulders. "Unhook it." His voice was thick with lust.

I reached behind my back, but my fingers were too numb to do anything.

"Allow me." He hugged me to him and undid the clasp. My bra dropped to the floor and I crossed my arms over my breasts. "Have a seat."

I backed up and sank down into the chair, the sticky blood of its last occupant coating the bottom of my arms. Cal knelt down and locked me in. I trembled and closed my eyes.

"Girls, I said go easy. He's engaged."

"Sorry." One of them giggled as a sharp sting erupted across my cheek.

Cal's hand turned into a blur as he slapped me again and again until I tried to loll my head forward to stop his attacks.

"Hold her head."

An attendant climbed up behind me and grabbed a fistful of my hair, pulling my head back so I had no choice but to see Cal.

"That was just foreplay." He balled his hand into a fist, his eyes sharp and focused. "Let's go all the way."

CHAPTER TWENTY-SIX
Sinclair

Her strength failed, her will dissipated, and no more screams passed her lips. Even when Cal took a scalpel and sliced across her left breast, she remained silent, her eyes open, though no spark lit them.

The whores on either side of me had finally given up trying to entertain me. All I could see was Stella, suffering in front of me while I sat in comfort. I only remained still because of her. She'd committed fully, sacrificing herself for Teddy. I had to see it through. For her.

The devils surrounding me would pay, but I couldn't take comfort in the promise of violence.

I had never prayed in my life. Perhaps when I'd been younger, before Brazil. But at no time in recent memory. I prayed as Cal hit her, lashed her body with his belt, split her lip and broke her nose. I prayed he would stop. I prayed she would recover. And I prayed for their deaths. The litany was on a loop in my mind, and it was the only thing that kept me sane.

Cal continued his expansive carving, ending the cut on her stomach at the edge of her jeans. He stood back and admired his handiwork as her blood oozed from the sweeping curved lines. Wiping the sweat from his brow with a bloodied sleeve, he stepped down from the platform. The attendant let Stella's chin drop to her chest.

"I think my masterpiece is done. What do you all say?" He scrubbed the blood from his hands with a towel as the crowd cheered, though their zest had died down over the hour of torture.

"Thank you. I take pride in my work. We have a delightful lunch prepared downstairs. Please make your way down, and I'll be there shortly after I get cleaned up. Don't worry, I still have enough left in me to carve the roast." He grinned and bowed as the applause swelled once again, and the guests began to leave.

Stella didn't move even as the attendant unbuckled her manacles. She sat as if she were still tied down.

"Sin, let's chat."

I finally stood, but forced my feet to take me to Cal instead of Stella. Everything inside me screamed and demanded vengeance.

Instead of snapping Cal's neck, I smiled. "Good work. You certainly have a knack."

"I knew you'd appreciate my art." He finished wiping the blood from his mouth, the bite marks along Stella's right breast and upper arms still red and angry.

Once the final guest left, Cal clapped me on the back. "What's it feel like to be the next Sovereign?"

"So, you've chosen?" I scrubbed a hand down my face, my relief for Teddy doing nothing to ease the burden weighing down on my mind, my heart.

"No, she chose." He pointed at Stella who sat like a pool of water, flat and motionless.

I peered into his taciturn eyes. "I'm not sure I follow."

He sank onto the nearest chair and let out an exhausted sigh. He stalled, wanting to provide more theatrics. I was desperate to grab Stella and run with her, get her help and save her. But, as she'd done from the moment I met her, she'd saved me, instead.

"The theme of the final trial is love for a reason. Every trial has its purpose. As Sovereign, you will tell your competitors that the purpose in the end is to break their Acquisition, to be the worst son of a bitch south of the Mason-Dixon."

"Yes?" I wanted to know. I wanted Stella more. The quicker Cal explained, the quicker I could get her out of here.

"That's not the trick of it, in the end. Think about it. Your mother, for example. She had a special relationship with her Acquisition. Still does, am I correct?"

"Yes." My gaze flickered to Stella, who remained impassive.

"You won't remember my Acquisition. She certainly had a special place in her heart for me. Redhead. Anyway—"

"Yes?" My impatience overflowed.

"She chose you. You who whipped her, allowed her to be raped, made her fight to the death, forced her through so many horrors. But still, she chose you. She chose to take your beating. Usually, the winner of this trial is the one whose Acquisition does the least damage to the Acquirer. No one knows that except the Sovereign of course, and it's a closely guarded secret."

I pinched the bridge of my nose. "What are you saying?"

"I'm saying the fact that you were able to mistreat Stella beyond all bounds of cruel and unusual, but that she is *still* loyal and protective, makes you the winner. She went one step further and actually took your punishment." He raised his eyebrows in chagrin. "That is unprecedented in trial history. You made her fall in love with you, even though you tortured her and even though she knew you could never love a peasant like her. You have twisted and broken not only her body, but her mind, her spirit. That's the sort of strength we need as Sovereign.

Congratulations."

No wonder Mother had won. Renee was devoted to her. How had I never seen it as the key?

He rose and popped his neck. "The coronation will be in a month at my estate. I'll take delivery of Stella then, as well."

"Delivery?"

"Oh, yes, forgot to mention. I'm taking Stella for a week or two before giving her to Dylan. I enjoyed our time today, but I want more of a private session. You don't mind, do you?"

My hands demanded I choke the life out of him. "No, of course not. I will turn her over then."

"Good man. I'm very pleased about your elevation, and I'll let Sophia know. Just keep it under wraps until coronation day. You know I love surprises." He grinned and turned to leave. "You coming to lunch? We don't want to start off on the wrong foot."

"I'll be down in a moment. Just want to get her handled so she doesn't bleed all over my suit."

"You are such a dandy." Cal laughed and walked out. As soon as he was gone, I jumped up to Stella and wrapped her in my suit coat.

When I picked her up, her head lolled back, her eyes still a glassy green. My chest burned as if my heart was being dipped in a vat of acid.

"Stella?"

She didn't respond.

"Stella, please."

Still no words as a tear rolled down her cheek. No, not hers. Another one landed at the corner of her lips, mixing with the blood there before moving down to her jaw. I blinked hard. My tears. The idea was so foreign to me. I hadn't shed a tear since Brazil, and now the floodgates were opened. Tears flowed down my face as I clutched her to me, her bloodied and broken body drawing breath but otherwise devoid of life.

I rushed through the ballroom and kicked the doors open, knocking an attendant on his ass as I rushed past. It seemed like days had passed since we'd been in the bedroom at the end of the hall, waiting to meet our fate. I pushed through the door and lay her on the bed.

"Is she okay?" Gavin walked in behind me.

"Get the fuck out." I picked the bloody strands of hair away from her busted nose and tried to gauge what sort of medical attention she needed. Not that I could give her any. I had to show my face downstairs. *Fuck!*

"There's a medic next door, fixing Bob up. I can get her in here."

"Get her. Now. Bob can wait." I turned back to her. "Stella, can you say something?"

She hadn't blinked. He'd hit her in the head so many times. I wanted to scream and rage and burn the entire fucking house to the ground. But I had no right. I'd just sat there, the whores pawing at my dick as Stella took hit after hit. For me. "Oh god, Stella, please."

"Move away from her." A woman's harsh voice cut through my misery. She wore bloody scrubs and had a flowery carrying case in one hand. "I said move."

"Can you help her?"

"Up. Go."

I stood, but wouldn't leave.

She pushed past me and inspected Stella's face, then opened my jacket and looked at the bloody wounds along her torso. "Jesus. At least she's not the worst I've seen today."

She set her bag on the bed and dug out a syringe. "Night night." She hit a vein, no problem, and let the meds fly.

Stella's eyes finally closed, and I was back in my mother's room as she screamed and railed until I drugged her to sleep. "Not her, please not Stella."

"I'll need to set her nose, clean her wounds, and bandage her up. Some of these cuts could use stitches, but stitches aren't my specialty." She dug several implements from her bag, including alcohol, gauze, tape, and what looked like a tongue depressor. "I tend to leave ugly scars. So if in doubt, I'll leave them out."

"Will she be okay?" Gavin stood at my elbow. I'd forgotten he was there.

"Mister." She shook her head, her black braids swaying. "I've seen some fucked up shit today that I hope I never see again for as long as I live. No amount of money is worth this. Don't ask me stupid questions like that."

She got to work as I stood glued to the spot.

"Why is she hurt?" Gavin shoved me back. "Why? I beat Bob unconscious. Brianne had to be pulled off Red. But you stand here without a scratch."

"Get off me." I couldn't see Stella.

"No. Tell me why!" He shoved harder until my back hit the fireplace.

I swung hard and fast, my fist crunching into his cheek. He fell away, and I rushed forward to Stella again as the medic dabbed her wounds with alcohol.

"Stella, please." I rested my hand on her shin.

"Motherfucker." Gavin got to his feet and brought his fists up.

The medic turned a harsh eye on both of us. "If you two are going to fight, get the fuck out. The last thing this poor girl needs is more violence."

I didn't give Gavin so much as a glance. "Don't try to keep me from her. I'll kill you." It wasn't a threat, only a simple fact. If he tried to come between Stella and me again, I'd pound his face into a bloody pulp.

"Mr. Vinemont?" Someone spoke from the hall.

"What?" I couldn't take my eyes off Stella as the medic wrapped a blood pressure cuff around her arm.

"Mr. Oakman is asking for you."

I ground my teeth so hard I thought they might crack.

"I'll stay here with her." Gavin walked around the

bed and sat next to her, taking one of her bloodied hands in his.

I wanted to kill him, to show Stella I could protect her. But that's what he was doing. Protecting her. I'd failed. I'd watched it all. I'd done nothing.

"Go." He didn't look at me when he spoke. He blamed me. He was right to. I was at fault for all of it.

I stared, wanting to will some sort of comfort into her as the medic listened for her heartbeat. I rubbed my eyes.

"Mr. Vinemont?"

"I fucking heard you." I whirled and walked to the door, but turned back before going through. "Don't let anyone touch her or hurt her while I'm away."

Gavin caught my gaze, hatred written in the narrowing of his eyes. "She'll be safe as long as you're gone."

I turned and left. The worst part was that he was right.

CHAPTER TWENTY-SEVEN
Stella

THE HOT BREEZE ROCKED the swing as I watched Lucius and Teddy toss a football back and forth in the yard. I stretched my arms above my head, ignoring the burn of pain that still sizzled from my healing wounds. Sin came out the front door, two glasses in his hands. He passed one to me, and I sipped as he settled next to me.

He pulled me gently into his side. "It's not too hot out here, is it?"

"No. I'm glad to be out of the house." I rested my head against his shoulder.

"Go long!" Lucius pointed to the tree line.

"I am long," Teddy called back.

"Longer than that, asshole. I can throw farther than a peewee league quarterback."

I laughed. Sin laced his fingers through mine as Lucius threw to a distant Teddy. He caught it, but had to dash up a few yards first.

"Fingers slipped." Lucius threw his hands up and turned around to look at us. "Fingers slipped. That's what that was."

"Sure." Sin nodded.

"You want to try it?"

"No." He hadn't left my side since we returned from the trial. I didn't remember much. From what I could tell, my faulty memory was a blessing. My nose was still swollen, and Sin had taken me to a plastic surgeon in New Orleans to repair the cuts. The scars would be barely noticeable, but I would always know they were there.

Sin watched over me day and night during the weeks since the trial, letting his prosecutor position go untended. Sometimes, it was as if he were afraid I'd disappear if he weren't looking right at me.

"Go on and throw the ball around. Show Lucius up." I pulled my hand away. He took it back.

"No."

"Don't want to embarrass him?"

He kissed my forehead. "Exactly."

The days were already growing shorter, the trees casting long shadows over the lawn. Sin rocked us slowly as the sun made its retreat down the sky. After a while, Lucius and Teddy, winded and sweaty, bounded onto the porch and collapsed into the rocking chairs. We chatted as the fireflies began to glow, an intermittent symphony of tiny lights.

"I think I'm going to go see what's cooking for supper." Teddy stood and made a show of rubbing his stomach.

"Try not to fuck her against the stove. It's dangerous." Lucius grinned.

Teddy's cheeks reddened, and he hurried into the house.

"That wasn't very nice." I shook my head at Lucius.

"He'll live."

"Yes, he will." Sin kissed my hair.

Lucius glanced to the door and then back at us. "He's gone now. Let's talk. I have all the goods collected and ready to be rolled into the estate as soon as the gates open."

"Stella, is your guy on the inside ready?"

"Quinlan, yes. I spoke to him earlier. He took the money and hired his own trustworthy people for the job. They know the score and will get out of dodge when it all goes down. Some of the attendants won't know, but he's promised to keep them out of harm's way when all hell breaks loose."

"How do you know we can trust him?" Lucius asked.

"We don't. But he's an ex-Marine, and his uncle runs a security firm. They're working together on this, and we're paying them both a small fortune. They won't get the money until the job's done."

Lucius seemed appeased and moved on. "The supplies?"

"Already loaded up in the caterer's vans, ready to go."

I'd been over the plan so many times in the past three weeks that it was in my mind like a well-worn path through grass. There was no missing it.

"I still think you should stay here." Sin sighed.

"No." I was going. I didn't care how many times Sin tried to talk me out of it. Besides, it would look fishy if he showed up without Cal's prize.

"Lucius, tell her she should stay."

"You'll get no help from me. She's right. She deserves to be there."

"She deserves more than that. Much more." Sin pulled me into his lap.

Lucius scowled. "If you're doing this, I'm out."

"We'll talk business later." Sin waved him away.

Lucius grumbled and slammed the front door on his way in.

"Are you tired?"

"No." I leaned against him and watched the fireflies spark. "I feel good."

"What hurts?" He ran a hand up and down my thigh, goose bumps rising under the thin material of my pajama pants.

"Nothing."

"Are you sure?"

"Yes. Stop worrying."

He kept rocking us at a leisurely pace. "I'll never stop worrying about you."

"I know, but I'm fine now. I'm healing. I want to get back to painting and walking and riding with you and Teddy. And mainly, I want you to stop feeling guilty." I kissed his neck.

"I don't think I'm capable of that."

"You didn't think you were capable of love, either."

He canted his head to the side, the stubble along his cheeks looking even darker in the low light. "Touché."

"You don't have to be careful with me, you know? I won't break."

"I can't hurt you." He peered down at me, worry wrinkling the skin near his eyes.

I nibbled at his neck. "Take me upstairs."

"No, you're still healing. I can't."

I twined my arms around his neck and pulled myself up to his mouth. I licked along his bottom lip and bit down on it.

"Stella." His voice lowered to a growl. "Don't."

"Make me stop." I kissed him and ran my fingers through his hair, pulling close to the scalp where I knew it would hurt.

He slid his hand up my thigh and gripped my ass, then lifted me so I straddled him. He kissed me hungrily, like he'd been starved for me. I caressed his tongue with mine and moved my hips back and forth over his growing erection.

He dug his fingers into my waist and moved me faster on top of him.

"No." He pulled away. "We can't. You're hurt."

"I'm not." I kissed down his neck.

He gripped the collar of my shirt and pulled it aside, the ugly red scar from Cal's cut curving around my collar bone. "You are."

"It's almost healed. Give this to me. Please?" I dropped my eyes. "Unless you don't find me attractive any longer, now that—"

"Don't be an idiot." He crushed my mouth with his, one of his hands tangling in my hair. Lifting me with ease, he walked to the door, his lips still pressed to mine, his tongue ruling my mouth.

I wrapped my legs around him as he pushed through the door and into the house. Making quick work of the stairs, he carried me to my bedroom and lay me down.

He pulled his shirt over his head. I stared at the broad expanse of his chest, the masculine V of his torso. I took the hem of my shirt and started to pull it, but he stayed my hands with his.

"I want to do it." He pushed my shirt up slowly, dropping soft kisses along my skin with each inch he exposed.

By the time he reached my breasts, I was clutching his hair and arching my back. He kissed around the bottoms of each, keeping his slow pace. He paid extra attention to my scars, his breath tickling me as his mouth sealed his love to my skin.

He kissed my nipples, still taking his time as my shirt moved higher and higher until he pulled it over my head and tossed it to the floor. His eyes were reverent as he kissed my lips with the same soft pressure he'd used on the rest of me. My thighs were on fire, and I wanted him, all of him.

He ended the kiss too soon and dropped to his knees, pulling my pants and panties off. Starting at my toes, he kissed up each leg. The gentle caresses multiplied and reverberated through my body until all I could think of was him.

Spreading my legs, he lay his palms flat against my inner thighs. His warm breath grazed my pussy, and he kissed my bare skin, up and down until no spot was left untouched. I jolted when he slipped his tongue inside me.

He hesitated. "Is it all right?"

"Better than all right. Please don't stop."

He gave me the devious smile—the one I once loathed and now loved—before diving back down. His stubble scraped against my thighs as he licked me from entrance to clit. I moaned at the overwhelming rush of sensation. He did it again and put his hands under my ass, lifting me to his face as he devoured me.

I clutched the blanket as he licked and sucked, his tongue darting inside me and then swirling around my clit. He groaned into me as I spread my legs wider, my body opening for him. He wrapped his lips around my tight nub and sucked.

I raised up on my elbows and met his eyes as he shook his head back and forth, his lips rubbing against me and his scruff prickling my most sensitive skin.

"Sin." I gasped and let my head fall back as he attacked my clit with his tongue again.

When he sank a finger inside me, I dropped back down on the bed. When he added another, I worked them like they were his cock. My hips moved to his rhythm, a slave to his fingers, his wicked mouth. I tensed as he gave me no quarter, every move designed to send me rushing over the edge and into the deep abyss of pleasure below.

My hips jerked, and I came, the release exploding through me as I rubbed myself against his mouth. His name rolled through me on a moan as my pussy convulsed again and again, the orgasm thumping through me as he continued fucking me with his fingers.

When I relaxed back onto the bed, he crawled on top of me and ran his fingers around my lips. I sucked them, licking myself off him before he kissed me and shared the taste. He rested his weight on his elbows, careful not to crush me. I didn't want careful or tentative. I wanted Sin.

"Fuck me." I yanked on his hair for good measure as he kissed to my neck.

"Stella, I'm warning you."

I pulled harder until he met my eyes. "Don't warn me. Fuck me."

He tangled a hand in my hair and pulled until I had to arch my back. "Is this what you want?"

"Yes."

He ran his lips down my throat and bit. "This?"

"Yes."

He thrust his hips against me. "This?"

"Yes, please."

He stood and removed his belt, tossing it on the bed next to me. Then he freed his cock and crawled back on top of me. When his tip hit my clit, I moaned and tried to kiss him. He pulled away and grabbed his belt.

"Hands together, over your head."

I arched an eyebrow. "No."

"Stella." His voice was gravel as he rested his weight on me and wrenched my hands above my head. He looped the belt around my wrist and pulled tight, then kept the slack in his hand. He kissed me hard, the way I remembered—the way I wanted.

I spread my legs as wide as possible, and he slid his tip down to my entrance.

He blinked and hesitated. "Am I hurting you?"

"Not enough," I breathed.

"Fuck, you were made for me." He thrust inside me halfway, pulled out, and then slid all the way in as I moaned.

He reached under me and lifted, moving me to one of the bed posters, his cock still inside me. He wrapped the free end of the belt around the wood and tied it in a loose knot. Then he yanked my hips down, the knot tightening and holding me in place as his cock surged even deeper inside me.

"I didn't want to hurt you." He settled on top of me and pumped slow and deep.

"I trust you."

He kissed me, just a taste. "I never want to lose that trust."

"You won't."

"I don't want you to go to the coronation. If I lost you, I don't know what I'd do."

"You aren't going to lose me." I captured his lips, kissing away his fear as he thrusted harder.

His tongue warred with mine, and he picked up his pace, making my pussy grow tighter with each impact. I raised my hips so every surge of friction caught my clit. He slid an arm under me and wrapped his fingers around my shoulder, taking complete control as he fucked me hard, finally taking what was his.

I moaned as he kissed to my neck and palmed my breast. He squeezed and then pinched my nipple as I pulled at my restraints. It was useless. I wanted to be caught.

"You're everything to me." He buried his face in my neck and nipped at my earlobe. "I can't be without you ever again. Promise me."

My heart—the one that had been betrayed, broken, and abused—suddenly beat with renewed purpose. I lived for him, for a life together outside the world of the Acquisition.

"I promise."

"Thank you." He dropped kisses along my jaw. His eyes glittered in the dim light as he took my mouth and ran his hand to where we were joined.

His thumb found my clit, and I lit up, every cell in my body focused on his movements. He swallowed my moan and stroked me insistently, demanding I come with each swipe of his thumb. My body tensed, the wave cresting. He must have felt it—he sped faster, his cock filling me again and again until my body gave in, my legs shaking and my hips locking as I came.

He groaned into my mouth and pressed deep inside, his cock kicking as I milked him, my orgasm rolling like waves crashing on the shore.

"Sin." I panted. My thoughts flew away, and he was the only one left.

He thrust once more and rested his head on the bed next to mine.

"I love you." His words were barely a whisper, but they spoke to me in a way nothing else ever could.

CHAPTER TWENTY-EIGHT
Stella

Farns shuffled into the breakfast room, his pace growing slower each day. Even as his age turned to infirmity, he refused to retire and simply live at the house. Though I wasn't sure if the earth might spin off its axis if Farns wasn't up at daybreak, dressed in crisp attire, and setting the house to rights from front to back.

"A messenger brought this." He handed a piece of parchment to Sin. The oak seal was unmistakable. Cal.

He broke the wax and unfolded the missive, his brows drawing down with each line he read.

"What?" Lucius glanced to the hall. "Say it before Teddy gets in here."

"All the last-borns have to attend the coronation. Even Teddy." Sin tossed the paper down on the table and leaned back in his chair, the heels of his palms against his eyes.

"Oh, god, we can't keep it from him." My appetite vanished, and I flinched when I heard Teddy's steps on the stairs.

"No, we can't. And I thought Cal would let him stay away. Fuck. We'll have to make adjustments."

Lucius pushed his chair back and rose. "I'll get in touch with Quinlan, let him know we'll have one more on the list."

"Do it." Sin nodded and gripped the arms of his chair.

Lucius disappeared toward the study as Teddy walked in. He wore a Led Zeppelin t-shirt and jeans riddled with holes. He yawned and stretched his arms over his head as he approached.

He was the heart of the family, a pure soul. Would the knowledge of the trials hurt him? I knew it would. I only hoped it wouldn't destroy him.

Sin grimaced, dread shrouding his features.

"Sin." I took his hand. "Let me. Go with Lucius and get the plan straightened out. I'll do this part."

"What part? What plan?" Teddy sat beside me.

Sin squeezed my fingers. "Are you sure?"

"Yes. I think it'll be better. Go on."

He rose and kissed me on the forehead before walking out, his steps stiff, worry sitting heavy on his shoulders.

"What is it now? Something bad?" The sleepiness had fled from Teddy's eyes, and only fearfulness remained.

How could I explain? I had to keep him grounded, give him just enough knowledge to know the score, but not too many details.

I began where it all started, where it would make the most sense. "There are seven rules to the Acquisition."

He paled. "It must be really bad if you're going to tell me."

"I have to." I took his hand and pressed it between my palms. "I don't want to, but Cal has demanded your presence at the coronation. So you're going to find out some things. I'd rather tell you now. Just the two of us. And I-I'm afraid. So I'll need you to help me. I don't want it to change you or hurt you."

"Tell me. I can take it." He scooted his chair back

and pulled mine around so we faced each other. "No matter what, I'll deal."

"The first rule, and the only one you truly need to know." I cleared my throat and gripped his hand tight. "Is that if an Acquirer loses, he has to kill the last-born of his line."

Teddy knit his brows together for a split-second before his eyes widened and his jaw went slack. "Me?"

I nodded. "If Sin were to lose, he would have to sacrifice you as punishment." The words were so harsh, so steeped in evil, but they had to be said.

He shook his head, disbelief and shock in the slow back and forth movement. "Oh, god. No wonder. No fucking wonder. And all this time, I've been blaming him."

"And you?" His eyes watered. "How long have you known? What did they do to you? What have you gone through for me?"

I leaned forward and pulled him to me, wrapping him in a hug as the pain washed over him like a pelting spring rain. "I would do it again if it meant keeping you safe."

A sob rocketed up from his lungs, and he clung to me. "I'm so sorry. God, Stella, I'm so sorry. I don't even know what to..."

"No. It's not your fault. You have to know that. You didn't set any of this up. It isn't your fault. I swear. I love you, and I never wanted you to know."

He shook, sob after sob breaking him down until tears wet my cheeks, too.

"It's okay. Shh." I stroked his hair and whispered what few words of comfort I could.

We sat for a long time as anguish poured from him. I recognized it all, the feelings he cycled through like gears in a car—anger, sorrow, fear, rage. I knew them by heart. I held him as Sin and Lucius milled outside the doorway, their faces set in grim lines of worry.

When Teddy's tears subsided, he let me go and cradled my face with his hands. "Thank you." His voice shook, but his resolve was certain. "Thank you, Stella. I can never repay you. Never."

"You already have." I smiled and wiped his tears away. "That was the bad news. I've got some good news, too."

I motioned for Sin and Lucius to come in.

"Good news?" Teddy rose and embraced Lucius and then Sin. The three of them stood together, brothers with a bond that could never break.

"Yeah, little brother. This is my favorite part." Lucius cracked his knuckles.

"We're going to kill them all." Sin spoke of mass murder with a gleam in his eye that would have chilled even the stoutest heart.

All I felt was pride. "We are."

"Good." Teddy nodded and stood straighter, the Vinemont steel strengthening his spine just as it did for Sin and Lucius. "I want them to suffer. For Stella. What can I do?"

Sin smirked and clapped him on the back. "I knew it was in there somewhere."

I stared up at them. I was caught in the web, surrounded by three deadly spiders, and there was nowhere else I'd rather be.

"I think that about does it." Tony clicked the tattoo gun off and sat back. "I can easily say this is the best work I've ever done. Here." He handed me a mirror.

Sun filtered through the glass panels in the spa room and lit the ink along my skin. I followed the swirls of vines curving gracefully from my collarbone, across my breast, down to my stomach, and ending with a flourish over my heart. "He's going to love it. Just don't tell him you saw my nipples or things might get ugly."

"Oh, I'm well aware. I could tell that night at the party with the masks."

I peered up at him. "You could?"

He dabbed some ointment along the fresh ink. "Are you kidding? He couldn't take his eyes off you. I thought he might take me out just for touching you. If that wasn't love, then..." He shrugged. "I don't know, maybe it was some sort of unhealthy obsession?"

I smiled. "A little bit of both."

"Sounds about right. He's a strange guy." He met my eyes and hastily continued, "I mean, I dig him. No offense meant."

"None taken. He's definitely strange." I sat up and pulled my t-shirt back on.

He leaned back and twisted one of the piercings in his eyebrow. "You sure you're okay? I know you said you got into a car accident, but the scars I covered—perfectly, I might add—look sort of, I don't know, intentional?"

"Don't worry. No one's hurting me. I promise." I smiled to reassure him. "It was a car accident."

He twisted the loop a few more times before dropping his hand. "Yeah, you seem like the sort of woman who gives as good as she gets." He packed up his tattoo gun. "Anyone else and I'd keep pressing, but I get the feeling you might put a hurting on me if I pry."

"Your instincts are spot on." I kissed him on the cheek. "Send Sin the bill. He'll pay up."

"He always does."

"And I'm glad you'll be far away from here when he sees our little secrets." I'd added in a couple of piercings especially for Sin, ones that he might strangle poor Tony over.

"Me, too." He shuddered, the tattoos along his arms dancing as he cleaned up his work space in the spa room.

I stood and stretched, ignoring the stings along my skin.

"Make sure you follow up with my aftercare instructions," Tony said as I retreated back into the main hallway.

"I'm all over it. Don't worry. And if I'm not, Sin will be."

The boys were in town finalizing preparations. I'd bowed out at the last minute, claiming I needed some "me" time. Sin didn't want to go without me. After a lot of convincing, I eventually shooed him out the door along with Lucius and Teddy. I hated for him to worry, but I was safe at home and wanted the new ink to be a surprise.

Laura bustled around the kitchen as I entered. She'd made a platter for sandwiches, so I fixed a ham and cheese and grabbed some chips from the pantry.

"How's Teddy been the past few days?" I tried to keep my tone nonchalant.

"A little distracted. Otherwise, fine." She hit some buttons on the dishwasher and turned to give me a smile. "You're looking happy today."

"I am. I got Sin a surprise."

"Oh, do tell." She walked over and leaned on the island.

I grinned and put my sandwich down. "Brace yourself."

She smiled and clasped her hands together. "Consider me braced."

I lifted my shirt, and her eyes went wide.

"Did those hurt?"

"Hell, yes, they did." I smoothed my shirt back down and ate some more of my sandwich as Laura stole a few of my chips.

"Do you think Teddy would like it if I did that?"

I laughed. "I'm beginning to think I'm a bad influence on you, and I like it."

A loud thunk sounded in the hallway.

"What was that?" Laura cocked her head to the side.

"I don't know. Stay here." I grabbed a knife from the

butcher block and walked into the dining room. I crept to the hall door, holding the knife at the ready. Peeking out, I saw Farns lying in the foyer.

"Oh shit, Laura!" I dropped the knife and ran to Farns. He lay on his side, blood running from a wound on his forehead.

He tried to sit up, but I pushed him down. "Don't move. Let us look at you."

"No." He pointed up the stairs, and his eyes swam. "Rebecca. Help her."

"Help her?"

Laura knelt and pressed a dishtowel to his forehead.

"Take care of him. I'm going to see about Rebecca." I darted up the stairs and dashed down the third floor hall.

Renee's sobs sounded clearly from Rebecca's room. I rushed through the door and stopped. The matriarch of the family lay still in her bed, her face turned toward the sun and her eyes closed. Renee sat next to her, gripping Rebecca's hand between hers.

"Renee." I walked over and rested my palm on her back. "I'm so sorry."

"Sh-she spoke to me this morning. It was her. The real her. She told me she loved me and the boys and to watch over you. And then she said she wanted a-a nap." Renee pulled Rebecca's hand to her lips and kissed it. "I thought she was sleeping. I didn't even notice." She stroked Rebecca's hair. "Please don't. Please come back." Her tear-filled pleas tore at my heart, but all I could do was be there for her as she cried.

I pulled a chair up next to the bed and sat as Renee smoothed Rebecca's hair and talked to her. Some of the most beautiful things I'd ever heard passed Renee's lips. The love between them was stronger than even I realized, and the well of grief inside Renee seemed to have no bottom.

After a while, Laura crept through the door. When she realized Rebecca was gone, she put a hand to her mouth. I stood and went to her.

"Farns?" I whispered.

"He's fine. Just came down the stairs too fast and slipped." She didn't look away from Rebecca. "I-is she?"

I nodded. "Go take care of Farns. I'll wait here with Renee."

She wiped at her eyes. "All right."

Hours passed before I heard the familiar roar of a motorcycle. Teddy had returned, Sin and Lucius likely with him.

"Renee, honey. I'm going to go tell them. I'll bring them up in a few minutes, okay?"

She didn't respond.

I left the room and headed for the foyer. Teddy was the first one through the door. The smile on his face faded as soon as he saw me.

"What? What is it?"

There was no other way to say it. "Your mom. I'm sorry, Teddy. But she's passed."

He looked up the stairs. "When?"

"This morning." I hugged him. "I'm sorry."

Sin walked in, Lucius right behind him. I went to Sin, his strong arms encircling me.

"Mom's dead." Teddy ran a hand through his hair and began to climb the stairs.

"What?" Lucius turned to me.

"She passed in her sleep this morning. Peacefully. Renee is up there with her."

Sin held me close, his heart beating wildly as if he'd been shot full of adrenaline. Lucius followed Teddy to the third floor.

"In her sleep?"

I swallowed hard. "Yes. She was kind to Renee this morning and then took a nap. She didn't wake up."

"Renee? How is she handling it?" He absentmindedly rubbed his hands up and down my back.

"Not great. I haven't been able to pull her away. Are

you okay?"

"I can't tell. My mother's dead, but…"

"It's all right to have mixed emotions."

"My problem is having emotions at all. You've changed me somehow. Before… Before, I don't think I would have felt this sort of, I don't know what it is. I can't put it in words." He sighed in frustration. "There's an ache where there used to be nothing."

I pulled away and met his eyes. "It's sorrow."

He stroked the back of his hand down my cheek. "I think so. And I always knew she would die. I assumed it would be in some horrible fashion." He shook his head. "But in her sleep?"

"It's a good thing."

"Yes. I suppose we should go up."

"I'll be with you the whole time. I'm here for you." I got on my tiptoes and kissed him. "Anything you need."

He squared his shoulders, took my hand, and led me upstairs.

CHAPTER TWENTY-NINE
STELLA

MY DRESS ARRIVED ON the morning of the coronation. Its emerald silk gleamed in the rays of sun filtering through my window. I walked around it, making sure it was perfect for the night. I would know for certain once Sin saw me in it.

After his mother's funeral, he'd gone to New Orleans for two days to clean up financial and legal matters concerning her estate. He was set to arrive at lunchtime.

I smiled just thinking about what he'd say about the dress. I drew it myself and sent the specifications to his seamstress. She'd whipped it up in record time. The bodice was a black corset with a neckline that skirted the tops of my breasts in a straight line. My vines would be on full display, and the back was low enough to show my scars. The skirt flowed out in deep green silk, with a slit up one thigh for easy access to my knife.

"Stella?" Sin's voice had my heart racing. He was home early.

I took off toward the stairs and flew down them. He caught me as I jumped into his arms from two steps up.

He laughed, the sound warming me more than a

summer sun. "I missed you, too." He kissed along my cheek to my lips and ran a hand to my hair. His tongue swept into my mouth, and he backed me into the wall next to the music room. He moved a hand to my breast and I squeaked when he ran his thumb over my nipple.

He broke our kiss and looked down. "What's this?"

"I..." Color rose in my cheeks, which was odd given that he'd seen and tasted every inch of my body. "I got my nipples pierced."

"You what?" He set me down and yanked my shirt up.

"Sin!" I tried to pull it back down and glanced around for Farns or Laura. We were, thankfully, alone.

"Jesus." He bent his head to my left breast and licked along the metal barbell.

My pussy clenched at the mix of pleasure and pain. "Ow. They're still healing."

"That's a *you* problem, not a *me* problem." He licked again and pulled my shirt to my collarbones. "Ink, too? This is beautiful. Here." He pulled my shirt up to my neck and caged my throat with his palm.

"Tony's work?" He inspected the vines and licked my other nipple as I made an *mmm* sound.

"Yes."

"He touched you?"

"He wore gloves."

His palm tightened. "He touched you?"

"He had to. But he knows I'm yours. He was a consummate professional the entire time."

"Mmhmm." He traced the vines with his index finger. "I love it, though I may still kill him for it."

"Sin, don't be mad—"

He rubbed the flat of his tongue along my left nipple, and I pressed my lips together to keep from moaning. Footsteps in the hall had him whirling, covering me with his broad body. I hastily lowered my shirt. Farns rounded the corner, a bandage still affixed to his forehead.

"How are you feeling?" Sin asked.

"Much better, thank you."

"Maybe we should have that talk again. The one about you taking it easy while bossing a younger man around."

"No sir. Not a chance. Not while there's still breath left in this beat up old body."

"It wouldn't be so bad." Once my shirt was straight, I walked over and squeezed Farns' bony elbow. "It's not like you'd be going anywhere."

"All the same, I prefer to continue my duties for as long as I'm allowed."

"Suit yourself. Come on, Stella, I have some estate particulars to go over with Lucius and Teddy."

I followed him down the hall. Laura had prepared an early lunch. We told her we'd be leaving in the afternoon and attending an all-night party. Teddy and Lucius sat at the table, Teddy chatting with Laura as Lucius spoke Spanish on his phone.

When we walked in, Teddy said, "We're going to need some family time, babe. I'll catch up with you before we leave this afternoon."

Laura's cheeks turned pink, but she nodded and went to the kitchen. Sin closed the door behind us, and Lucius ended his phone call.

"What's the word?" Lucius popped a cheese straw into his mouth.

"Mother's estate is taken care of. I checked her holdings in the city—all the safe deposit boxes are secure. She left it all to me, but I saw fit to divide the estate equally three ways. However, the business won't be quite so easy to divvy up, so all three of us will remain on the board. Also, I kept the house for myself, because I can."

"That all sounds fine by me." Lucius nodded.

"Does that mean I'm rich now?" Teddy asked.

Sin smirked. "Oh, forgot to mention, your third is held in trust. Lucius and I are the trustees."

"Aw, shit." Teddy took an angry bite of his baguette to the point it was almost comical.

"Good one, Sin." Lucius laughed.

"Now, let's get down to more pressing business." He sat at the head of the table. "I've checked with Quinlan, and everything is on schedule. He's adjusted arrangements to add Teddy; otherwise, the plan is the same."

A knock sounded at the door.

"Yes?" Sin barked.

Renee poked her head in. Though her eyes were ringed with dark circles, her hair was fixed and her clothes clean and neat. I dropped by to see her more frequently over the few days after Rebecca passed. She made a habit of sitting by Rebecca's grave under an oak near the levee, often taking a blanket and lying in the shade for hours.

Sin, Lucius, and Teddy were grim for the brief funeral, but Rebecca's death seemed to bring as much relief as grief for them. Renee, however, was inconsolable. The love she'd shared with Rebecca—even when it was twisted and ugly—was one that even death couldn't snuff out.

"What can we do for you, Renee?"

"I'd like to help, if I can."

Sin nodded. "Come in."

She closed the door behind her and came to sit next to me. I held her hand under the table as Sin continued.

"Once Quinlan gets everything in place, I'll give my coronation address. Lucius, Teddy, and Stella will stick close to me. I don't want to lose sight of any of you. Not for a second. When things start to happen, it will go quickly. There's no room for error. Teddy, you'll handle helping the last-borns and Acquisitions out. Lucius will remain hidden and aid Quinlan. Stella will warn Brianne and Gavin. And that's all we can control."

"What can I do?" Renee asked.

Sin tapped his fingers on the table. "Until you, we didn't have anyone here at the house who could keep an eye out. If things turn out badly, we'll regroup here in a hurry and then scatter. All of us are packed and ready to go should the need arise. Just be ready. If we don't show back up by daybreak, you will need to take Farns and Laura and get as far away as you can. I've already set up my bank to wire money into your account should that happen. I was going to leave instructions, but now you know."

"I'll kill anyone who tries to set foot here." Renee squeezed my hand.

"It won't come to that."

"Are you going to kill them all?" Her voice rose.

"We're going to make a run at it."

"Good. I hope they rot in hell." The acid in Renee's voice reinforced my own conviction that we'd made the right choice. Not that it mattered. Right or wrong, we were committed.

"We could still fail." Sin ran a hand through his dark hair. "Even though we've planned it all right down to the last detail. If anyone gets wind of it, we're dead. Everyone at this table knows the stakes. One misstep, and it's all over before it even began."

"I'm all in." I held his gaze.

"I wish you weren't."

"I'm going." I didn't want to have this argument again, but I would. Nothing could keep me from bringing the Acquisition down, and I wanted to be there when it crumbled.

He sighed. "I know."

"To the death. Theirs or ours." Lucius stood. "That's the way it's got to be. I think everyone is on the same page."

Sin rose. "Let's go get ready. Make it look good. We don't want to tip anyone until the right moment."

"I got this. And I'll even tie your bow tie for you." Lucius smirked at Teddy.

"I can tie my own tie."

"And end up looking like a circus clown? Dead giveaway."

"Dick." Teddy stood.

I laughed and got to my feet.

"Oh, and one other trifling detail I shouldn't overlook." Sin walked to me and dropped to one knee. He pulled a ring from his pocket. It had the biggest emerald I'd ever seen, surrounded by diamonds.

My heart seemed to stop and I couldn't catch my breath. I stared down at him, my mind spinning as I tried to understand what was happening. The sharp lines of his face softened and his eyes glimmered as he offered the ring. I covered my mouth with one hand, disbelief rolling through me like a turbulent wave.

"Will you marry me?"

I grabbed the back of the nearest chair. "Are you serious?"

"I don't get on my knees for anyone—except you." He lifted the ring higher, and the gems caught a ray of sun and scattered a prism of light against the dining room wall.

"Smooth," Teddy whispered.

I stared into his eyes, his soul laid bare. He was the one I needed, the man who loved me more than his own life. It was all written there in the deep blue, the open heart, and the proffered ring.

I held out my shaking left hand. He kissed it and slipped the ring on my finger. My heart upped its pace to a hectic beat as he rose and pulled me to him. He hesitated before giving me the kiss I would kill for.

"I think you forgot something," he whispered against my lips.

I smiled and wrapped my arms around his neck. "Yes."

CHAPTER THIRTY
SINCLAIR

I PULLED THROUGH THE gate and sped past the line of cars.

"Is that wise?" Stella smoothed her dress down. She didn't need to. Everything about it, about her, was perfect.

"I'm the new Sovereign. If anyone has a problem with it, they can take it up with me."

"Good point." She held her left hand out and admired the ring.

The Vinemonts owned several priceless gems, but this one spoke to me the moment I saw it in the safe deposit box in New Orleans. It had been in my family since the 1920s, and had never looked more stunning. She was born to wear it. My chest swelled with pride that she liked what I'd picked for her. Then again, I always did have impeccable taste.

I pulled up to the valet in front of whoever had been patiently waiting and got out. An attendant helped Stella from the car.

"This is the one." I handed the attendant my keys.

The attendant stopped and nodded, recognition firing in his eyes. He whistled two notes—the signal—to let me know he understood. Quinlan's men were in place.

I helped Stella to the curb, and we climbed the stairs. We were two different people since the first time we'd done this a year ago. A cool wind whipped around us, and Stella's skirt flowed to the side as I wrapped my arm around her bare shoulders. She trembled.

"Are you all right?"

"I'm perfect. I can't wait, to be honest."

I smiled at her bloodlust, and we continued to the top of the stairs. Dropping my hand to her waist, we entered the chateau.

Cal stood in the foyer greeting guests with his usual aplomb. "Hello gorgeous," he said and shook my hand. "Stella, you look nice, too." He laughed and took her waist.

My hands fisted, the need to destroy him rising like a ship on an ocean wave.

"I can't wait until I get you home, beautiful." He kissed her neck, and then held her at arm's length. "And what's this? New ink?"

"I had her branded a bit more. Just so everyone knows I had her first." I kept my tone cold, though my hatred seethed, red and smoldering.

"I'll take your sloppy seconds any day. Go on in. Your seats are on the stage. Where's Teddy?"

"He's arriving separately, but he'll be here."

"Perfect!" Cal slapped me on the back and waved us toward the ballroom.

Stella walked ahead of me, her red locks cascading down her back in a soft wave. I took her elbow and guided her through the groups of people, each of them whispering about us, each of them dying to know who the Sovereign would be.

We entered the ballroom—this time devoid of the enormous oak in the center. A stage stood along one wall. Red, his younger sister Evie, and Brianne sat in a huddle, as did Bob, his brother Carl, and Gavin. Three seats to the left of the podium remained empty.

Servers whisked by with drinks and hors d'oeuvres. Every so often, one of them would whistle from high to low, assuring me that the preparations were in order.

"Have I mentioned how beautiful you look?" I whispered in Stella's ear.

"You may have mentioned it about a dozen times. But it can't hurt to hear it again." She smiled. That simple turn of her lips, nothing more than a reaction to stimulus—I lived for it. Her happiness was as necessary as the air in my lungs.

We made our way through the chattering throng toward the stage.

"Sin?" Sophia's voice clawed at my eardrum.

I spun, keeping Stella shielded at my back. "Sophia."

I turned my head and whispered, "Wait for me by the stage."

"Okay." Stella backed away.

"Sin, where have you been? We were supposed to brunch on Sunday with Mother." Her displeasure was eclipsed by mine. I hated the sight of her.

Even so, I masked my disgust. "My apologies, but my mother passed. I should have sent word."

"She's dead? Yes, you should have sent word," she hissed. "Now it will look like I didn't care."

"When I'm Sovereign, will that matter?"

She opened her crimson lips, closed them, and then re-affixed a smile to them. "You're right." She kissed me on the cheek, and I wondered if her lips were still warm from being wrapped around Ellis' cock. Not that I cared. Her lips would be forever stilled within the next few hours.

"Sin." Teddy walked up and took Sophia's hand, kissing the back of it.

"I'm glad to see at least one of the Vinemont men has manners." She smiled, her dark eyes taking Teddy in from head to toe.

"When I see a beautiful woman, my first thought is to

kiss her." He shrugged, his boyish charm now an act, but just as convincing as the real thing.

"Oh, you flatter me. Keep it up." She shifted her gaze to some point behind Teddy.

I followed her line of vision to Ellis.

"Excuse me for a moment." She walked around Teddy and beelined for her lover.

Teddy shifted closer and eyed the crowd. "Where's Stella?"

"In front of the stage." I turned and scanned for her. My heart chilled when I realized she was gone.

Guests milled around, and I pushed through them until I stood at the stairs. She wasn't there.

"Fuck!" I couldn't breathe, couldn't think.

"We'll find her. Calm down," Teddy leaned this way and that, trying to see through the mass of people.

"Welcome!" Cal's voice carried over all others as he made his way to the stage.

"We don't have time." I wanted to scream for her, to knock down anything that blocked the path to her, but I couldn't.

Cal waved us on. "Come on fellas, get up there. Where's Stella?"

"Powder room." Teddy lied almost as easily as I did.

"We'll have to start without her. Shame." Cal pushed us up the stairs ahead of him.

At the top, I turned and scrutinized all the faces. I finally found hers, a look of horror on it as Dylan dragged her into a side room, his hand clapped over her mouth.

CHAPTER THIRTY-ONE
Stella

I SCREAMED AS DYLAN threw me to the floor in a small sitting room off the ballroom. His weight crushed down on top of me, and he pinned my hands to the floor.

"No one here to save you now." He smiled as I tried to free my hands.

I should have been afraid. I wasn't. Anger boiled over, scorching my insides with naked hatred.

"Get the fuck off me."

"Shut up." He let one hand go and slapped me. "I wanted to get my taste before Cal. I'll have you after, too. But something about being inside you first just does it for me." He pushed his hips into me for emphasis.

"You're fucking pathetic!"

He backhanded me this time, his knuckles busting my lip.

I spat my blood in his face.

He wiped it away with the back of his sleeve as I inched my hand down to my thigh where my blade waited. Cal's amplified voice came through the door clearly as he went over the trials of the year and built up to announcing the victor.

"I'm going to rip you apart for that." He yanked my dress up and fumbled at his zipper.

"I'll kill you." I palmed my knife.

He stopped and wrapped his large hand around my throat. "I could snap your fucking neck right now. I should. You deserve it."

Thunderous applause erupted from the ballroom and I swung, stabbing him in the side over and over before he even realized I'd done it.

"What are you—?"

I bridged up, shoving him off me. He clutched his side and brought a bloody hand to his face.

"You cut me." He shook his head in disbelief as I got to my feet.

"That's not all." I aimed a kick at his face and delighted in the sickening crunch his nose made during the impact.

He fell back sputtering. The applause died down, and his cries grew louder. I had to shut him up so he could bleed to death quietly. I kicked him in the side of the head with all my strength. He went limp.

I wiped my blade on the window curtain and stuffed it back down in the garter on my thigh. My hands were steady, my heart in a calm rhythm. I dabbed my busted lip on the inside of my skirt and traced the outline of my lips with my finger to wipe away any smeared lipstick.

Opening the door, I saw Sinclair at the podium. He spoke of history and the importance of tradition, but his eyes were fixed on me—his future. I gave him a nod to let him know I was okay and pushed my way through the throng before climbing onto the stage and taking my seat next to Teddy.

I glanced at Gavin and Brianne. They both watched Sin. I hadn't had a chance to warn them. Dylan had grabbed me soon after Sin began speaking with Sophia.

Red cradled Evie in his arms as she sobbed, and Bob's brother cried quietly to himself. Teddy rested his arm along the back of my chair as the faceless mob in the darkened ballroom stared up at us.

"You okay?" He whispered.

"I could take them all on, bare handed. I'm that okay right now." Getting the best of Dylan shot me into the stratosphere, especially when his was only the first blood that would be spilled tonight. I'd killed a man, and instead of regret, all I felt was triumph.

"And now, I'd like to thank my Acquisition, Stella Rousseau. Without her, this win wouldn't be possible. I'd also like to thank Red and Bob, and let them know their sacrifices are appreciated. Bring the knives." He waved toward an attendant who climbed the stairs and gave long, curving knives to Red and Bob. Red's hand shook as he took the blade, and Bob grabbed his with a chilling nonchalance.

The crowd began to chant. It started as a whisper in the corner of the room and grew until the entire room filled with the word "blood" on a never-ending loop. Sin whistled two notes, the sound carrying across the speakers and over the sounds of the continuing chant. Red held his sister, the knife shaking in his hand as he gave me a vindictive glare. I shook my head. *Wait*, I mouthed to him. His eyes narrowed.

Doors along the back and sides of the ballroom opened, and attendants wheeled in several carts covered with black cloths. They spaced them out amongst the guests and then retreated back through the doors. I couldn't see it, but I knew lengths of chain were being affixed to all the exits. There was no escape for any of the people below. A small, hidden door behind the stage remained unbarred. That was it.

Sin held up a hand and the chant died down. "Patience. I have one more official act before the blood will be spilled."

Cal stood at the foot of the stairs, his brow wrinkled in confusion at the change of plan.

"As you all know, being Sovereign comes with amazing benefits. I take a cut from each of you every year. My wealth grows and grows, and I have the power to end whichever one of you I see fit. Sovereign is a time-honored role, one that is coveted beyond all others. Wouldn't you agree?"

Some of the guests applauded, though I could sense unease begin to build. I wanted to smile, but kept my face impassive.

"The reason we have a Sovereign is, of course, to prevent infighting and to consolidate power in one principal place. But have you ever wondered what would happen if there were no Sovereign?"

Whispers rippled through the crowd.

"That would lead to a power vacuum. That would mean the strongest of you would be the next Sovereign. There are plenty of people in here who could claim the throne—Cal, for instance; he's strong. Sophia, his daughter, very smart and wily. Look at your neighbor. Would they take it from you? Your chance to be Sovereign? Would you let them? Or would you claim it for yourself and have everything you've ever dreamed of?"

Sin let the crowd ruminate for a moment. One of the guests pulled the sheet from atop a cart and a collective gasp sounded from everyone close enough to see what was there.

"As some of you have discovered, there are weapons scattered throughout the room. Knives, hatchets, hammers, bats, daggers, axes—you name it, it's there."

All around the room voices rose, and even in the glare of the spotlight, I could see people snatching weapons from the carts.

"Now, look around you. Who will reign? You best decide quickly, because my first act as Sovereign is to banish the Vinemont household from the nobility forever."

Cal sputtered and shook his head as Sin continued.

"This is *your* chance. You want to reign? Take it. You want the spoils? Take it. You want to decide who lives and dies? Take it. Because if you don't, someone else will. Pick up the knife and strike down anyone who tries to take what's yours. There is no Sovereign anymore, except whoever is strong enough to claim it."

The stage lights went out and the room became steeped in gloom. Screams erupted from all sides.

Cal groaned and fell forward, a dagger glinting in his back. Teddy jumped to the floor and yanked a cart full of guns from beneath the stage and sent it skittering into the crowd.

I darted to Gavin. "There's a door behind the stage. Go. Take Bob's brother."

Bob tried to get up, too, but Gavin punched him in the side of the head. He fell to the floor and began to cry, the sound drowned out by the screams.

"You're staying." Gavin kicked him in the stomach and led Carl down the back of the stage.

"Brianne, go." I pointed to where Gavin had disappeared. She rose and followed, though she seemed to have no idea what was going on.

"Evie, you too."

She clung to her brother. I pulled my knife out and shook my head at Red. I couldn't let him go.

He glowered and tried to dislodge Evie. "Go sweetheart. I'll be all right."

She wouldn't budge. "No."

Gunfire erupted, and Sin grabbed me. "We have to leave, now."

I pointed my knife at Red. "Take her and go."

He picked her up and fled down the back stairs as more gunfire ripped through the air.

"Stella, now!"

I surveyed the room, a mass of bodies caving in on itself. Some ran for the doors and screamed to be let out. It made them easy targets, and they fell in heaps as their former friends and allies fought to claim the throne. Every time someone fell, or a cry of agony pierced the air, I felt a sliver of comfort. I wanted to stay, to watch all of them suffer.

Judge Montagnet tried to scramble up the stage steps, his eyes wide and a bloody slash on his cheek. I tightened my grip on my blade, but a young man behind him swung swift and sure with a double-sided axe, almost severing the judge's head completely. The man yanked the axe free and climbed to the platform. Sin pulled out a revolver and fired two rounds. The man fell backward as others began to rush the the stage.

"Let's go." Sin threw me over his shoulder and dashed down the back stairs.

I got one more glimpse of the gratifying chaos before he carried me through the hidden door. Quinlan swung it shut behind us, and he and another larger man chained and barred it. The noxious scent of gasoline filled the air, and rows of gasoline cans lined the carpeted hall, a stark contrast to the hand-drawn walls and ornate chandeliers.

Sin put me on my feet. All eyes turned toward the door as pounding sounds and screams poured through it. The cries were silenced one by one.

I covered my nose, a futile attempt to avoid the gasoline fumes, and looked down the hall. Red lay on the floor in a puddle of crimson. Lucius stood over him, a bloody knife in his hand.

I nodded. "Good."

Evie cried on Gavin's shoulder as the screams rose and fell within the ballroom. Brianne clung to Carl, her stare far away. Gunfire continued sporadically, the stately chateau devolving into a slaughterhouse floor. My heart sang with each life that was snuffed out, their blood slowly dousing the rage burning inside me.

"It worked." Teddy ran a shaking hand through his hair. "I can't believe it worked."

Sin whipped me around to him and pulled me into a

kiss. I closed my eyes and reveled in our victory, in the turmoil and death beyond the door, and most of all in the man I loved.

"We need to get out of here." Lucius knelt and wiped his blade on Red's pant leg.

"Quinlan, are we good here?" Sin asked.

"It's ready to burn."

Sin pulled a roll of hundreds from his inner suit pocket. "Make sure no one gets out alive."

Quinlan took the money. "Not a problem. Everyone's cleared out, and I've got men with eyes on this place."

"Thank you." I met Quinlan's eyes.

"After that last thing, in the fort." He shook his head. "This was my pleasure."

"Come on." Lucius pulled Teddy down the hall. "We have to go."

Sin scooped me up and ran with me, my heels clattering to the floor. Gavin, Evie, Carl, and Brianne followed. Quinlan and the large man brought up the rear.

We burst out into the cool night, but Sin stopped and set me on the ground.

"Stella gets to do the honors. Give them to her."

The larger man pulled a book of matches from his pocket and handed it over. I turned the matchbook over in my hands, amazed at how light total destruction could be.

I opened the pack and pulled out a single match, the tip green. With a single flick of my wrist, the head flamed, a bright orange burst in the evening gloom. Time stopped, and only I and the flame existed, both burning, both bent on annihilation. I threw it, the flame flickering in the light wind. It bounced off the door, landed on the carpet, and then multiplied into a snakelike inferno. Orange flames raced down the hall in a whoosh, the carpet catching and the walls bubbling.

Quinlan slammed the door, and Sin scooped me up again and ran to the cars waiting for us.

"You." He pointed to Gavin and then a car. "That one. Key's in the ignition. Money's in a bag in the trunk. Get far away from here. Take them with you."

Sin tucked me into the passenger side of his sports car.

"Wait." I got to my feet and dashed to Gavin, wrapping my arms around his neck.

He held me close. "I got your back."

"I got yours."

"You did it. I can't believe you did it. You burned them the fuck down."

"Be safe."

"You too."

"Stella!" Sin banged on the hood of his car.

I gave Gavin one more hard squeeze and ran back to Sin. He dropped into the driver's side, waited for Teddy and Lucius to pull away, and then tore down the drive.

The gate was wide open, and we followed Lucius's taillights down the main road, away from the chateau, and back toward home. *Home.*

I looked at Sin, his jaw set tight and his eyes flicking to the rearview.

"It's over."

A loud boom rumbled through the air. I craned my head back. Smoke rose over the trees, blotting out the stars and hazing across the moon. An orange glow marked the Oakman estate, fire wiping the slate clean.

Sin shifted into another gear, speeding faster, and took my hand, bringing it to his lips.

"I would gladly kill a thousand more for you."

"Let's hope we don't have to. Do you think anyone will come for us?" We'd discussed it before, but tonight we had just tried to get through the coronation alive. This was a whole new reality.

"I don't think anyone's left to retaliate. If they do, we'll be ready." His tone was full of malicious promise. He kissed my hand again, his gentle lips at odds with his dark words.

"The police?"

"Anyone who's left will kill any investigation into the Acquisition. The governor won't want anyone digging too deeply into this *tragedy*. Besides, every sheriff from the surrounding parishes was in the crowd."

I relaxed back into my seat, staring ahead as we raced off into the night. Into our future, while the world of the Acquisition turned to ash behind us.

CHAPTER THIRTY-TWO
Stella

"No, to the left." I put my hands on my hips. "No, Teddy, your other left. And they're really going to let you operate on people?"

He laughed and adjusted the star atop the Christmas tree more to my liking. "How about that?"

"It looks straight to me."

"The top is cocked to the left." Sin wrapped his arms around me from behind.

"No it isn't." I ran my hands over his arms.

"Yes, it is. Angle it to the right more, Ted."

Teddy looked at me for permission.

"Fine, to the right. See how that looks."

He tweaked it and stood back on the ladder. "I've only changed it five times so far."

"See, now it's perfect. Like you." Sin kissed my neck, and I sighed.

Teddy climbed down and pulled the ladder away. Sin reached over and hit the lights. The tree glowed white, the lights glittering amid the silver and gold ornaments.

"Beautiful. Also like you." He nibbled at my ear, sending goose bumps running down my arms.

Teddy sank into an arm chair and threaded his fingers behind his head. "This is pretty much my best work yet."

Laura walked into the library and clapped. "Oh my god, it's perfect!"

I smiled. "It was all Teddy."

"Liar," Sin whispered in my ear.

I melted into him, leaning back as he held me. He was everything; I couldn't even fall asleep without him now. He kept the nightmares at bay—the faces, screams, and flames. He'd given up his position in town and focused on the sugar business. Where he went, I followed, though I drew the line at returning to Cuba.

After the coronation night, the news ran several stories about the "tragedy in the bayou," the fast-moving fire that had trapped many fine and upstanding members of Southern society. At first, it seemed like coverage would never end, but after a couple days, the world just seemed to move on.

The house was on high alert the first month, hiring Quinlan's men to keep watch at the front and back gates. But after a while, it appeared the entire power structure had collapsed, leaving no one to retaliate.

Fall turned to winter, and as Christmas approached, I wanted to change our history, mold the season into a happy time.

Laura walked to Teddy, who pulled her into his lap.

She protested. "Stop. Not in front of them."

Teddy scoffed. "Stella and Sin don't care. They're practically doing it standing up over there."

She laughed as he ran his hands around her waist and pulled her down to his mouth.

"Jesus, that tree is overdone." Lucius walked in and plopped down on the sofa, drink in hand as always. "Did you raid the north pole or something?"

I arched an eyebrow. "Shut up. It's gorgeous."

"If you say so." Lucius saluted me with his drink and downed half of it in one go. "Farns would have a heart attack if he saw it, for the record." Lucius kicked his feet up on the coffee table.

"Well, then it's a good thing we sent him on a vacation to a sunnier clime." I refused to let Lucius bring down my Christmas spirit.

Teddy came up for air. "Lucius, don't be such a dick. It's Christmas."

I walked to Lucius and pulled his glass away. "I think what we need is food instead of alcohol. Maybe it will improve your mood."

He glanced to Sin and then stared at my chest. "I'd love to tell you what would improve my mood, but Sin probably wouldn't like it."

"Don't talk to her like—"

"Sin, it's fine. He needs to eat. The liquid diet makes him grouchy. I'll go get some snacks from the kitchen."

"There's a roast on the stove." Laura started to get up.

"No. Stay. I'll make a plate and bring it. Lucius and Sin, play nice while I'm gone. Laura and Teddy—" I smiled. "—carry on."

I hummed "Last Christmas" as I entered the kitchen. Renee stood in the pantry, her back to me.

"Oh, hey, I was wondering where you were. We just decorated the tree. I'm going to take some—"

She made a strangled noise and fell forward.

"Renee!" I rushed to her and turned her over. A knife protruded from her chest. I drew air into my lungs to scream, but Dylan lunged from the darkness of the pantry and clapped a hand over my mouth.

He shoved me until my back was against the island, his knees straddling me.

"Miss me?" He licked my cheek and pressed something metal against my chin.

"If you make a sound, I'll pull the trigger and splatter your brains on the ceiling. Nod if you understand me."

I nodded, too afraid to blink. His hand crushed my

lips, but the gun barrel was still foremost in my thoughts.

"You're coming with me. I own you. See, I'm the Sovereign now. You're going to serve me until your cunt is worn out and your will is broken. Then I'm going to spill your blood for all to see. Like christening a boat. I'm going to rebuild it all." A crazed light burned in his eyes. "And your boys in the library? They'll be punished, too. But you're the prize, the one I want. They'll try to come after you. I'll kill them and make you watch." Spit flew from his lips, and he almost vibrated with excitement.

"Come quietly, or I'll kill them all now. So what's it going to be? Will you behave and come with me?"

I nodded.

"Do you promise, Stella?"

I nodded again.

"I'm going to take my hand off your mouth. Make a sound and I'll kill you. No hesitation." His soulless eyes made me believe every word.

He pulled his hand away slowly. I took a shuddering breath, but didn't make any noise.

"Good girl. Now get up." He pulled me to my feet and leaned close to speak in my ear. "I'm going to fuck you as soon as I get you where no one will hear you scream. Keep that in your mind. Hold onto it for me." He pulled me away from the island. "Out the back door."

Pushing me ahead of him, he shoved the barrel between my shoulder blades. Blood pooled around Renee as her unseeing eyes stared straight ahead. I walked past her, biting back my grief, and turned toward the rear of the house.

The door from the hall opened and Teddy walked in. "Stella, Laura sent me—"

The gunshot deafened me. Teddy fell to his knees, crimson spreading along his stomach as he stared up at me.

"Teddy!" I whirled and knocked the gun from Dylan's hand, and then darted to the knives lined up along the wall over the stove. I pulled two down as yells erupted in the hallway. Dylan ran. I followed.

His feet thundered down the back steps and out onto the lawn. I couldn't let him get away. He was fast, but I was faster. His bulk slowed him down as I sprinted after him, his blond hair glowing in the bright moonlight. Everything inside me was numb—everything except the need for vengeance.

I gained on him, my feet sure on the grass as he ran past the garage toward a car parked under the oaks. I pushed harder until everything burned. When I finally caught up with him, I cut a slashing arc across his back.

He screamed but kept running. I shoved my hand out, embedding a knife in his thick torso. He slowed and stumbled. I slashed him again and dropped to his knees, only a few yards shy of his car.

I circled to his front and kicked him so he landed on his back, the knife penetrating deeper. Bloody bubbles rose from his lips as I settled on top of him.

Someone yelled my name. I stabbed downward. Dylan screamed weakly. I withdrew the knife and did it again. I stabbed and stabbed until Sin grabbed my wrist and pulled me to my feet.

"Stop. It's over. Stop."

"Renee? Teddy?" A car reversed out of the garage and squealed tires, passing us and almost knocking us over with the draft.

"Renee is gone. Teddy—" His voice broke.

I dropped the knife and wrapped my arms around him.

"Lucius took him."

"I left Dylan alive. This is my fault." I shuddered, everything shaken all the way down to my soul.

"No." He stroked my hair as Laura ran out the front door and collapsed on the stairs, head in her hands. "You didn't do this."

"Renee." A flash of her kind smile on the first day we

met struck me like a slap in the face. "Are you sure? Maybe she—maybe..."

"No. Shh. She's gone. I'm sorry."

I stared down at Dylan, blood covering his throat and face. Pulling back, I looked down at my red hands, the blood seeping into my shirt and jeans. I shook even harder.

"You're in shock. Come inside."

"We need to go to the hospital. We have to help Teddy."

Sin locked his arm around my waist and guided me to the porch. "We will, but we can't take you like this."

"We have to—"

"Lucius has him. We'll leave as soon as you're okay." His voice remained calm as he hurried me up the front steps.

"Laura, I'm going to get Stella cleaned up. Pull my sedan around. We'll all go to the hospital as soon as we're done."

Sin picked me up and carried me to my bathroom. He turned on the shower and stripped me. All I could do was stand, my teeth chattering. He stripped his clothes and got in with me.

The red bloom on Teddy's shirt spread larger and larger in my mind. His wide eyes full of pain and surprise. "Do you think Teddy—?"

"I don't know." He hastily lathered a washcloth.

The blood sluiced down into the drain, a crimson river that would never run clear again.

I covered my face with a shaking hand. "It should have been me."

"Don't say that." Sin pulled my hand away. "Never say that. We'd all be dead without you. Either from the hell of the Acquisition or Dylan's bullets."

"But Teddy—"

"No!" He slammed his fist into the tiles hard enough to break one. "Never wish yourself away from me."

He crushed me to him, our battered souls clinging to one another as they had done from the start. "Never."

EPILOGUE
Stella

"Teddy, come in. It's time for lunch." I called loud enough for the dark-haired toddler on the lawn to look up at me.

"Mommy!" He grinned and did his best to navigate the grass toward me. Lucius ran up behind him and scooped him into his arms, tickling him as they barreled through the sunny morning.

I rubbed my stomach, the twins growing inside me apparently engaged in a fistfight. I turned as Lucius stomped up the stairs behind me.

Teddy giggled like a maniac. "Again, Unky Lusus!"

"Lunch first."

"Mommy's a buzzkill, little man." Lucius set him on his feet in the foyer. He toddled off toward the kitchen. I may have been his mother, but he knew Laura had all the snacks.

"When are you going to pop?"

"Two weeks. You know that."

"You keep telling me that, and I keep disbelieving that you can *still* be pregnant. Huge, is all I'm saying."

"Beautiful, he means." Sin came down the stairs and

gave me a kiss. He peeked down the hallway and saw Teddy.

Giving me a grin, he turned and crept along behind his son, then grabbed him up and blew raspberries all along his stomach as he giggled.

"Are you sure they're both girls?" Lucius matched my lumbering pace toward the breakfast room.

"That's the word at the doctor's office." I trailed my fingers beneath my mother's portrait that hung in the hall. I'd painted it from memory, and her smile greeted all guests to the house.

"Do you think maybe you could name one Lucia or something?"

"Not a chance." I eased into the breakfast room. Lucius pulled out a chair for me, and I sat, my feet thanking me for the brief respite.

"Here." He scooted out the chair next to me, and lifted my feet up.

I leaned back and closed my eyes. "Thank you."

"Welcome."

Sin came through from the kitchen and started rubbing my shoulders.

"He's not eating sweets, is he?"

"Not really. Laura knows he's supposed to eat lunch first. She only gave him a handful of jellybeans." He kissed my forehead and kept rubbing.

"That's sweets." I threw my hands up. "Whatever. No one listens to the preggo lady around here."

"Yes we do." He dug his thumbs in, unwrapping my tight muscles like a Christmas present.

"I'm just irritable."

"We know." He laughed and kissed me again.

"Twins are your fault."

"You may have mentioned that a couple hundred times. Though, I don't think it's true."

Sin moved around and sat opposite me, putting my feet in his lap. He knocked my house shoes off and rubbed my swollen feet. "Spread your legs a little more."

I tilted my head at him. "What?"

"You heard me."

"I did but—"

"Do it." He used that tone—the one that sent a thrill through me every time.

I slowly opened my legs.

"Pull up your skirt more."

"Sin." I shook my head.

"Stella. Do it now." He dug his thumb into the bottom of my foot.

I grabbed the material and pulled until my skirt hit mid-thigh.

"Much better." He continued rubbing, his gaze vacillating from my eyes to between my legs.

My body warmed as he watched me. "You're a bad man."

"So I've been told." He switched feet. "As soon as Teddy's down for a nap, I'll be going down on you."

My temperature kicked up a notch. "Bad, bad man."

He shrugged. "What? I can't give my pregnant wife the special attention she deserves?"

One of the babies kicked what must have been a vital organ. I groaned and rubbed my belly with a vengeance. "Twins are all your fault."

"Actually they're not." Teddy walked into the dining room, his green scrubs making him look older.

I closed my legs and wrinkled my nose. "What do you know? You're not even a real doctor yet."

I huffed as he leaned down and pecked me on the cheek.

"Okay, you're right. It *is* all Sin's fault."

"Much better. I thought you were in rounds or something all day?"

"Nope. Got done this morning. Wanted to come by and see little T. And check on you, of course."

"I'm fine. I mean, I would like to have my body back

to myself, but other than that, I'm good."

"I could do like a check or something. See how your cervix is dilating—"

"Don't even think about it." Sin squeezed my foot tighter.

"Teddy was kidding. Right?"

"Yeah, kidding. Little T in the kitchen?"

"He takes after his namesake. He's in there charming Laura right out from under you." I smiled up at him.

"That's my man." He pushed through the door to the kitchen.

Sin rubbed my feet for a little while longer. "Have you thought any more about names?"

"Yes." I set my feet down and leaned forward, resting my head on his chest.

"I know we discussed lots of different ones, but I've been thinking… What about Rebecca and Renee?"

He stayed silent and pulled me closer.

"If you don't want to, that's okay. Those names obviously carry some baggage. But I thought it would be—"

"I love it." He tilted my chin up and pressed his lips to mine.

Little Teddy toddled in, both uncles hot on his heels.

"Mommy, jay bees!" He held out a hand with two jellybeans stuck to it.

"I see that." I shook my head.

He ran to Sin, who picked him up and sat him in his lap. Sin whispered in his ear. Teddy's eyes lit up, and Sin pointed at me. "Tell her."

"I love you, Mommy." His smile, so much like his father's, was infectious.

"I love you, too."

Sin cupped his hands around Teddy's ear and whispered again.

"Daddy love you, Mommy."

"I love Daddy, too."

Laura bustled in from the kitchen with lunch, and before long we were all laughing at big Teddy's and little Teddy's antics.

I lay my head on Sin's shoulder, and he pulled me close. The long shadow of the Acquisition no longer darkened our doorstep, and the nightmares were nothing more than ghosts.

ACKNOWLEDGEMENTS

Thank you, reader, for giving me your most valuable asset—your time. This has been a dark and twisted journey, one I'm glad you've taken with me. This story is over, but there are more to tell. I hope you'll come along with me on some new adventures—some dark, some light—in the near future.

There are so many people who helped this series go from a dream to words on a page. My family, who let me run off for days on end to get this story out of my head. My friends, who encouraged me to keep writing. And the readers who chatted with me, made fabulous art, or wrote beautiful reviews.

Thank you to Mr. Aaron for going over just how depraved I could get and working through different scenarios for Acquisition payback. Thank you to Sloane Howell, my first line of editing defense and my writing bestie. Thanks to Jeff, for doing the heavy lifting on comma placement and my overuse of the word "but." Thanks to Rachel at The Saucy Owl for being my beta guinea pig.

Thanks to Neda, who is awesome at PR and life in general. Thanks to my Acquisitions, the most supportive bunch of readers a gal could have. Thanks to Vivian at Beaute de Livres, Terilyn, SueBee, The Literary Gossip, Irene, the PinkLadies, Leia, Warhawke, Jabberwocky, Kay, Shhluts, Heather, PopKitty, Agents of Romance, GetYourSmutOn, WhoSheReads, Samantha, Sissy, Lin (my first fan ever), Stacey Broadbent, and every other blogger, reader, supporter, or person who has sent me a note or just followed me on social media (if I left anyone out, I'm sorry, but the Oscar music started playing and they dragged me off stage).

Readers and book lovers like you are what keep me writing. You keep doing you, and I'll keep doing me. And we can all dream that we keep doing Sin.

ROMANTIC SPORTS COMEDY BY CELIA AARON & SLOANE HOWELL

Cleat Chaser

Kyrie Kent hates baseball. She hates players even more. When her best friend drags her to a Ravens game, she spends the innings reading a book... Until she gets a glimpse of the closer—a pitcher who draws her like a magnet. Fighting her attraction to Easton Holliday is easy. All she has to do is keep her distance, avoid the ballpark, and keep her head down. At least, all that would have worked, but Easton doesn't intend to let Kyrie walk so easily. When another player vies for Kyrie's attention, Easton will swing for the fences. But will Kyrie strike him out or let him steal home?

***

EROTICA TITLES BY CELIA AARON

Forced by the Kingpin
Forced Series, Book 1

I've been on the trail of the local mob kingpin for months. I know his haunts, habits, and vices. The only thing I didn't know was how obsessed he was with me. Now, caught in his trap, I'm about to find out how far he and his local cop-on-the-take will go to keep me silent.

Forced by the Professor
Forced Series, Book 2

I've been in Professor Stevens' class for a semester. He's brilliant, severe, and hot as hell. I haven't been particularly attentive, prepared, or timely, but he hasn't said anything to me about it. I figure he must not mind and intends to let me slide. At least I thought that was the case until he told me to stay after class today. Maybe he'll let me off with a warning?

Forced by the Hitmen
Forced Series, Book 3

I stayed out of my father's business. His dirty money never mattered to me, so long as my trust fund was full of it. But now I've been kidnapped by his enemies and stuffed in a bag. The rough men who took me have promised to hurt me if I make a sound or try to run. I know, deep down, they are going to hurt me no matter what I do. Now I'm cuffed to their bed. Will I ever see the light of day again?

Forced by the Stepbrother
Forced Series, Book 4

Dancing for strange men was the biggest turn on I'd ever known. Until I met him. He was able to control me, make me hot, make me need him, with nothing more than a look. But he was a fantasy. Just another client who worked me up and paid my bills. Until he found me, the real me. Now, he's backed me into a corner. His threats and promises, darkly whispered in tones of sex and violence, have bound me surer than the cruelest ropes. At first I was unsure, but now I know – him being my stepbrother is the least of my worries.

Forced by the Quarterback
Forced Series, Book 5

For three years, I'd lusted after Jericho, my brother's best friend and quarterback of our college football team. He's never paid me any attention, considering me nothing more than a little sister he never had. Now, I'm starting freshman year and I'm sharing a suite with my brother. Jericho is over all the time, but he'll never see me as anything other than the shy girl he met three years ago. But that's not who I am. Not really. To get over Jericho – and to finally get off – I've arranged a meeting with HardcoreDom. If I can't have Jericho, I'll give myself to a man who will master me, force me, and dominate me the way I desperately need.

***

A Stepbrother for Christmas
The Hard and Dirty Holidays

Annalise dreads seeing her stepbrother at her family's Christmas get-together. Niles had always been so nasty, tormenting her in high school after their parents had gotten married. British and snobby, Niles did everything he could to hurt Annalise when they were younger. Now, Annalise hasn't seen Niles in three years; he's been away at school in England and Annalise has started her pre-med program in Dallas. When they reconnect, dark memories threaten, sparks fly, and they give true meaning to the "hard and dirty holidays."

Bad Boy Valentine
The Hard and Dirty Holidays

Jess has always been shy. Keeping her head down and staying out of sight have served her well, especially when a sexy photographer moves in across the hall from her. Michael has a budding career, a dark past, and enough ink and piercings to make Jess' mouth water. She is well equipped to watched him through her peephole and stalk him on social media. But what happens when the bad boy next door comes knocking?

Bad Boy Valentine Wedding
The Hard and Dirty Holidays

Jess and Michael have been engaged for three years, waiting patiently for Jess to finish law school before taking the next step in their relationship. As the wedding date approaches, their dedication to each other only grows, but outside forces seek to tear them apart. The bad boy will have to fight to keep his bride and Jess will have to trust him with her whole heart to make their happy ending a reality.

F*ck of the Irish
The Hard and Dirty Holidays

Eamon is my crush, the one guy I can't stop thinking about. His Irish accent, toned body, and sparkling eyes captivated me the second I saw him. But since he slept with my roommate, who claims she still loves him, he's been off limits. Despite my prohibition on dating him, he has other other ideas. Resisting him is the key to keeping my roommate happy, but giving in may bring me more pleasure than I ever imagined.

***

Zeus
Taken by Olympus, Book 1

One minute I'm looking after an injured gelding, the next I'm tied to a luxurious bed. I never believed in fairy tales, never gave a second thought to myths. Now that I've been kidnapped by a man with golden eyes and a body that makes my mouth water, I'm not sure what I believe anymore... But I know what I want.

About the Author

Celia Aaron is the self-publishing pseudonym of a published romance and erotica author. She loves to write stories with hot heroes and heroines that are twisty and often dark. Thanks for reading.

Printed in Great Britain
by Amazon